START FROM HERE

SEAN FRENCH

PICADOR

First published 2004 by Picador
an imprint of Pan Macmillan Ltd
Pan Macmillan, 20 New Wharf Road, London N1 9RR
Basingstoke and Oxford
Associated companies throughout the world
www.panmacmillan.com

ISBN 0 330 43455 1

9 8 7 6 5 4 3 2 1

A CIP catalogue record for this book is available from
the British Library.

Typeset by Intype London Ltd
Printed and bound in Great Britain by
Mackays of Chatham plc, Chatham, Kent

TO NICCI

All I can say is that this isn't the way it was meant to be. This wasn't the plan. I know that it isn't the best moment to assess it – the plan, my life – lying awake at four with a warm, scarred body lying next to me, breathing in and out, in and out. I sometimes lean over to check, the way mothers are supposed to with a new baby, stupidly worried that the breathing may have stopped.

The birds wake me in the morning. I thought the dawn chorus was a figure of speech, but I've discovered that out here it really exists. It's a scientific mystery, but it happens: a mob of whistles, hoots, screeches until the sun comes up.

At four in the morning you shouldn't think about your life. Do anything else instead. Get up. Have a bath. Go for a walk. They say the dawn is beautiful out here.

That's the other point. If this wasn't the plan, then what was the plan? There wasn't a plan, but what should the plan have been? Where was I meant to be? Anywhere but here. What was I meant to do? Anything but this. I think about the past because if I can put it all together, maybe I will understand why I'm lying in the bed I'm lying in, why I'm lying next to the person I'm lying next to. Maybe that's all it's good for.

So at four in the morning I remember it all over again. That's a problem as well. I'm tired, so tired. It's dawn and I feel I am the only person in the world who is awake. Sometimes when I'm telling myself the story of my life – silently, inside my head, so I don't wake her – I feel that I wasn't in the story I thought I was in. But it could be that if I had been in the story I thought I was, then I might not have ended up here. And it's where I want to be, I think. Which is a good thing, because from any other point of view, it looks remarkably like a fuck-up.

In the dark I think of other things. I think of the future, and that can make me cry. I try to keep to the past. The past is difficult enough.

1

You don't know it, but you may have talked to me. You wouldn't remember, but it's possible. That time the phone rang while you were watching TV or pouring a mug of tea. You answered. A voice – it may have been my voice – asked for you by name, though the name may have been slightly wrong. If your real name is something like Ferdinand James Robinson and everybody calls you Jim, I would still have asked for Ferdinand Robinson. Because the companies buy these lists. That time you filled out a form because you had a chance of winning a car. That time you sent off two tokens for a free oven glove decorated with a scene from *The Lord of the Rings*.

You forgot all about it but your name and address and financial details were filed and archived and became a commodity to be sold on until it appeared on my screen as one of the three or four hundred names I had to throughput during every eight-hour day.

Yes? you said, caught by surprise. I asked you if you would be interested in a free assessment of your window frames. Now that I come to think about it, I probably didn't put it as directly as that. I informed you that I worked for a company that was conducting market research in your area and could you spare a couple of minutes to answer some questions. Maybe you said that you didn't have time because your child was in the bath. Then I asked what would be a convenient time. At that point you might just have slammed the phone down. That was the response I liked most. I just clicked the No Further Action icon. Another one down. As if I cared. It wasn't my fucking double glazing I was trying to sell you. I was just on five seventy-five an hour for a two-week contract. You didn't want too many NFAs on your screen. They had Parameters for that. They had Parameters for everything. If your NFAs rose above thirty per cent or whatever it was, you were hauled in and asked the reason why.

If you did agree to help with our market research, I asked you if you would be interested in a free quotation for double glazing. If you said you were interested, what I really felt like saying was, If you want double glazing, then why the fuck don't you get off your arse and sort it out yourself? Do you really think that you're going to get the best deal from someone who just rings you at random? But I only felt that the first few times. After that you were just a number on a screen. And I was just one of three hundred people in headsets in a giant space in a warehouse in Hendon or the Isle of Dogs or Edmonton or the Elephant and Castle.

It might not have been double glazing. It might have been a cable connection or it's even possible that you called me to arrange your mobile-phone agreement or to ask why your airline tickets hadn't arrived. The terminals had a small mirror attached. You were instructed to look in the mirror and smile before pressing the button for the next call. Customers can always hear on the phone when you're smiling, we were told. Hello, I'm Mark, thank you for calling whatever cowboy outfit I was working for at the time. What can I do for you?

I hope you weren't one of the people I rang to tell you that you'd won a holiday. That was the only one I walked out of. I couldn't bear any part of that one. I've heard people say that they couldn't be a salesman because they couldn't deal psychologically with having doors slammed in their face. When you're selling by phone, it's only a metaphorical door and it's all very detached but you'd still see the occasional woman sniffing pathetically a couple of terminals along. She'd either be gone after an hour or the next day she'd be like the rest of us.

But when I rang people to tell them they'd won a holiday, the slammed-down phones were the good ones. The next best were the ones who said, This is one of these time shares, isn't it? Or, understandably, one of these *fucking* timeshares. Even though the caller was going cold, we had a set answer to that. There was a set answer to everything. I'd say: As part of your prize, we would like to give you our special presentation of a unique investment opportunity.

It started to get painful with the people who got excited about the idea of having won a prize. You'd hear them call other members of their family. What was that? Two weeks in Spain. Did we win it? Just like that? Yes, sir, congratulations. So when can we go?

5

Then, gradually, you would hear their enthusiasm sour as they discovered the special conditions attached to the prize. They would have to attend the presentation. Yes, yes, they might say, but what about the prize? The two weeks in Spain, free flights and hotel? There was no catch? Of course not, the answer went. The only condition was that they must spend the two weeks in our designated hotel and pay in advance in full for dinner in the hotel restaurant for the full two weeks.

It was at this point that three-quarters of the remaining people finally cottoned on: This is one of those timeshare things, isn't it? I continued with my set speech but it didn't feel good. Even they weren't the worst. The worst were the ones who stayed excited all the way through, who kept shouting to other members of their family, who said they'd never won anything before and that they couldn't believe it. When I told them about eating their dinners in the hotel every night, they just said, yes, yes, as if it was an insignificant detail, this meal they were agreeing to pay for at an unknown price. And the presentation they had to attend in order to collect their tickets, they were excited about that as well.

I imagined them arriving at some crappy conference centre for the presentation and then finally getting a twisty feeling in their stomach and thinking of the friends and neighbours they'd told about it and slinking away. I meant to ask one of the supervisors if, in the end, a single person had ever actually got to Spain, and had those two grim weeks of having an awful dinner in the hotel every fucking

night at some farcical price; but I didn't. The third day I just
went out for lunch and didn't come back.

It was the biggest fucking shitty job of all the jobs you
could imagine that weren't actually dangerous or involved
getting stuff on you. But there were compensations. You
didn't have to get up early or stay late. There was nothing
difficult. It was in London. The pay was crap but at five
seventy-five an hour times eight hours times five days times
the two weeks of a contract, that added up to four hundred
and sixty pounds. You're not exactly going to make massive
pension payments out of that, but it was a nice chunk of
money to get in your hand.

To be honest, though, I've got to admit that I'm a bit like
those lazy bastards who are not entirely against the idea of
getting double glazing. What they're against is the idea of
walking out of the house and arranging it for themselves.
They'll sit at home and if they never get the double glazing,
then there's all that money saved. If somebody rings and
suggests a free quote, then that's good too. All right, so they
haven't gone round the superstores of London and compared the different brands, but what's to compare? Don't
they all just keep the draughts out? What I always thought
of about double glazing was that when I was a kid, there
was a guy in a double-glazing ad and he'd stand in his
double-glazed house with a feather in his hand. There'd be
this helicopter going full blast on the lawn outside and he'd
drop his feather and it would flutter delicately to the floor.
See? he would say. It was meant to show how good the
double glazing was, even with a helicopter outside. But then

7

the guy in the commercial committed suicide. Not in the commercial itself. He killed himself in real life. They whipped the commercial off straight away. It's the strictest rule in TV. When someone in a commercial dies, they don't keep showing it as a tribute. They pull it instantly. But it was too late. I've associated double glazing with death ever since; violent death at that.

The point I was making is that I'm passive. There was a Chinese saying somebody told me once: if you sit by the river for long enough, the body of your enemy will float by. It takes some thinking about, but the basic meaning of it is that things will sort themselves out in the end. If you chill in your armchair for long enough, someone will phone you up and offer you double glazing.

At the end of a day of being glued to a headset and being paranoid about the idea that one of the managers was listening in to check we were being nice enough to the customers, most of the time everybody was just too shagged out to do anything and we all crawled away like victims of a disaster. But every so often we'd all go to the pub and one of the managers might buy you a drink and you were supposed to fall down on your knees in gratitude. This particular time we were in a pub that was down by the river and was consequently decorated with old oars and fishing nets and those wheels with knobs around the rim you steer boats with. I was talking to one of the managers, a gentleman called Selim. In fact, I mustn't misrepresent him. I must do justice to the full dignity of his title. His official designation, which you could read on a badge on his chest, was

Operational Systems Manager. As befitted his standing, he wore a grey suit and a sober tie. The rest of us were in all sorts: tracksuits, jeans, combat gear, shell suits, everything you could think of.

He bought me a pint and stuck to orange juice himself. He looked around the pub, which was crammed with the human debris of our shift. He shook his head.

'What a shower,' he muttered.

I just grunted something meaningless and sipped my beer. I had my own thoughts on the subject, but I wasn't going to share them with Selim.

'You're one of the better ones,' he said.

'That's not saying much.'

'What do you mean?'

'This isn't exactly the most motivated workforce of all time.'

'They do what we ask. But you do a bit better.'

'Have you been listening in?'

'We check the figures. Your figures aren't bad.'

'It's all just chance. It just depends which names you get. Skill doesn't come into it with those people who just swear at you and slam the phone down.'

'There's no such thing as chance,' said Selim. 'It all evens out in the long run. Who was the man who said, "A salesman is the only man who knows exactly what he's worth"?'

'A wanker,' I said, before I could stop myself. 'I'd like to see him working on our shift.'

Selim frowned. I don't think he liked bad language.

'You're too good for this job,' he said.

'I'm not.' I suddenly had this horrible feeling that he was going to offer me a proper job at CC5 Ltd, which was the name of the organization I was working for that fortnight. The idea was completely grotesque. When it came down to it, we were all in it for the money, what there was of it. That was the accepted deal. We didn't expect any favours or any respect from the company and they knew they weren't entitled to anything more than the bare minimum from us, the exploited proles. But the managers like Selim were an exception to this. They were like a cross between preachers and prison-camp guards. When they talked about phone manner or throughput they got a glow in their eyes like something in a horror film. I hurried to correct him.

'If you think I ought to stay on at CC5, then I'd better tell you . . .'

'No, no,' said Selim. 'I didn't mean that at all. I was just thinking that you're someone who ought to be thinking about a career. I mean this . . .' He looked around with an expression of distaste. He looked like a farmer surveying a crop that had failed utterly. 'You might as well be flipping burgers. You should think of the future. You can't build a career in this place.' He pulled another face. He had the most incredible repertory of disdainful faces. 'These call centres are going to be finished in a few years. They'll all be in India. They're a tenth of the price and you can find people who speak proper English.'

I took another sip of my beer and looked over Selim's

shoulder. There was an interesting-looking girl who worked three screens to the left and two down from me. Once or twice we'd caught each other's glances, raised eyebrows at each other to show how we were united in despising CC5 and everything it stood for, and I wanted to grab a word with her before she left the building.

'I've never really given much thought to my career,' I said.

'You should,' said Selim. 'How old are you, Mark? Twenty-four? Twenty-five?'

'Twenty-six.'

He gave a sharp intake of breath and shook his head.

'It may seem fun now,' he said. 'But it won't seem so much fun when you're thirty.'

'It's not that much fun now.'

'Of course not,' said Selim.

I was halfway down my beer and I should say straight away that I've not got much of a head for alcohol. I get very speedily disinhibited and I suddenly felt pissed off. I'd been pissed off pretty solidly for the previous week, but now I had someone to express it to.

'For example,' I said. 'Have you ever looked at this whatever it is we work in? I can't believe it was ever meant to be an office.'

'It was originally designed as a storage facility.'

'A storage facility, right. Well, it's a dump. Has CC5 ever thought of making it a moderately bearable place to work in?'

Sean French

'What for?' said Selim. 'Maybe it's meant to be a dump. If an office is too pleasant, then people get attached to it. They want to stay.'

'Wouldn't that be a good idea?'

'If they stay, you have to give them holidays and pay their pension. The company starts to depend on them, they depend on the company. That's not what CC5 is there to do.'

I drained my beer.

'This is starting to sound a bit too much like a committee meeting,' I said. 'And much as I'd like to stay and discuss company policy, there's someone I need to . . .'

'I've got a friend over at Wortley,' Selim said.

'What's that?'

'It's an insurance company. I've a friend who works there. Human resources. I put people in touch with him.'

'Sorry, Selim, I'm not interested.'

He took a card from the top pocket of his suit and handed it to me.

'Don't be an idiot, Mark. You'll be doing much the same work you're doing here and you'll be paid twice as much. And there are probably pot plants in the office. It's a good company.'

I sighed, one of those big sighs that he was meant to notice, and took the card and put it in my pocket. He gave me a fatherly pat on my shoulder and moved across the room to buy a drink for some other poor sod.

I did go over to the girl, my near-neighbour at CC5. She was even better looking without her telephonic apparatus wrapped around her head. She was called Julia and she let me buy her a drink. She was in conversation with someone who was obviously a complete no-hoper who she'd worked with a few contracts ago over in Limehouse. I talked to her about the awfulness of the CC5 office and she said it wasn't worse than the last few places she worked in. I asked where she lived. She said Harlesden. I said I lived in Balham. She said they were a long way apart. She was already calculating how long it would take for her to get from my place to her place. That was an especially good sign. I asked her what sort of things she got up to after work. She finished the last of her large gin and tonic and said that unfortunately she had to rush because she was meeting her boyfriend.

There ought to be rule that people should have to wear the information on their lapel badge to save wasting time. Julia Whatever, Call Operator, Has Boyfriend.

So I drew a blank there. But I did phone Selim's friend. I thought it might turn out to be some fake, but it didn't. He invited me to come over on the Monday my contract ended. I turned up at a huge modern building by London Wall. I expected it would be an aimless sort of chat but Selim's mate, Phil, had clearly done this before. He gave me a form to fill out and then a personality test. It looked more like an entrance exam for primary school. It was like three triangles and a square: which one is the odd one out? And there were psychological questions as well: If the man opposite you has a stain on his tie, do you a) tell him? b) ignore it? You find a five-pound note in the street. Do you a) keep it? b) hand it in to the police? I wanted to discuss the finer points of some

13

of these questions. For example, had anybody in history ever lost a five-pound note and then gone to a police station to report it missing? Phil told me just to fill out the form. Half an hour later he told me I had a job in the claims department of Wortley Insurance Ltd.

2

You still might have talked to me but this time it was definitely *you* who wanted something from *me*. The back wall of your house had fallen down. Your husband had tripped on the stairs and he was in a coma. You'd had a head-on collision in Reading, the car wouldn't move, it was pissing down with rain, you were in a blind panic and what the hell could you do? It was pretty depressing, if you stopped to think about it. Every call was the worst day of someone's year, or the worst day of their life. I then spoke to you in a calm voice. There was no trick to that. I didn't think there was anything morally wrong with it either. You weren't ringing up for somebody to start crying with you. There was a procedure. I would find an approved garage and they would come and get your car and give you another one and life would go on.

Selim was right. It was better. It was more human. There weren't just pot plants. There was a fluffy brown carpet and a coffee machine in the corner. There were posters on the wall of families with small children clutching furry pets, of houses, of cars. Mike, the Resource Supervisor, pointed them out to me. Look at them, Mark, he told me. They're what we're about. Downstairs there was a cafeteria. There'd been a cafeteria at CC5. Upstairs. We were downstairs, away from the light. But the cafeteria at CC5 didn't serve food. It was a space where you went with your sandwich and your bottle of water.

There were only a hundred and twenty of us in the room now, so we were a bit less like a termite colony and more like some slightly higher form of life. Rodents, maybe. There was a bit of a view, although because I was new I didn't get one of the good terminals by the window. I was in the middle. I was a good distance from the window but I got a look on my way over to my desk in the morning and on my way out in the evening and there wasn't much to see. Just office buildings opposite. But there was light, real light from the sun, and that reached me even in the middle of the office.

The most obvious difference was that we had to wear suits. When Mike told me this the first time we met, I made a token protest.

'We're on the phone all day,' I said. 'It wouldn't make any difference if we were naked. They wouldn't know.'

The problem with dealing with Mike was that he had a procedure. He was like me when I was back working the call centres. You're given a line for everything.

'But *you* would know,' he said. 'When you're on our time, you're representing Wortley Insurance. The customer-service agents in the claims department are as much representative of Wortley as the Chief Executive. Perhaps more so. For the customer who requires our services, you are the voice of

Wortley. And I believe that deep down, the customer knows if you're dressed for business. Also, we constantly have customers and business partners visiting our premises and we don't want them wandering in here and finding you all dressed for the beach.'

'I was just asking,' I said. 'I don't mind wearing a suit.'

And my starting salary at Wortley was almost twice what I'd been earning before. Twenty grand, five weeks' holiday, and for basically doing the same job. Easier, if anything, because I wasn't trying to hassle people about things they weren't interested in and I didn't have to meet some ridiculous throughput target day after day. A guy two rows along told me about a bedsit over between Camden Town and King's Cross, so I was able to move my clothes and my music out of my Balham shithole. It was great. There I was, working the phones from nine to five-thirty, with overtime on the weekend whenever I wanted. After a fortnight I could do the job in my sleep and I was back to sitting on the bank of the river, waiting for a body to float by.

Telephone sweatshops are a good place for meeting women. For a start, women make up about two-thirds of the staff. Mike said it was about communication skills and empathy. Sometimes when he was in his preacher mode he would urge the male staff to cultivate their female side. There'd generally be a guffaw at the back. When our customers call us in their time of trouble, he would say, remember, you are their best friend, you're the neighbour over the fence, you're their old mother, you're the good Samaritan who doesn't pass by on the other side. These people don't have friends to turn to, most of them. You're their friend. It was quite moving, from some points of view.

Two rows to my right and one back was Sonia. Like every woman in the room, she wore a suit with a skirt, not trousers; and like most of the women, she had her hair tied back tightly, in a bun; and like quite a lot of the women there, she wore black stockings. I guess you could add a third reason for wearing a suit to Mike's two, which was to take all of our minds off the subject of sex and sexual attraction. But these incredibly severe uniforms had completely the opposite effect on me, especially when I was going through the usual checklist of paint damage and witnesses and the other party's insurance details. It gave me something to look at.

Sonia had light-brown hair and pale skin. She blushed easily, or at least when she blushed it showed vividly on her cheeks. I saw this the first time that I caught her eye. She had a soft voice, so most of the time I couldn't hear her talking on the phone. But this time Chas, who occupied the terminal on what you might call the hypotenuse between us, was out of the office, and that afternoon she got into a long and involved conversation. Even though I was taking call after call, I quickly gathered that she was dealing with a sewage problem. A raw-sewage problem. We saw a lot of that. In my first week with Wortley there was flooding in a village in Worcestershire. The drains got backed up and raw sewage was ejected onto the High Street and into people's homes. That basically means turds and bog paper and probably tampons and whatever else people shove down their toilets. The expression 'raw sewage' is meant to stop you thinking of the turds but for me the word 'raw' just got me thinking about things you cook and eat, and I'd rather have just thought about the turds.

Sonia was talking to a householder who was having a major raw-sewage problem. There were new carpets and there was furniture and a dog and raw sewage everywhere. Sonia was trying to take down the exhaustive details, but the customer was apparently in a confused state and Sonia kept having to read passages back over the phone. At first she tried to do this in a mumble but apparently the customer was deaf or it was a bad line and she was clearly being constantly told to speak up, and so this quiet-voiced young lady was having to virtually shout about spreading brown stains and putrescence and faecal matter and unidentified objects floating through the door.

She was looking round guiltily and I caught her eye and smiled and I saw that she was blushing like a demonstration in a biology lesson of what blushing involves. A purple stain was spreading across her cheeks. She looked away.

One of the benefits of a real cafeteria was that it was a way of meeting your workmates, sitting down next to them with your tray and starting to chat. Our exchange of glances had given me a classic opening line. You've probably already worked it out for yourself. The next day I saw her sitting at a table with a friend. I came across and asked if the seat next to her was taken. She said it wasn't.

'Hi,' I said. 'We're almost neighbours.'

'Oh, yes,' she said.

'I really like it when you talk dirty.'

She looked startled.

'What are you talking about?' she said, glancing over at the woman opposite her, who looked puzzled as well. 'What do you mean?'

Like virtually all classic opening lines, it was a complete disaster. I had to embark on a ridiculously laborious explanation of how I'd overheard her conversation about the sewage.

'Oh, that?' she said, not smiling at the memory. 'Yes, it was pretty tricky. The man we did the insurance with had a heart attack last week. He's in intensive care. I had to talk it all through with his wife and she was in a very distressed state.'

'Which makes it even less funny,' I said.

'What?' she said.

'Not that it was even funny in the first place. I guess it's not possible for something to be less funny than not funny at all.'

It wasn't apparently going well, but at least we were talking and I painfully managed to steer the conversation into another direction about how I was still quite new to the company and I asked her how long she had been there and then we were away.

The point of the body in the river is that it's not entirely about sitting on the bank and doing nothing. Lots of strange

things drift down rivers, and you have to recognize the body
when it floats past. For that moment, I have to move forward
four or five weeks. It was a rainy Sunday morning and I
was lying in the bed of my now not-so-new Camden flat
with Sonia Vaughan. She was pale all over her body, as if
she'd never been out into the sun. The nipples on her small
breasts stood out, although they were only the lightest of
pinks. Her pubic hair was a shock of red, quite different
from the hair on her head.

Her skin fascinated me. There was something very
slightly creepy about it. I thought of veal calves that were
reared in the darkness and lapped desperately at the bars of
their cages because they were so desperate for the iron that
was withheld from their diet. I thought of baby mice, when
they are just born and haven't opened their eyes and have
no fur, just that naked pink skin. There was nothing creepy
about Sonia herself. Out of the office, out of her suit, she
wasn't quiet or shy or disapproving. She smoked and drank
and had a gang of friends.

But even now in the closing stages of our relationship –
she didn't know that they were the closing stages, by the
way – even now I loved stroking that impossibly smooth,
soft skin and thinking that one day soon I would never be
able to have that sensation again.

The original plan had been that we would get up and go
to the market but the rain was splattering on the window as
if we were driving into it, so I got up and made some coffee
and toast and brought it back to bed where she was lying
half asleep. I found that odd. She looked so efficient and

brisk in the office at her screen, but in the morning in my bed she looked as if she was made of dough.

'Mmmm,' she said, biting off a piece of toast and then taking a gulp of coffee before she'd swallowed it. 'That's nice of you. Take your dressing gown off. Get back into bed.'

'When I've drunk my coffee,' I said. 'I'm cold.'

'I'll warm you up.'

'When you've finished your coffee.'

'You sound quite prim when you say that.'

'I'm not,' I said.

'You're worried that I'll spill coffee on your bed.'

'I wouldn't say I'm worried about it. I mean, worry's not exactly the right word.'

We munched the toast and sipped coffee in silence for a moment. I looked round and caught Sonia looking at me.

'What's that?' I said.

'What?'

'You were looking at me with a suspicious expression.'

'I was thinking about you.'

I wasn't sure I liked the sound of that.

'What were you thinking?'

'I was thinking about what you ought to do. I mean at work.'

'Is there something I'm doing wrong?'

'Not really, but that's not what you want to be doing: sitting at a desk handling claims all day.'

'What's wrong with it?'

'Aren't you ambitious?'

'No. I'm happy with what I'm doing. The job is a doss and I get well paid. Look at this flat. You should have seen the pit I had in Balham. You wouldn't have enjoyed lying in bed in that place on a Sunday morning.'

'You should go and see someone.'

'You mean a doctor?'

'Stupid. Someone in management. Go and tell them you want to do something better.'

I thought for a moment. This wasn't what I'd planned at all.

'Why don't *you*?' I said.

'I don't want anything better. In about six months I'm going to save up some money and then I'm out of here. I'm going to do some travelling.'

I took the mugs and plates over to the sink. Sonia was impressively undomesticated. In a month, I'd literally never even seen her rinse out a mug. I came back to the bed and she pulled my dressing gown off me, giggling because the cord had become all tangled.

'You see,' I said, 'the problem is that I've never thought of myself as working for an insurance company.'

'Shut up,' she said, and ran her hands down my chest. 'Do you want to talk about insurance or do you want to fuck?'

'Fuck,' I said.

And we did. It was that good morning sex where you seem to feel it all more than you do at night. Except that about halfway through I started to imagine that I was with Christine, a girl whose monitor is about three rows behind

23

Sonia. She was larger than Sonia, with bigger breasts, and I thought how different it would feel if I were fucking her. Then I became paranoid that I would call Sonia Christine. Maybe I already had. I got so worried that when I came, I didn't use her name at all, just moaned something unintelligible.

'So you reckon I should talk to Mike?' I said afterwards.

'What? Oh, that? No, don't bother with him. He's got no power. He just wants to keep the phones working.'

I leaned over and stroked the skin on her stomach and on the underside of her breast. That skin, where it was softest.

'Should I get in touch with human resources? I could apply for some managerial job.' She started laughing. 'What?'

'I can't believe I'm having this conversation,' she said. 'I should have kept my mouth shut.' She took my hand firmly. 'Look. Show some initiative. Find someone in management who's got some power and go and bang on their door.'

'What? Really?'

'Try it. Either they'll kick you out and forget about you or they might be impressed. Oh, there's one other thing.'

'What's that?'

'I think I'm falling in love with you.'

It took me a bit of time to make sense of what she'd said. I wasn't prepared. My brain was still expecting careers advice. When my brain finally did compute, it said to itself: Oh, shit. I said nothing.

'Sorry,' she said. 'I shouldn't have said that.'

I still didn't reply.

'I can't believe it's a big shock. We've been together enough.'

I had to say something.

'I wanted to talk about that,' I said. 'I've noticed the stuff in the bathroom. The toothbrush, that stuff in the cupboard. Your knickers in the drawer.'

'Is there a problem?' she said. 'I've been staying overnight. What am I meant to do in the morning?'

'We should have talked about it,' I said. 'It's like you're secretly moving in. Suddenly you'll be there.'

'And wouldn't *that* be awful,' she said. She gave a huge gulp and I saw that her eyes were glistening.

Quite suddenly she threw the cover back and got out of the bed. I looked at her pale, slim body and it made me ache for her more than at any time since we'd met. It took a serious effort not to stop her and say it was all right.

'It'll only take a few minutes to get it all,' she said as she put her bra on before her knickers. It seemed an oddly loveable, intimate thing to do, to be shouting at me while reaching behind to fasten the clip. She went to my drawer and pulled out a pair of knickers, brandished them at me as if it signified something, and then pulled them on. I watched her put on her jeans and a T-shirt and a pullover. She had to sit on the bed to pull on her socks and shoes. Then she was in the bathroom, rattling things loudly as they were thrown into a plastic shopping bag.

She came back into the bedroom. She had a bag over her shoulder.

'I think that's everything,' she said, then stopped, searching for words. 'You . . .' I thought she was going to say something rude but she didn't. 'I'm sorry,' she said. 'It was probably my fault. I was probably pushing too hard. I always seem to, I . . .'

She choked and wasn't able to say anything. She looked so sad and lovely and I thought of her on the phone talking about shit and I wanted to say something of comfort to her, but mainly, of course, I wanted her to go. I just managed a sort of shrug and she went.

At this point, of course, the proximity was a problem. But Sonia was a woman who could show determination on her own behalf, as well as mine. When I came in to work the next day, she had already managed to swap terminals with a rather striking Asian woman called Meera and she was far, far away to the north-east.

3

The eighth floor smelled of money. It might as well have been lying around in piles on the floor. Everything was better than on the second floor. Things you wouldn't think it was possible to be better. Better door handles and magazine racks. There weren't normal offices either. The minions were dotted around in a semi-open-plan way, but the executives were around the edge in offices. Even these had glass walls. You'd have to go to the executive washroom to pick your nose. It would probably be worth it, though.

I walked around the perimeter, trying to look as if I knew where I was going. I came to the door I was looking for. Darryl Wingate. Divisional Manager – Underwriting. This was one of the good offices, on the corner, wall-to-wall windows. It was such a good office that there was a sort of pre-office you had to go through to get to it, a filter, to filter out people like me. A woman was sitting at a desk. Wingate's secretary, except that she was probably called something like an executive personal assistant. She was very neatly dressed. She wore a patterned scarf fastened around her neck with a little gold clasp, the sort that air stewardesses wear.

27

'Hello, can I help you?'

'I'm Mark Foll,' I said. 'I'd like to see Mr Wingate.'

'Have you got an appointment?'

She knew I didn't have an appointment. She had the appointment book. She *was* the appointment book.

'I work downstairs. I just wanted to have a quick word with Mr Wingate. It'll only take a minute.'

'Mr Wingate is in a meeting.'

'I'll wait and then it'll just take a minute.'

'Mr Wingate is leaving for another meeting immediately afterwards.'

'I could talk to him very briefly just between the two meetings.'

'That's quite impossible. Really, what is it you want, Mr . . .'

'Foll,' I said. 'Mark Foll.'

My palms were starting to sweat and I had an impulse to murmur an apology and leg it back down to the second floor. But it had taken me days and days of steeling myself and daring myself to get this far. I had to stick it out. On the other hand, I'd told the floor supervisor downstairs that I was going to the toilet. There was a limit to how long I could be gone. If I was much longer they'd send dogs out for me. Then the inner door opened and two people stepped out. The first was a woman who looked about my own age, maybe even younger. She wore a dark suit with a skirt, black shoes. So far, so like virtually every other woman in the building, but her hair wasn't tied back in any way. It was blonde and so fine it would have been hard to tie up.

And she wore glasses, but it took a second to spot them because they were the narrow kind, without any frames.

Behind her, escorting her out, was the man I took to be Wingate. He was older, with greying hair and a greying face. His jacket was off and so I got a clear view of his shirt, which was striped, like a pyjama jacket. It shimmered painfully. No tie in the world would have gone with that. His didn't. It just floated in front of it in a hopeful sort of way.

'So is it daughter's day?' I said.

He looked round and noticed me for the first time.

'What?' he said.

That was meant to be an ice-breaker and we were meant to then go on to discuss my future career prospects. But there was an awesome silence. I clearly had to expand on my comment.

'You know, daughter's day,' I said. 'When I was at school, they had a day every year when fathers brought their daughters to work with them. Kind of to encourage them. A feminist thing.'

Wingate and the woman looked at each other in some sort of disbelief.

'I know what daughter's day is, but did you mean . . .?' He looked at the woman again. 'Who are you?'

'Foll,' I said. 'Mark Foll.'

'Yes?'

'I work in claims. On the phones.'

'You're on the wrong floor,' Wingate said. 'You need to take the lift back to the second floor.'

'No, no,' I said. 'I wanted to see you. I want to talk to you.'

'What about?'

'I thought maybe when you two are all done, we could talk.'

'Can I introduce you to Donna Kiely?'

'Hi, Donna.'

I held my hand out. She didn't take it.

'She's our General Manager.'

'That sounds important.'

'Important?' said Wingate. He'd gone a bit red in the face. 'What did you say your name was?'

'Foll,' I said. 'Mark Foll. Claims department.'

'Wait there,' he said and retreated into his office. I heard the sound of him talking on the phone. This was a bit awkward, just me and Donna and Wingate's grumpy assistant standing in an office without much to say to each other. I hate silences. I have to fill them.

'Probably gone to call security,' I said. 'They can't throw me out. I work here.'

She didn't say anything. Fortunately Wingate came back in.

'I just phoned claims.'

'See?'

'The supervisor told me you'd gone to the toilet.'

'Yes, that's right. You see, I had this problem. I wanted to come and see you. But if I did it out of hours, or at lunchtime, you wouldn't be here. But if I did it in office hours, I'd have to explain why I was coming to see you.'

'And why are you coming to see me?'

'You mean you want me to tell you now?'

'Yes.'

'What? Now?'

I looked at Donna Kiely. She was biting her lip. One of those nervous habits.

'Yes, now.'

'It'll sound a bit stark.'

'Stark?'

'Stark. Too stark.'

'Just tell me. Or go away.'

'I want to have a more interesting job.'

When I had gone over this scene in my mind in the preceding days I had imagined various kinds of reaction and I'd planned responses accordingly. But I didn't expect what happened. There was an explosion next to me. Donna was laughing. It took some time for her to be able to speak.

'Are you for real?' she said finally.

'What?'

'Did the guys in the office hire you? Are you suddenly going to start singing or take your clothes off?'

'No,' I said. My cheeks were starting to feel hot. I wondered if I was making a complete idiot of myself. Was this going to be a funny story she'd tell? This buffoon who walked in without an appointment and talked crap.

'This is the way you apply for a promotion, is it?'

'I want to do something different.'

There was a silence. I could see Wingate's jaw flexing, about one flex a second.

'How long have you worked here?'

'Just over two months.'

Wingate gave something between a snort and a sigh.

'Two months?'

'A bit more.'

'Have you thought of talking to your supervisor?'

'What can he do?'

'He's your bloody boss.' He glanced across at Donna. 'Sorry. Shall I sack him or just chuck him out of the window?'

'What for?' I protested.

'For being an idiot.'

'Look, I was just asking.'

Various glances were exchanged. Wingate's assistant had long since sat back down at her desk and was pretending to be getting on with some work. I saw Donna nod at Wingate.

'Talk to him,' she said. 'It took some nerve to come up here.'

'Fine,' said Wingate. 'Fine. Come on through.' He looked at Donna. 'Shall I catch you later?'

'I'll sit in, if that's all right. I don't want to miss this.'

'Fine, fine, let's have everybody in. Margaret?' His assistant looked round. 'Could you call down to claims? They may think that Mr Foll is having some sort of medical emergency. Tell them he's here.'

We processed through. It was great. It felt like I'd won something. The view from Wingate's office was fantastic.

'Is that the real London Wall?'

'What?' said Wingate.

'Out there. I guess that London Wall means the old city wall. I wondered if that was part of it.'

'I don't know,' he said. 'Now, could you sit down there?'

I sat in a chair that directly faced Wingate's desk. Donna sat on the sofa by the wall, out of my eye line. Wingate picked up a pen and tapped it on a notepad. It gave a muffled, unsatisfactory sound.

'So?' he said. 'What have you to say? Or do you just want me to give you a better job?'

'No, I've been thinking about it. I deal with claims over the phone. You know, little crashes, fires, things spilled on carpets. Not factories being burned down, nothing big like that. But anyway, even over the phone, just talking to these people, it's obvious that about a quarter of the claims are pretty dodgy and about half of those are bloody dodgy.'

'That's no problem,' said Wingate. 'If a claim is false, we don't pay out on it.'

'It is a problem. What I'm saying is that there's a whiff of dodginess about it. I mean, I can't tell over the phone that they've deliberately tipped the coffee over an old rug so that they can buy a new one. Or that a bike that they say has been lifted from the shed was actually given to their nephew for Christmas. I'd have to go there and look. What I'm saying is that I could guarantee to save this company more than my yearly salary.'

Wingate had a very slight smile on his face, but at least now it wasn't a bastard smile. It was more like amused.

'How would you do that?'

'Instead of just sitting in the office settling the claims over

33

the phone, I could go over and take a look. I can absolutely guarantee that five, ten per cent of claims would just collapse if I put my head round the door.'

Wingate stopped tapping his pen and started drawing a circle on his pad.

'I'm sure you would, Mark. I'm sure you know as well that this is an idea that's occurred to people before. We have claims assessors who do exactly that.'

'Yes, but I'm talking about the claims I deal with over the phone. Nobody checks those.'

'I don't want to get bogged down in a discussion about procedure, Mark, but I think some of the claims are assessed. We send someone round to check car repairs. And I assume that your supervisor selects some of the claims for further assessment.'

'But what have you got to lose from the offer?' I said.

Now Donna spoke for the first time.

'What about the people you piss off who are making genuine claims?'

'They'll get their money.'

'You're the only person they'll ever meet from Wortley, and you've been snooping around making them feel bad. They might renew with someone who won't hassle them.'

'There'll just be a few.'

'Also, there is a certain percentage of people who treat a few minor claims as a perk of the policy.'

'That's dishonest.'

'Maybe. But we factor it into our charges. Do we lose them as well?'

'I don't know.'

'And then there's the cost of you traipsing around London like Sam Spade. How many cases could you investigate in a day? Four, maybe? Instead of forty. So as well as paying you, we have to pay someone to do your job while you're on the road losing us customers. Does that sound like a good deal for us?'

I thought Donna was wonderful. I was completely in love with her.

'There's two sides to it, of course,' I conceded.

Donna leaned back in her sofa, looking relaxed, having made her point. She had surprisingly large breasts for such a slim woman. Large eyes as well, behind those rather snazzy glasses. It made her expressions very appealing, even when they were disapproving ones.

'I'm sure there are other things I could do,' I said.

Wingate put some very severe-looking steel-framed glasses on and looked at me over them.

'What sort of qualifications have you got?'

'The usual, a degree.'

'In?'

'Business studies.'

He gave a snort.

'Where?'

'You wouldn't have heard of it.'

'Try me.'

'Cleoford University.'

'Cleoford?'

'You wouldn't have heard of it,' I said. 'It's in Shropshire.

It's not very good. But look, Mr Wingate, this business isn't about what you know.'

'What the hell are you talking about? This business is entirely about what you know.'

'I meant to say that this business isn't about *who* you know.'

'Really? Mr Foll, I think that the first thing you should be aware of, as Ms Kiely said, is that the claims department is the friend of our policy-holders. We're not trying to put them in prison or cheat them out of their money.'

'I appreciate that . . .'

'We're not a branch of the legal system, we're a proprietary insurance company. Do you know what that means?'

'Not exactly.'

'Well, you bloody well ought to. It means we have shareholders. Do you know what that means?'

'What?'

'I'm saying this with my boss sitting over on the sofa, so you'd better believe me. Wortley Insurance Ltd has one duty above all. Do you know what that is?'

I felt like I was trapped in a nightmarish unending exam. But I couldn't just say no to everything. Anyway, I knew this one.

'To sell insurance.'

'No, it is not. Our main duty is to maximize shareholder value. Nothing else matters. I don't know what I'm doing here having this conversation. I was going to say that we do have a career path in this department, with mentoring and

36

in-house training and CII but I would literally stake the life of my children that you have no idea what that stands for.'

'Something insurance,' I said.

'Brilliant,' he said. 'Mr Foll, do you know anything at all about insurance?'

'I'm sorry,' I said. 'But I didn't come here to have an argument. And I know I'm not an accountancy expert. Basically I'm just sick of talking on the phone all day. I wanted to have more fun.'

'Fun?'

'It should be fun. Well, it should, shouldn't it? Miss Kiely, do you have fun?'

She was biting her lip again.

'Yes, Mark,' she said. 'I think I have fun. What about you, Darryl? Do you have fun?'

'Some of the time,' he said, but not looking as if he meant it.

'It should be exciting,' I said, feeling that things were finally going my way. 'Because what we're doing is calculating that, as a whole, the risk they're all facing isn't as serious as they think. So they are paying us just a bit too much money to be safe, and we make a profit.'

There was a pause now. Wingate was screwing his face up in concentration.

'No,' he said. 'That's not true. You've got it completely wrong. What we're doing is spreading risk. Everybody benefits from this. Look, it's . . . well, look, I'll tell him the pig story.' He looked at Donna. 'You know the pig story?' She rolled her eyes. Clearly she knew the pig story. 'I was told this story on my very first insurance course. There were eleven men and they each owned a pig. One of the pigs suddenly died. The man couldn't afford the ninety pounds to buy a new pig so he gave it all up and went and got a job somewhere else. So the remaining ten men went to see a wise man. They told him about the dead pig and they were worried it could happen to any of them, so what could they do? He asked if they could afford ten pounds for a new pig. They said yes, so he made the following proposal: "All right, each give me ten pounds. If one of your pigs dies in the next year, I'll buy a new pig." They all said yes to that. In the next year one of the pigs did die. So the wise man bought a new pig to replace it. That man had a nice new pig for his ten pounds. He hadn't lost anything. The wise man had made a profit of ten pounds. So nobody suffered. Except for the pig.'

'And the other men,' I said.

'What do you mean?'

'Nine of the men paid their ten pounds and didn't get anything for it.'

'They got peace of mind.'

'What if two pigs had died? Did the wise man have enough money for that?'

'That was his risk.'

'What if there had been an outbreak of swine fever and they'd all died? He wouldn't have looked so wise then.'

'It's just a story, that's not really the point.'

'I hope he checked up on the pig.'

'What?'

'The man might have been tempted to sell the pig, slaughter it and then get the insurance as well. If the man were really wise, he'd insist on getting the dead pig.'

'Shall we leave the fucking pig story?' Wingate looked over at Donna. 'I'm sorry.'

Donna smiled.

'Why don't you send him out with Giles?'

'Giles?' said Wingate. 'Are you sure?'

'It would get Mark out of the office. If that's what he wants.'

'Great,' I said. 'That's great. Who's Giles?'

Wingate gave a great grunt. He held up his hands in some sort of surrender.

'All right, all right,' he said. 'I'll phone him.' Donna stood up and nodded at him and left the room. He looked back at me. 'Mark, go back downstairs. We'll be in touch. It'll be a couple of days.'

'Thank you,' I said. 'That's so great. That's fantastic. Thank you so much.'

'Just go,' he said, but then gestured to me to wait. 'One moment. Daughter's day? She's only about three years younger than me.'

'It was just a joke.'

'Go.'

As I closed Wingate's door, I saw that Donna was still there, signing something for Margaret. We stepped out into the corridor at the same moment. This was just so my lucky day, I couldn't stop myself.

'Thanks so much, Miss Kiely,' I said. 'I'm really grateful.'

'Good,' she said, and turned away.

'By the way . . .'

'Yes.'

'I wondered if we could maybe meet for a drink. You know, to talk about it. You could tell me about things. Maybe.'

To do her credit, she didn't flinch. She didn't change expression at all. So I couldn't tell at all what she was going to say.

'Are you insane?' she said. 'Are you hitting on me? Here? After that?'

'It was just a drink.'

'I'll tell you what,' she said. 'Maybe you could babysit for me and I could go out for a drink with my husband. It's *Ms* Kiely, by the way.'

'That would be a possibility.'

'Except that after that performance in there, I'm giving you a go with Giles, but if you think I'd let a chancer like you be in charge of my children . . .'

And she was gone. She was ten times more beautiful, even than she'd been back there in Wingate's office.

4

When I came back to the sweatshop on the second floor, it looked different. A dial had been turned down so that the colours were dimmer. It was just a bit out of focus. I sat down at my terminal, put my headset on, took the first call and, in the best way, I felt a little drunk and I could see that everybody else was stone cold boring sober. Suddenly the job was fun because I knew that in a week's time I'd be gone and everybody else wouldn't and some other poor bastard would be sitting in this chair.

At the end of the day I made sure to finish just a little bit early so that I could see Sonia on the way out. I caught her by the arm.

'I did what you said.'

'What do you mean?' she said.

'I did it, I did what you said. I went to see Darryl Wingate. And this woman, Donna, was there. She's very high up.'

'What did they say?'

'It was great. It worked out really well. They've arranged this other job for me. I'm going out on the road with someone.'

'That's great, Mark. I'm really happy for you.'

She turned and left me there. It hadn't been the way I thought it would be. I thought she'd either give me a big hug and say she was proud of me and let's go and have a drink to celebrate. Or else that she would flare up and make a scene. I'd looked at her face to see some signs of grief. Bloodshot eyes or perhaps gaunt, hollowed cheeks as a sign that she'd been starving herself. She looked just the same as ever. Her manner had gone all the way back to the way it was to that first meeting in the cafeteria. A bit more disdainful, perhaps. Were her cheekbones just a little bit more pronounced than normal? For some reason I hadn't noticed before what a striking face she had, like a smoothly sanded mask made out of white clay. That was what made the blushing so visible. I'd noticed the blushing. I hadn't noticed the face. Funny that, with all the time we had spent naked together. In fact we had spent almost all our relationship in bed. During that fairly short period we'd sometimes vaguely planned to go out to a club or a movie but it always seemed simpler to miss out the middle bit and go straight to bed. That's what I should have said to Sonia when she said she loved me. That's one of my problems. I'm always either blurting out the thing I shouldn't have said or else about three days later suddenly remembering what I really meant to say. It's just that Sonia threw me when she talked about loving me. I did have a feeling that she was going to say something big but I thought it was going to be that we should go away for the weekend or that I should meet some of her friends. Love was something else altogether.

What I would have said if I'd managed to gather my

thoughts and had about an hour of preparation is that we couldn't say we loved each other because we'd never had a conversation. That sounds stupid but I think it's almost completely true. We had that misfired talk in the cafeteria with my classic line. We must have made arrangements on the phone. See you at eight, that sort of thing. But the funny thing is that looking back I was unable to remember a single thing she'd said. I don't mean a single clever or funny or emotional thing, I mean a single thing. I should have said: How can we be in love when we've never talked? Except that might have seemed crueller than saying nothing. I don't know. I don't know about these things. It generally seems to work out fairly badly either way.

What I remembered was her body, that soft white skin that wasn't like anything I'd ever felt before. And the odd thing is that I started to forget that as well. I'd thought so much about the whiteness and the softness that the Sonia-ness, the skinness, whatever, just got lost. I could feel it running through my fingers and then it was gone. So I was just left with some ridiculous memory of whiteness and softness, like a commercial for something.

Anyway, who knows what we would have found out if we had really talked? Maybe she would have turned out to be incredibly boring or she would have started telling long, unfunny jokes. I knew someone like that. She was called Angela, and until I went out with Angela I thought it was only men who told jokes all the time. I wish I couldn't remember anything Angela had ever said.

In general, my last days in telephone claims were not a

massive success. I don't want to give the impression that I was expecting tears and leaving presents and a party with bunting and balloons. The turnover in that room was pretty constant and most people in the room didn't know I'd arrived. There were a few people I saw for a drink, a few others I sat with in the cafeteria, a couple of people I nodded to occasionally and couldn't quite remember their names. Probably the only person who cared one way or the other was Sonia and she would just be glad to get me out of her eye line. Because even though she had moved way away behind me, when I looked in that direction there was still a clear line of sight through about forty terminals. It was a geometric freak, like an eclipse.

Then there was Mike. On Friday afternoon I was on the phone as usual settling a complicated motor claim. Our client had been driven into from behind by a woman on the school run in a four-wheel-drive job with one of those ridiculous grilles on the front that is designed to fend off herds of water bison or something. The grille had remained immaculate but the rear of our client's Saab had been mashed. It should all have been completely simple. One of the cast-iron laws of insurance is that the person in the car behind is always wrong. And the woman behind, being a nice woman, had admitted responsibility anyway, so it should all have been settled straight away. But the car had been towed to the nearest garage, which wasn't approved, and they'd started work on the bodywork already without a proper quote, so it took a bit of straightening out.

As I was winding it all up, I saw that Mike the supervisor

was standing over me. I knew that on a fairly random basis, the company's secret police listened in on our phone calls, which must have been the world's most tedious job. But it was a bit off-putting to have your supervisor eyeballing you while you're trying to make arrangements with an apprentice panel beater in deepest Somerset. Finally I replaced the receiver and Mike still hadn't moved. Didn't he have a job to do?

'It was a complicated thing,' I said. 'You don't want to hear about it.'

'Congratulations on your change of job,' he said.

'Thanks, Mike,' I said.

'Why didn't you tell me about it?'

It was a bit sad, really. Mike wanted to know why I hadn't told him that I wasn't happy in the department. We could have discussed it and sorted the problems out. I was going to say that I didn't want to sort my problems out. I didn't have any problems. I just wanted to work somewhere different. He went on to tell me that it didn't make him look good, someone from his department going over his head and saying they weren't happy.

I couldn't take all this suffering and guilt. First there was Sonia and now I had rejected Mike's little kingdom and undermined him in the hierarchy.

'I'm tired of just hearing voices on the phone,' I said. 'I want to go out into the world and actually meet some people.'

'We'll see,' said Mike, sounding angry and sarcastic now, instead of pathetic, which was easier for us both to handle.

45

'Customers have only had to hear your voice up to now. We'll see what happens when they have to see your ugly mug as well.' With that he was going to march off but then he stopped. 'I forgot. You report to Giles Buckland on Monday morning. Eight-thirty. Third floor.'

'Wanker,' I said. But very much under my breath and when he was about ten yards away with his back to me. You never know who can lip-read.

5

One of the things about all these offices with glass walls is that it presumably provides some incentive to keep them moderately tidy. But this clearly hadn't worked with Giles Buckland. His office was staggering. I had arrived at twenty minutes past eight, just to be sure, and I didn't even think of going inside. I couldn't see any floor. Where a floor should have been, it looked like a model of downtown Hong Kong constructed out of piles of books and files and envelopes. I looked around and I could see only one area of neatness. On the wall there was a shelf with very expensive-looking hardback books: *Charlesworth's Mercantile Law*, *Tables for Assured Lives*, *Witherby's Dictionary of Insurance*, *Legal Aspects of Insurance*. They were glowing and new and looked entirely untouched.

'You're admiring my office,' a voice said behind me.

I looked round and saw a man who looked about forty. He was carrying a shoulder bag under his arm. The broken strap was trailing behind him. He was wearing a dark-blue suit and a tie, but it looked as if he had made an effort not to. The tie was pulled down loosely and although the man was quite big, the suit was bigger. He had a big face as well.

Everything about Giles Buckland – because it was obviously him – was large. Large hands, brown hair flapping down over his forehead.

'Dr Foll, I presume.'

'What? I'm not a doctor.'

'I do not love thee, Dr Foll. The reason why I cannot . . .' He paused. 'I'll have to think about that one. You were looking at my office. You think it's the most disorganized room you've ever seen.'

'I don't know about *ever*,' I said cautiously.

'Did you know that some people say that bebop was invented by jazzmen who wanted a kind of music that white musicians couldn't steal?'

'I've never listened to jazz.'

' "They can't steal it if they can't play it." That's like my office. They can't interfere with my work if they can't get into my office.'

'Who's "they"?'

'I don't know. Them. The suits. But there is a way in. Look.'

It was actually pretty impressive. With a sort of balletic delicacy Buckland tiptoed through the chaos and reached his desk without toppling a single pile. He turned around and leaned back on his desk.

'Have you heard of Hereward the Wake?'

'No.'

'He was a Saxon prince. He retreated into the East Anglian fens to escape William the Conqueror. There was only one route to his refuge. But he was betrayed by a monk, who led

his enemies along that secret route, and Hereward was killed.
Are you that monk, Mr Foll?'

'Mark.'

'Are you that monk, Mark?'

'I don't really . . .'

'Never mind. Never mind. This all looks disordered but it
is actually an organic arrangement. I can put my finger on
any document within seconds.'

He rummaged around on his desk and grabbed what
looked like a small desk diary and slid it into his jacket
pocket. Then he tiptoed back across his office. I wasn't sure
if I ought to look or not.

'I'm Giles Buckland,' he said, holding out his hand.

'Yes, I know.'

'Have you brought sandwiches?'

'No. Nobody said.'

'Oh,' he said.

'Have you got any?'

'Yes, but those are for me.'

'I didn't mean that. I guess I can buy some.'

'Maybe,' Giles said. 'It depends where we end up.'

Giles sounded mysterious but it isn't as if we were going
up the Amazon. We weren't going to a world without sandwich bars.

'Where are we going?'

'I don't know yet.'

'I don't normally have much lunch.'

'Then there's nothing to worry about.'

There was a slightly awkward silence.

'So what do we do?'

Giles didn't answer immediately but looked at me with narrowed, suspicious eyes.

'I wonder why they sent you to me? Did you do something wrong?'

'No.'

'I'm not a mentor, you see. They only sent one person before. It didn't work out. After a week he asked to be moved.'

'What happened?'

'He was an ambitious man, I think. He kept talking about the fast track.' Giles suddenly looked cheerful. 'I don't think he thought this was the fast track.'

'I said I wanted to have fun. Maybe they wanted to punish me for that.'

'Fun?' said Giles, now looking very thoughtful. Almost tragic. 'You're going to see life at its very worst. Widows, fires, atrocious crimes, floods, infestations. I can't promise you fun.'

'I didn't really mean fun. I wanted to get out and meet people.'

'All right. We'll pop up the corridor and collect the claims files and then we'll go out and meet some people.'

'Just like that?' I said.

'Why? Is that a problem?'

'Aren't you going to teach me anything?'

Giles looked completely stumped. He ran his fingers through his hair.

'No, I don't think so. It's all pretty obvious, really.'

Giles led me down to the car park where we got into his incredibly smart silver executive-style BMW that was completely at odds with him and his office and everything about him. He seemed puzzled by it himself.

'They give me a new one every year. I'm the face of the company. Did they tell you that?'

'They didn't say what you were.'

'We're the interface between Wortley and the general public. We're the policy-holder's friends.' He fastened the top button of his shirt and then pulled up his tie. It was a slight improvement. 'Get in, get in.'

Giles was a better driver than I had expected. It's just that he seemed to have so much else on his mind. At first he seemed preoccupied by the idea that he had to teach me something, so at odd intervals he would insert a random fact about insurance assessment.

'You see,' he said suddenly, 'it's not just a matter of the claim itself. We have to make a judgement about the level of insurance. If the property or whatever is underinsured, then we scale down the compensation accordingly.'

'What if it's overinsured?' I asked.

'Same thing,' Giles said. 'Unless it's a valued policy allowing for insuring above the value. But we won't see that in the sort of place we're visiting together. I'd just warn you that this is all going to be routine. I'm a bit worried about what you said about wanting fun. It's preying on my mind.'

'But as I said . . .'

'I joined this company eight, nine years ago, and I used to go around with this man from the old school. He had

51

amazing stories about the days when he started out. The firebugs, people setting fire to their warehouses for the insurance. Having, of course, flogged off the contents before doing so. Jewish lightning, he called it. I had to say to him: "Ron, I'm a Jewish person. You can't say that to me." He was a terrible old Nazi. But what I really wanted when I joined, I wanted it to be Chicago in the 1920s. I wanted it to be all shysters and grifters and ambulance chasers and banana-peelers.'

'Banana peelers?'

'These flop artists would carry around their own banana-peel. They would drop it outside a greengrocer's and pretend to fall on it. There was even a subcategory that suffered from brittle-bone disease. The X-rays would show a horrendous fracture and they would immediately be offered wads of cash not to sue. English insurance came as a terrible disappointment after that. It was high drama if some old woman had poured tea on the cat.'

'But . . .'

'Then there was fake involvement in real accidents. A trolley car would crash with a truck and immediately a dozen quick-thinking citizens would clamber into the wreckage. Instead of helping the victims, they would lie there groaning and sue the trolley company. Actually, it has got more fun recently. Ever watch TV in the day, Mark?'

'Not so much.'

'About every second commercial shows a man in a suit promising they can get money for you if you've stubbed your toe in the last five years. Consequently, I can promise you you'll spend about half of your time on the phone to Islington Council telling them to fix a cracked paving stone in Upper Street. How's your numeracy?'

'I got a maths GCSE.'

'GCSE? That's after my time. Means nothing to me. What's a quarter of a fifth?'

'What? Er . . . a twentieth, isn't it?'

'Excellent. What's a fifth of a quarter?'

'That's still a twentieth.'

'Yes. I should probably think of something a bit different. What about maps?'

'My geography was weak.'

'There's a street map in the glove compartment. We've got to get to Portondown Road. It's somewhere along here.'

We pulled up outside a terraced house on the corner of Portondown Road.

'The files are in the back,' said Giles. 'Reach them over, will you?' I got them and he told me to keep hold of them myself. 'We're starting with something simple.'

6

Paula Renton was a large harassed-looking woman, with long curly brown hair.

'I'm sorry,' she said, 'I really didn't expect anybody actually to come round about this. It was just a coat.'

'It's a formality,' said Giles. 'For claims above a certain amount we like to do it in person. It's old-fashioned, I suppose.'

'Come through. I'm sorry, we're in the middle of break-fast. It's complete chaos.'

We followed her down the hallway into the kitchen where two very small children were at the table tipping food over themselves.

'Chloe, for goodness' sake, look at you.'

We teetered in the middle of the kitchen while Paula Renton ran round us pushing chairs under the table, wiping faces, clearing away dishes, washing up, scrubbing surfaces.

'We'll only be a minute,' Giles said.

'It was the most stupid thing. I was just going out and Chloe was sick absolutely everywhere, over everything. Including the coat, which needless to say is the only good bit of clothing I've got. My husband bought it for me.'

I looked around the scene of disaster in the kitchen.

'That's the deal, is it?' I said. 'Your husband buys you nice coats and you deal with this.'

'Not any more,' she said, glancing at the children. 'He er . . . we're separated.' The boy was rubbing yoghurt in a circle on the table with the palm of his hand. 'Jack! Stop that! Anyway, I put the coat in a binbag. I was going to take it to be cleaned. And the childminder thought it was rubbish and put it outside and the bin men took it before I realized. So . . . I know four hundred pounds is a lot. It's certainly a lot to me at the moment.'

'Don't worry . . .'

Giles paused because there was the sound of the front door opening. Paula looked confused.

'Who's . . .? Oh, she must be early.'

A young woman walked confidently into the kitchen as if she owned it.

'Hi, Paula.'

She looked round at us and waited to be introduced.

'This is Sally,' said Paula. 'She looks after the children. These two men are here about the coat.'

'Oh, that,' said Sally, laughing. 'I'm sure you've heard it was completely my fault. Well, my boyfriend's . . .'

'It's all right, Sally,' said Paula weakly.

'Your boyfriend's?' asked Giles.

'That's right. It was crazy. I was just dropping them off at the station and that's where Chloe was sick on Paula's coat. It was like a vomit explosion. So we shoved it in a bag and I took it back to my flat and I was going to sort out the cleaning while Paula was away. And then Guy, who's my lunkhead of a boyfriend, put the bag outside with the bins downstairs. It was really bad luck because our bin men only come about once every two weeks, and they're usually on strike anyway. And when they do come, they hardly take anything away. But by the time I ran down after it, they'd whipped it. Beautiful coat as well, beautiful. So, Paula, shall I get on with things?'

'Sure, Sally,' said Paula quietly.

We stood in silence while Paula helped Sally to hustle the stained and sticky children out of the kitchen.

Giles looked over at me.

'Can I have the file, please?' he asked, almost in a whisper. He turned to Paula. 'You know that this is a household policy?'

Paula had gone fiercely red. She was blinking quickly.

'I didn't . . .' she said. 'I wasn't sure.'

'If you'll just sign this release,' he said. 'Revoking the claim.'

He handed her the form, with a pen. She signed it.

'There,' she said. 'I'm sorry. I don't know what to say.'

Back in the car, Giles asked me to check the next address.

'That was a bit unfair,' I said.

'Why?'

'What did it matter which bloody doorstep the binbag was left on?'

'It matters because it was excluded by her household contents policy. She knew that. That's why she lied about it.'

'Didn't you feel sorry for her? She obviously didn't have much money. She's lost her husband and now she's lost her coat.'

'If she had been properly insured, she would have been compensated. For the coat, at least.'

'Or if her childminder hadn't come in early.'

Giles smiled as he started the car.

'At least she has the satisfaction of being an honest woman again.'

'That is so, so . . .'

I choked.

'Pompous?' said Giles. 'She was perpetrating a fraud. We could have reported her to the police. Now read the map.'

The next case was fairly similar except the house in Highbury was about fifty times as big. Mrs Furneau was a very elegant woman. She looked about the same age as Paula but she clearly didn't spend much of her life chasing after small children. She made us tea and then sat down with us in the upstairs living room. The downstairs room was uninhabitable.

'It was the silliest thing,' she said. 'I was fiddling with the radiator, and suddenly water was spraying everywhere. Honestly, it was like something out of a Keystone Kops film. I tried to tighten the knob-thing and it just seemed to make things worse. By that time it was like Niagara Falls. So I rang up this wonderful man Jimmy who lives around the corner and does all of that sort of stuff for us. I managed to get through to him finally and he was pretty quick, but it still took him about fifteen minutes to get here and I was there filling saucepans desperately, but even so it was all just ruined. And it ran down into the kitchen in the basement as well. There was just brown water everywhere. I didn't realize that. The water in the radiators is sort of rusty, and it's got stuff in it as well. The really silly thing is that Jimmy arrived and just did a little twist on the pipe and it all stopped straight away. Apparently there was a twisty thing round the side that I couldn't see. I feel awful, as well, because we only had carpets put in there a couple of months ago. Charlie – that's my husband – he'll absolutely hit the roof.'

'Not to worry, Mrs Furneau,' said Giles in his warmest manner. 'At least it will make the costs easy to establish.'

'Yes. I hope so,' said Mrs Furneau. 'I dug out the receipts. Here they are.'

She passed a sheaf of them. Giles glanced at them and passed them over to me. The figures almost made my eyes water. At first I thought there must be a decimal point missing. Now she was going to spend that sum all over again. Or rather, Wortley Insurance was.

'By the way,' said Mrs Furneau. 'When I rang your office to report it, I was put through to some girl and she was saying something about having to get different quotations for the work. Is that really true? It would be such a bother.'

'Don't worry about that, Mrs Furneau. I'm quite happy if the people who did the work for you before do the work. But if you could arrange for them to come and make an estimate, and then if you could phone me, I'll send young

Mark here along and he could be there and take down the details. Would that be all right?'

He handed his card over to her.

'Yes, of course. That's very sweet of you. I'll look forward to seeing you, Mark. You've both been so kind. And there's just one other thing. Do you think it could all be settled quite quickly? I was so hoping the carpet could be replaced before the boys are back from school.'

I couldn't stop myself from blurting out:

'You mean by this afternoon?'

'No, no,' she said. 'They come back at Easter.'

'I'm sure that will be no problem, Mrs Furneau,' said Giles, glancing at me. I couldn't tell whether his look was one of anger or deeply subdued amusement.

'Is there a penalty for being an upper-class idiot?' I said after we had left Mrs Furneau.

'Not unless it's in the policy,' said Giles, inspecting his lunch, which was arranged in a Tupperware box. Although it was only March, it was warm and sunny and we were sitting on a bench in Highbury Fields. I'm not really much of a lunch person. I had bought one banana from a rack outside a shop. I nibbled at it without feeling really hungry.

'Don't you feel that it's unfair?'

'What? Life?'

'That Mrs Furneau. She was pissing around with the radiator valve and then couldn't switch it off. It was completely her fault. And did you see how much that carpet cost? There are parts of England where you can buy a house for what Mrs Furneau, or presumably her bloody rich husband, spent on carpeting one floor. Then that really poor and very nice woman lost her coat and didn't get compensated at all. I mean, forget insurance. Just as a human being, don't you think that's incredibly unfair?'

'Did you read the policies in the office?'

'You know I didn't. We picked them up on the way out.'

'I checked through them over the weekend. It may be that Mrs Furneau was stupid. But she's insured against being stupid. You would need to show that she had opened the valve of her radiator deliberately in order to collect the insurance. Do you think that's likely?'

'Course not.'

Giles had opened a small plastic container and was eating the contents with great relish.

'You know, my wife is a master, or mistress, of salads. This is one of her masterpieces. Tomato, cucumber, spring onion, fennel, avocado, feta cheese, sun-dried tomato. Here, try some.'

He held out a clump out of it on his fork. I took a bite. I'd just eaten my banana, so it tasted weird.

'That's great,' I said.

'Do you know what you are, Mark?'

'No, what?'

'A philosopher. Or a theologian, even. Do you believe in God, Mark? If that's not a rude question.'

'I don't know,' I said. 'I'm not sure. A sort of God, maybe.'

'I wonder what God thinks of Mrs Renton and Mrs Furneau? Perhaps he believes that we should have given our shareholders' money to alleviate Mrs Renton's relatively straitened circumstances. Or perhaps he is preparing rewards for her in eternity. On the other hand, he might be preparing to consign her to eternal damnation for being a liar and criminal and a divorcee. What do you think, Mark?'

'I wish we'd given her the money for her coat.'

'You see, I'm not a philosopher, Mark. I'm not even a businessman.'

'What are you, then?'

'I'm not sure. But when I was your age I wasn't working in insurance. I was a scientist.'

'What sort?'

'Oh, I don't know, biology, zoology, that sort of thing.'

'Why did you change?'

'Got tired of it, I think. Didn't like it any more. But I'm still a sort of scientist, in a way. I like gambling. Do you like gambling, Mark?'

'I used to play a bit of poker at uni.'

'Poker?' said Giles, as if I'd mentioned a particularly delicious kind of food. 'Dangerous game, poker. Too dangerous for me. Too much psychology. Ever heard of the three most important rules of life? What were they? Don't sleep with a woman whose problems are worse than your own. That was one of them. Never managed that. It's certainly not true of my wife, so far as I know. Never play poker with a man called Doc. Can't remember the third. Blackjack's my game. I'll tell you about blackjack some time. But what I was

61

starting to say is that we're gambling with our customers, Mark. We're betting against them. We're betting a small amount of money that something won't happen. If it does happen, we have to pay them a large amount of money. But if you lose, you don't try and change the rules, and you don't whine about it.'

'What if the other person cheats?' I asked.

'You saw that this morning. Now, this afternoon we should be seeing something that will probably be more to your taste. Also I'll be able to introduce you to one of our loss adjusters.' He looked at his watch. 'He'll be there already.'

'There's one other thing,' I said.

'What's that?'

'You seem very different when you're with those women from the way you are the rest of the time.'

'Oh, dear. Really? You mean, fawning, obsequious, oily, that sort of thing.'

'No. Just different.'

He gave a sad-sounding sigh.

'Customers. That's what we're supposed to call them now, isn't it? When we're with customers I sometimes feel like a drunk man pretending to be sober.'

I wasn't so sure about that. I thought that Giles Buckland was a bit more of a businessman than he let on. We drove down the Balls Pond Road towards Hackney. Using the map I guided him through a complicated series of twists that brought us to the mews street that ran along the back of

Cheston High Street. Giles explained to me on the way that there had been a fire in a fabric shop that had also burned down a storeroom at the back. There had been moderate damage to the interior of the shop but the storeroom and its contents were totally destroyed.

As we got out of our car, I was amazed at how little damage there was. The back of the shop was a terrible mess, of course, but the buildings on either side were completely untouched. We were met by two men in suits. Giles introduced me to Peter Stenecki, the loss adjuster. Stenecki was tall, dark-skinned, with hair cut right to the scalp, so there were only dots to show that he wasn't bald. Stenecki introduced us to a paunchy, double-chinned man called Matt Fender. He told us that he was chairman of the holding company, whatever that meant. Fender seemed quite cheerful. He took us through the rubble and the charred beams as if he was rather proud of it all.

'It's a bloody mess, that's what it is,' he said. 'You should have seen it the day after. Wet and smoking and smelling like I don't know what. Mind yourselves.' This last was as he stepped over a black oily puddle. 'The shop's not too bad. The fire started at the back and mainly burned itself out there, and then the fire brigade arrived about five hours late and did their stuff on the last of the embers.'

'Is that true?' said Giles to Pete. He shook his head.

'There was some delay. It wasn't significant.'

He led us through into the shop itself, which was now boarded up at the front.

63

'Most of the damage was done by the firemen with their silly hoses and their axes. It's mainly a paint job through here.'

'What did you have in the storeroom?'

Matt Fender looked as if he had sucked deeply on a lemon.

'Oh dear,' he said. 'That was not good. Bloody awful luck. A whole lot of deliveries had come in from all over the place. You know, ready for the spring collections.'

Giles looked around the shop.

'The spring collections?'

'One of our big times of the year. The whole lot up in smoke.'

'How did the fire start?'

Fender gave an eloquent shrug, proclaiming innocent bafflement.

'All I know is what the fire people and the police told me. There's always boxes and packing cases out the back. It's what the dresses come in. Sometimes people sleep rough out there. They might have made a fire, and the whole lot went up. Or it may have been kids.'

'Yes,' said Giles reflectively. 'Will you give us a moment, Mr Fender?'

'Take as much time as you want, gents. I've got some calls to make.'

We walked out of the front of the shop onto the High Street.

'It's not exactly the King's Road, is it?' said Giles.

'It's a right old bit of dodginess,' said Pete.

'What's he asking for?' said Giles.

'Twenty-five for rebuilding the storeroom, another twenty for the contents.'

Giles gave a short laugh.

'What do you think, Mark?'

'Me?'

'What are your impressions?'

I looked round to make sure that Fender wasn't nearby.

'He's a wide boy, if ever I saw one,' I said. 'This is the rag trade. It's classic, isn't it? You're having a few cash-flow problems, so you shift your dresses out of the warehouse, knock them down for cash. Then torch the warehouse, get the insurance for the building and the dresses you've already sold, and you're laughing. He seems pretty happy to me.'

I saw that Giles and Pete were both smiling.

'Well, that's Nipper of the Yard's theory. What do you think, Pete? You got here this morning.'

'I was on it yesterday afternoon as well. I talked to the police and the fire investigator.'

'What did they say?'

'Nothing much they could say. It's just like Mr Fender said. The boxes behind the warehouse were set alight. But no traces of fuel or wood shavings.' Giles sniffed and Pete continued. 'There was a pile of cardboard with a few wooden crates mixed in. You didn't need to be in the boy scouts to get a fire going. That cuts both ways, obviously. Some winos might have made a fire to keep themselves warm. Got out of control.'

'There've been warm days recently,' I said.

'The nights have been cold, though. Have you seen invoices for the dresses?'

Pete gave a sour smile.

'I've seen invoices. But who knows what invoices they are? You wouldn't believe this company. It's broken up into so many pieces it's almost impossible to work out what's what. This isn't Marks and Sparks.'

'You know, I'm going to find the gentleman who sold this policy and I'm going to give his nose a tweak. What were the figures again?'

'Twenty-five and twenty.'

There was a long pause. Giles was frowning, deep in thought. It was a couple of minutes before he spoke.

'Wait here,' he said.

He walked back into the shop. The two of us watched as he talked to Matt Fender.

'What do you make of Giles?' Pete asked.

'I only met him this morning,' I said. 'But he doesn't seem like other people in the firm.'

Pete pulled a face and I was going to ask him something but then I saw Giles was coming back.

'Thirteen and seven,' he said, as he joined us.

'What? Just like that?' said Pete.

'Yes, yes, otherwise it'll go on for ever. Bring the papers into me and I'll sign off on them. Then I'll cancel the policy.'

Pete left us and Giles took several very deep breaths.

'Are you all right?' I said.

'You know the feeling when you're about to be sick?' he

said. 'I don't know whether it's better to be sick or to do the things that are supposed to stop you being sick.'

'What are they?'

'Looking at the horizon. I don't think Cheston High Street has a horizon. What was the next file?'

'Something about a greenhouse.'

7

I'd had plans for the flat. This wasn't a question of knocking
walls down and putting in joists. The place didn't belong to
me. It was owned by a friend of a friend of someone who
was working in Amsterdam for a couple of years. But it
needed something doing to it. It was not on the face of it an
impressive place to live. It wasn't somewhere to invite the
boss and his wife and get the doilies out on the dining table.
All that I'd done in that flat was to sleep, wash and have sex
with Sonia. I'd never attempted to prepare a meal more
complicated than toast or a cup of coffee.

But the location was fantastic. I could walk up to the
supermarket or Camden Lock or the veg market in a few
minutes. There were some clubs nearby. It was never going
to be a place to invite six people back to but I could imagine
it as perfect to bring one person back to. A good scrub down
would have been a start. A vacuuming would be better than
nothing. I had a glowing image of myself spending a week
doing the place up. I would be like a man in an advertisement for ... well, the sort of thing I was doing at the
moment. I'd be up a stepladder putting up the wallpaper,
and a beautiful blonde, except that she'd be wearing dunga-

rees to show that she's domesticated, would be bringing me a mug of coffee. Put the torn lampshade and the browny-green curtains and the ancient carpet with a hole half covered by a scrawny rug, put all of it in a skip and replace it with bright new things in pastel colours and it would be quite a dinky little top-floor flat.

I never even got around to the vacuuming. Worse than that. Hanging over the sofa, there was an awful old picture of a boat sailing into a sunset that looked as if it had been knitted. The very first moment I walked into the room, I was irritated not just by the badness of the painting but the fact that it was hung very slightly askew. It made me feel queasy every time I looked at it. All I needed to do was to pull a chair over, stand on it and straighten the bloody picture. Then that little bit of my life, at least, would have been sorted.

I never did. I never seemed to have the time. I should explain a few things. I'm not the sort of person to hang around the office. I mean, if work was enjoyable, they wouldn't call it work, would they? Sometimes, I'd be in the office, in a lift or walking through the front entrance, and I'd imagine someone from outside, an ordinary person, looking at me and that crowd of insurance employees and just assuming that I was one of them. It made me laugh. The idea of a career at Wortley was a joke, as far as I was concerned, but it was a well-paying joke. I'd been thinking of Sonia and what she'd been planning and I thought she had the right idea. My grandfather went to work in the local car factory when he was about fifteen and he worked there solidly until he was made redundant in his late fifties. Then he sat in his special reclining chair watching TV until he died. That's all changed now. No one works like that any more. Not if they've got any sense. My plan was to work for a year or two, build up a stash of money, then throw in the job and go abroad until it was spent.

I certainly didn't want to hang around the Wortley office. The problem was that Giles Buckland was a weird sort of teacher. In fact, I'm not sure that he was any sort of teacher at all. He hardly told me anything, at least not about insurance. He'd sometimes tell me about some beetle he saw. He was mad about beetles. That was from when he'd been a scientist. He hardly ever explained anything. I just had to pick it up as I went along. I noticed even on that very first day that he never referred to the files, even though we had to bring them along. He'd always read through them before and he remembered all the details. So after a couple of days I thought I'd have to do something about it. Usually after we'd been out, I'd have stuff to finish up back at the office, doing some filing, phoning surveyors and loss adjustors and checking appointments.

That took me through till seven or eight. I'd get hold of the claims forms and photocopy them. Then I'd call up the policies they referred to and print them out. I'd take all that home with me and grab a pizza or some chips and a few cans of beer and read through them, get them in my head for the next day. And reading through an insurance policy isn't just like looking at the sports pages. I don't mean that it's technical. That was all easy after a couple of days. It's just that it all hinged on a particular word, or a thing that was disallowed or whatever. I was never done before midnight.

I'm not quite sure why I did it. It just made more sense when I was standing there next to the broken window of a shop front or a burned-down garden shed or whatever. It's like looking at a forest. Whenever I've looked at a forest, I've always thought it would be more interesting if I knew what kind of trees they were, which one was an ash or beech. Pine trees. I can recognize those.

Not that I got a kiss on the cheek from Giles about it. A couple of days after I'd started going through the policies the night before, he asked me some renewal date and I told him without opening the file. He gave me a funny look and took the file himself and looked at it, as if I'd been playing an incredibly boring practical joke on him. As if I was suddenly going to say, April Fool, it actually fell due on the twenty-eighth. Ha ha. He looked in the file and just gave a grunt, a sort of hmm, and then just went on with it. No wink. No pat on the back afterwards.

He didn't really respond to what I said either. He'd quite often ask me what I thought, and I'd say something. Sometimes he would just carry on as if I hadn't said anything at all, as if it had just been the sound of a door squeaking, and I think those were the times when I was wrong or stupid. If he replied, then that must have been when it made some sort of sense.

It didn't bother me. What I liked about it was travelling into weird bits of London I'd never thought about: anywhere you can think of inside the M25, industrial estates, lock-ups, mansions, Underground stations, ruins, mashed-up cars, hospitals, any place you can imagine where something bad can happen. We'd sit there while women cried and cried, and we'd meet plump men in suits who'd start making demands and present us with forms and threaten us with lawyers. Some of it was accidents that had happened the day before. There would be women who had just got back from the hospital and the undertakers would be on the phone and the flowers would be arriving. There were times when the ground would still be hot from the fire. Other times we'd be dropping in on a case that had been going on for years.

A lot of the time Giles would have a cheque in his inside pocket. We'd have a few words, the client would sign along the dotted line, we'd hand the cheque over and be on our way in less than twenty minutes. Another time a lorry driver had fallen asleep on the motorway and there was a massive pile-up and fourteen people were killed. You probably read about it. For that one we went to a preliminary meeting with people from about five different insurance companies. And that was just about the procedure for appointing engineers.

Only a couple of them really stick in my mind. One time we were going to see a wife about her husband's life policy. He'd just died of a brain haemorrhage. We'd parked in this road of huge houses in Hampstead, just up from the heath. Normally, Giles didn't say anything beforehand, but this time he stopped on the front steps as if he'd forgotten something.

'Did you read the policy?' he said.

'Yes.'

'Did you think there was anything funny about it?'

I didn't answer straight away. If Giles was asking that, he must be suspicious. But I couldn't think of anything.

'It's just a completely standard life policy. Nothing else.'

'Really?' he said. 'Oh well.' He looked up at the tall house with a gloomy expression. 'I hate these ones.'

There's a look that people get when something terrible has happened. I remember hearing stories of people whose hair turned white overnight. I don't know if that's really possible but there's a greyness people get, not in their hair but in their eyes. They look as if they've had very fine lines chiselled into their face. Isabel Fry was just like that. When she spoke, her voice trembled. Her features were blurry. I think she'd been crying just before we arrived and she'd made the effort to compose herself just before we were due. She asked us to sit down and she talked.

'They said it could be years,' she said. 'Five or six or even longer. I asked the specialist. He said that people sometimes went quickly but it wasn't very likely. The average was three or four years and some people were alive for seven years or even longer. That seems so far off. And it's stupid, but you start thinking that maybe they'll find a cure by that time. They're doing so much research, aren't they? Robin was so determined. They were going to put him into a clinical trial. They were going to do a special kind of surgery. It had some funny kind of name. I can't remember it.'

'Stereotactic?' said Giles.

'Yes, I think that's it. How on earth did you know?'

'I'm very sorry about your loss,' he said.

'We never even started the treatment.'

That we. As if they were doing the treatment together.

'It was going to start next week. It was last Sunday. He started having a fit. He'd done that before. All of a sudden he just went quiet. I dialled 999 but they were so long getting here. I've got a son who's a doctor. Do you know, he always said that you should never have an accident on a Sunday. He says that junior doctors are in charge and by Sunday they're exhausted. That's when they make mistakes. The ambulance came quite quickly but they couldn't revive him.'

'I'm terribly sorry,' said Giles. 'I'm sure they did the best that they could.'

Then he did something that was very unusual for him. He turned to me and asked: 'Mark, can I have the file?'

I passed it across. He laid it on a coffee table in front of him and opened it.

'And now,' he said. 'We have your husband's policy. Assigned to you.'

'Yes,' she said faintly. 'I didn't know anything about it. Our solicitor rang yesterday and told me about it. I didn't know.'

Giles adjusted the document carefully, as if it was really important that it lined up perfectly with the edges of the red cardboard file.

'I'm very sorry, Mrs Fry,' he said. 'But would it be all right if I used your bathroom?'

I tried not to let it show on my face how startled I was. It was a totally bizarre and insensitive time to suddenly go off for a piss. Maybe Giles really was nervous.

'No, of course. There's one in the basement and there's one at the top of the stairs, on the landing.'

Giles got up and left. It was especially embarrassing because I was then left alone with Mrs Fry. I consider myself quite good at keeping a conversation going. I'm not really the bashful type. But this really was beyond me. First I said in an awful mumbling sort of tone that I just wanted to say how sorry I was about her loss. She said thank you and that was it. I would even have been pleased if she had blathered on a bit more about her husband's treatment and all that. At least that would have filled the silence. But I guess that she thought that if she was going to give a grief-stricken monologue, she ought to give it to the organ grinder rather than to his monkey. It was definitely not-in-front-of-the-servants time and she looked fairly composed. I thought about opening one of the files and reading it, but that would have made it look as if I was bored. I felt I couldn't even look around the room. I just kept a feeling of concern on my face until it started to hurt.

Giles was a long time as well. This wasn't just a splash on the porcelain. I began to think that he must have amoebic dysentery or that he had climbed out of a back window and legged it. Finally, after about fourteen hours, I heard him coming down the stairs. He sat down, adjusted the file once more, and started talking as if he hadn't been away.

'Normally we wouldn't trouble you at this time,' he said.

75

'But we have certain guidelines. One of them, obviously enough, is if a life policy-holder dies shortly after the commencement of a contract.' He picked up the paper, as if he needed to check the date. 'And your husband took out this policy relatively recently. Last November, in fact.'

'I didn't know that,' she said.

'This is painful, Mrs Fry, but the reason for this guideline is that we then have to assess whether any pertinent information may have been withheld when the policy was signed.'

There was a silence that was even worse than the one when Giles had been out of the room. I couldn't believe what was going on and I don't think Mrs Fry could either. I saw her jaw muscle flex. She looked less blurry now.

'I'm sorry, Mr . . .?'

'Buckland.'

'Mr Buckland. Are you accusing my husband of having lied?'

Giles didn't look embarrassed or upset. He just seemed puzzled, as if it was all a bit odd.

'Mrs Fry, I'm considering whether your husband might have omitted anything material when he arranged his policy with us.'

'Omitted?' she said. 'Are you saying that my husband was a liar? He's been dead two days. I don't know where to start. My husband died very quickly after being diagnosed with a brain tumour. You know that. I told you. I cannot believe that you've come here two days after his death and accused him of deception.'

Still looking puzzled, Giles reached into his left jacket pocket, the one closest to me, and took something out that I couldn't see. He held it up. Now I could see.

'Do you know what this is?'

'No,' she said. 'Not from here.'

It was a plastic pill container. Giles stood up, walked across the room and handed it to her. She looked at it.

'What's this?'

'You must recognize it.'

'I'll have to get my glasses.'

'It's dexamethasone,' said Giles. 'It's a steroid that's used for reducing the swelling around brain tumours.'

'Is that my husband's?'

'It has your husband's name on it.'

Very lightly, he took it from her hand and walked over and gave it to me.

'What's the date on it, Mark?'

I looked at it.

'The third of November,' I said.

Isabel Fry's face was chalk-white, her eyes flickering this way and that, as if she was looking at something we couldn't see.

'Mrs Fry,' said Giles. 'I'd like you to save us all trouble and embarrassment. Please, I have a release form I would like you to sign.'

'He took a medical,' she said. Her voice sounded like someone speaking while they were hypnotized. 'He told me. You made him have a medical. They didn't find anything.'

'They didn't find anything, because the routine medical

doesn't include a CAT scan. Please, Mrs Fry, let's not make this any more distressing. Please sign the form.'

Isabel Fry stood up.

'I can't believe it,' she said. 'You were rummaging in our medicine cabinet.'

'Well . . .' said Giles, looking shifty for the first time.

'In our *bedroom*. I told you about the bathrooms downstairs and on the landing. But you went into the bathroom in my . . . in *our* bedroom. You went and rifled through the medicine cabinet.'

'Well . . .'

'I should call the police . . .'

'I apologize, Mrs Fry. It wasn't ideal behaviour, but I . . . I wanted to avoid embarrassment. I wanted to bring this to a close without involving doctors and the hospital authorities.'

'I'm going to have you struck off . . .'

'Mrs Fry . . .'

'Get out of my house. Now. This moment. You two *disgusting* men. You filth. How you can live with yourselves, I cannot imagine. I am going to call the police, Mr whoever you are, and I'm going to call my lawyer and I can promise you that you, and you too . . .' That last was at me. I almost crapped myself. 'You will both be out of a job. I will see you both in court.'

We were hustled out onto the front steps and the door slammed behind us. We walked down onto the pavement.

'That was better than I expected,' said Giles, rubbing his hands together.

'Better?' I said. 'How the hell can that be better?'

'I thought that maybe she didn't know anything about it, but she did. That's the way some people react when they're in the wrong. They shout and bluster and get angry and self-righteous. It would have been much worse if she'd just been quiet and sad. Not that it matters much either way.'

When we came back to the office at the end of the day, there was a hand-delivered message waiting. It was from Mr J. H. Waldron, Mrs Fry's legal representative. He said that if we would, at our convenience, forward the release form to him, it would be signed and returned.

8

A day or two later I was sitting with Giles in a cafe on High Holborn. We had half an hour spare and we were grabbing a coffee. I had to ask him about Mrs Fry, to ask him if he felt upset by it. He just gave a shrug.

'Is it just like a game to you?' I said.

He took a sip of his coffee, delicately, testing the heat.

'You said you wanted fun, Mark. Isn't it better than taking claims over the phone?'

I was still uncomfortable and it showed because Giles asked me what was up.

'I know your argument,' I said. 'About how they're being dishonest and need to be checked up on. But there's this expression you get, it's a sort of innocent look like an animal that's about to pounce.'

'You think I enjoy my work too much?'

'You're so good at this,' I said. 'I'm surprised you haven't been promoted.'

He looked puzzled.

'Funny, isn't it?' he said. 'I'm good at this, so why don't they get me to do something I'm not good at? You've asked the wrong question, Mark.'

'What question should I have asked?'

His expression turned sardonic.

'You should have asked, why do I put in so much effort when it hardly matters to Wortley one way or the other?'

'So what's the answer?'

'Because I enjoy it.'

'But if you understand the system so clearly, wouldn't you rather be higher up than . . . you know.'

Now he smiled.

'Scrabbling around at the bottom?' he said. 'Is that something you've been thinking about, Mark? Do you want to climb the Wortley ladder?'

'I don't know,' I said. 'I've never done anything like this. I've always just done the odd bit of work, grabbed the money, scooted off. I'm too young to find work interesting.'

Giles gave a grunt and looked at me through narrowed, suspicious eyes.

'You didn't answer my question,' he said.

'I don't know the answer,' I said.

'You've got to recognize the moment when it comes,' he said. 'The readiness is all.'

He meant I must recognize the body when it floated past. And so the job I particularly remember from that time was an advertising agency in Clerkenwell that was almost walking distance from the Wortley office. Giles looked rueful as we walked along Clerkenwell Road.

'I've always wanted to live somewhere like this,' he said.

'A little flat in the middle of town. You could wander out to a little coffee bar whenever you felt like it. You're up the road in King's Cross, aren't you?'

'Camden.'

'Excellent. Your flat must be worth a fortune.'

'I'm just staying there. Belongs to a friend of a friend.'

'Oh,' said Giles, quite cast down. 'But I suppose it's handy for coffee bars.'

'I guess so,' I said. I wasn't quite sure what it was with the coffee bars. I assume that Giles connected it with some tacky old image of the good life, of Vespas and cappuccinos and *La Dolce Vita*. We walked along past the photographic labs and clock repairers and jewellers until we came to a bright shiny new building, metal and glass, and things sticking out at strange angles. The companies occupying the building were incised on what looked like a bronze tombstone just inside the main entrance. Dalby Douncy Pountain were on the third, fourth and fifth floors.

The burglary had been the night before and the police had spent most of the morning there. I had phoned ahead earlier and arranged to meet one of the officers. At reception there was a beautiful girl with blonde hair, cut short, which made her look like an elf. I'd got used to the look people gave us. She looked at us expectantly. We could have been two more detectives. Everybody's interested in the police. Or we could have been clients. But when Giles said we were from Wortley Insurance, you could see the interest drain out of her face and we became invisible. It reminded me of the way I'd felt ten years earlier about anybody over the age of about thirty. It didn't matter to me whether they were old fogies who asked me what my favourite subject was at school or whether they pretended to be in touch and asked me what 'bands' I was listening to. I wasn't interested. I just wanted them to go away.

The beautiful receptionist was like that. I felt like I should have a card printed and I'd hand it out whenever I saw that expression. It would say: 'This isn't really me. I'm disguised as an insurance man but in real life I'm completely different. Just look at my face and you'll see.' Or I could wear a sandwich board. I don't think it would have made much difference. She just told us to take a seat.

Too many minutes later a man came through. You could tell that he worked in an advertising agency because of his suit. It was an ironic suit. It was green, but not just any green. It was the kind of green you have on snooker tables. It was an amusing suit, but the joke would wear off, and you just knew that the person who would wear one like that would have about thirty other completely different ones at home.

He was neither Dalby, Douncy nor Pountain. We probably weren't worthy of their attention. He was called Jem and he took us upstairs to see the damage. I expected to find lots of men in white coats sprinkling chalk dust on window sills and other men taking photographs of the crime scene. But there was just one bored-looking man in an ordinary suit like ours. He was Detective Constable Maguire.

'This is our design and layout section,' said Jem. 'It's where we have most of our computers. We've got computers everywhere, but these are the good ones. As it were.'

'Did they take them all?' asked Giles.

'On this floor,' said Jem.

'What about the floors below?'

'The fire doors are locked and alarmed.'

'So how did they get in?'

'They came up the back fire escape,' said Maguire. 'They knew what they were after. In and out in a few minutes. They must have had a van in the alley behind.'

'Who did this?' asked Giles.

'There's no mystery about these guys,' said Maguire. 'There's a gang been doing this over the last couple of years. They hit offices where there are high-end machines, rip them out of the wall and they're gone.'

I looked around and I could see that it was pretty brutal. There was plaster on the floor and exposed wires where they'd been pulled away. Nothing subtle about their way of working.

'They've done the same thing in Covent Garden,' continued Maguire. 'They did one in Waterloo. Another in Shoreditch. Places where the security isn't too heavy. Not like the City or Canary Wharf.'

'It doesn't sound as if you're hot on their trail,' I said.

I thought I'd put my foot in it but Maguire looked completely unconcerned.

'It's not my case,' he said. 'I'm just standing in for someone today.'

'So what's the damage?' said Giles.

Jem had a piece of paper ready in his hand.

'We've drawn up an inventory of what's missing,' he said.

This was a scene I'd got used to. There'd been a burglary and nobody cared. Maguire didn't care because it wasn't his case. Dalby Douncy Pountain didn't care because they were going to get a set of nice new computers. Wortley Insurance didn't care because this was in line with a projected payout rate, calculated by actuaries over previous years. And the burglars were happy as well. Everybody was happy. Giles nodded at me.

'Give it to him,' he said.

Jem handed me the paper. There was a typed list of models and serial numbers.

'So it was just the ones in here?' said Giles, as if it hadn't been made tediously clear.

'That's right,' said Jem. 'Here and in the annexes at the end. That's where the two department chiefs work. I think it's all pretty straightforward.'

'That's right,' said Giles. 'Mind if we look around, just to see if there's any other damage, that sort of thing?'

'Do you still need me?' said Maguire.

'We won't be a minute,' said Giles.

He started walking around the office, looking around, occasionally crouching. He wandered to the window and looked out. I assumed that he would be recommending stringent changes to the rear access. What he called the stable-door bit of the job. I started to wander around as well, doing my impersonation of the very professional insurance investigator. I thought how all offices are basically alike. It may be a high-class place like Dalby Douncy Pountain, with designer lampshades and desks that look like sculptures. Or it can be a council office in the back of beyond with an assortment of funny old desks and chairs that look as if they were rescued from a skip. But you still have the coffee machine in the corner and the notice boards with postcards pinned up, some half-covered-up fire-warden instruction and a bit of newspaper that's been stuck up there because the person in the story 'amusingly' has the same name as someone in the office. On this particular notice board I stopped to read a news item about a man called Christopher Marsh who had been arrested for harassing women over the telephone. He had phoned them and pretended he was conducting a survey about varying breast weights. Varying on the same women, that is. He would get them to remove their bras and hold each breast in turn to determine which was heavier. Someone had circled the name 'Christopher Marsh' in red ink and written: 'No end to your talents, Chris!'

Giles was still pottering around at the window so I walked over to the annexe. There were two small spaces with lockable doors screened off from the rest of the office. As reported, the connecting cables were hanging off the desk. I started walking back towards Giles and the others, and then I stopped. Something was buzzing in my head. An irritation rather than a headache. What was it? I looked over at the mess in the office, the plaster on the floor, the ripped-out sockets in the wall. Then I walked back to the annexe. I stood there for a minute looking at the cables draped over the desk. One of them was coiled neatly round. I looked at this list that Jem had given me. There were twenty-two computers listed altogether and four printers. Two of the computers were identified as coming from these two offices. I took out a pen and put crosses next to them.

I walked across to where Jem was standing, looking as if he had more important things to do somewhere else. Anywhere else.

'Who does your computers?' I asked.

'What do you mean?'

'Who installs them? You don't go out and buy them at PC World yourself, do you?'

'No, it's a company called Byte Part. That's spelt B-Y-T-E. You know, always the puns.'

'Right,' I said, smiling. 'That fire door you mentioned. Where is it?'

He pointed.

'Over there.'

'It's not locked now, is it?'

'Not during the day.'

'I'll just take a look.'

I walked across and pushed it open. I wasn't interested in the fire exits. I wanted to get to the floor below without encountering that irritating girl at the reception. She probably wouldn't remember me anyway. But I wanted to have a bit of fun. I walked down some concrete steps and pushed open the first door I came to. I was in a virtual carbon copy of the floor above. Except that this office was crowded. Probably some of the people from upstairs had had to move down. I smiled at a girl sitting at a desk close to me.

'Hi,' I said. 'I'm from Byte Part. I do your computers. Do you know where the new computers are?'

She shrugged.

'Sorry, I don't know anything about that sort of stuff. Ask Don over there.'

I walked over to Don, who was on the phone. He noticed me standing in front of his desk and covered the mouthpiece of the receiver with his hand.

'Yes?' he said.

'I'm from Byte Part. I wanted to check on the new computers. The ones that were brought down this morning.'

I suddenly felt a ripple of nausea. I'd been so stupid. For all I knew, maybe there were only two people working at Byte Part and Don knew them. Maybe there was only one. But Don just pointed behind him and said:

'Over there, in the corner.'

'Cheers,' I said.

There they were crammed on a table, waiting to be put somewhere. I hardly needed to bother, but I checked the serial numbers stamped on the labels behind. They were the same as those on my list. I had to stop myself grinning like an idiot. As I passed Don's desk, he called out at me.

'Everything all right?'

'Fine,' I said.

'Are you going to . . .?'

I walked away without looking round. When I came back through the fire door, Giles walked up to me, looking irritated.

'Where the hell have you been?'

'You can cross two of the computers off the list,' I said.

'What do you mean?'

Jem was lurking nearby so in a low voice I explained what I'd done. Giles's expression was bemused at first, and then a smile spread across his face.

'The bastards,' he said. 'The greedy little bastards. They were really down there? You saw them?'

'Yes.'

'You're sure they're the right ones?'

'I checked the serial numbers against the list.'

Giles shook his head.

'I don't believe it,' he said, then caught my eye. 'By which I mean that I do.' He turned round. 'You.'

'Jem,' said Jem.

'Jem,' said Giles. 'Do Dalby and the rest of them actually exist?'

'Of course,' said Jem indignantly.

'Then get one of them up here.' Jem looked puzzled and started to say something. 'Now.'

He scuttled away.

'What are you going to say?'

'Say?' said Giles. 'I don't know what I'm going to say but I know what I'm going to do. I'm voiding the contract.'

'What's that mean?'

89

'It means we're not paying them a penny.'

'What about the computers that really were stolen? There *was* an actual burglary.'

'Doesn't matter.'

Douncy was a woman. She was called Helena Douncy and she swished into the room in a beautiful black suit. It didn't disarm Giles at all. I was really impressed. He got very angry indeed while staying amazingly quiet. At first Helena Douncy was puzzled and said it couldn't be true. Then Giles waved the piece of paper in her face and offered to march her downstairs to check for herself. Then she said there must be some sort of mix-up. Giles then said that if she said one more word, he would call Detective Constable Maguire over and there would be two investigations instead of one. Helena Douncy didn't say anything for a while.

'There were only two,' she said.

Giles's eyes were locked on Helena Douncy's face but his next words were addressed to me.

'Mr Foll. Will you note that Ms Douncy stated that there were only two computers in her company's fraudulent insurance claim.'

'Fraudulent?'

'I'm voiding the insurance contract.'

'What? The whole thing?'

'That's right.'

'I'm going to have to talk to our lawyers about this.'

'That's no problem,' Giles said. 'We'll expect to hear from them by the close of business tomorrow or we'll call in the police. And you'd better not tamper with the evidence. I mean tamper with it again.'

Giles didn't say anything more to me until we were back walking along the Clerkenwell Road.

'That wasn't bad, Mark,' he said.

It was the nicest thing he'd ever said to me.

9

At the end of the next day, it was almost seven, I was back at the office going through some forms when I felt a tap on my shoulder. It was a woman I'd never seen.

'Are you Mark Foll?'

'Yes.'

'Ms Kiely would like to see you.'

'Tomorrow?'

'Now. Come with me, please?'

We went up in the lift. I asked what it was about but she just shrugged. She took me through a series of doors that ended in a large office with Donna Kiely sitting at a desk at the far end. The windows went from the floor to the ceiling. It was dark but still spectacular.

'The views get better,' I said. 'I mean the higher you get.'

She put a pen down.

'It is the old city wall, by the way.'

'What?'

'You were curious. You asked Darryl Wingate about it.'

'Oh, right. That's good. By the way, I ought to say, Ms Kiely, that I'm sorry about, you know, that thing, when we last met. At the end of when we met. That last thing.'

'You know, I actually gave you some credit for it as an attempt to pull something out of the ashes of disaster. In some insane sort of way.'

'Right. So is that it?' I started to turn back toward the door and escape.

'I just got off the phone with Gil Pountain. As in Dalby Douncy Pountain.'

'I didn't meet him. I only met the woman. Helena Douncy.'

'Did you ask her out?'

'No, it didn't really seem . . .'

'Opportunity gone begging, Mark. Anyway, he was grovelling to me for a solid twenty minutes. Have you ever had a senior figure in the advertising industry grovel to you?'

'No.'

'It's pathetic to listen to. And not only did he grovel to me, but there'll also be a humble letter to Giles and one for you as well. You should frame it.'

'Right. So has the contract been – what was it? – voided?'

'No,' she said. 'That was what the grovelling was about. They've cancelled the claim, they've made a payment to cover our expenses, promised to improve their security arrangements. In return, we'll maintain the cover.'

'Does Giles know?'

'I've only just sorted it out. I'll tell him tomorrow.'

'He was pretty pissed off with them.'

'He's had his fun. That should be enough. I'll square it with him. He already told me about you.'

'That's nice of him.'

'That was a good call, Mark.'

'I couldn't believe it,' I said. 'I mean, if someone had just taken the bloody computers home. Then nobody would ever have known.'

'If they'd done that, they would have been admitting to themselves that they had something to hide. They saw it as just like helping yourself to a couple of pens from the stationery cupboard. Like we all do.'

'I'm never in the office,' I said. 'I don't know where the stationery cupboard is.'

'You're in the office now.'

'I was just sorting some stuff out for tomorrow.'

'Are you busy? Have you got to get somewhere?'

I thought for a mad moment that now she was going to ask me out for a drink. As a sort of reward.

'No,' I said.

'There's someone I want you to meet. I'm afraid we're going even further up.'

We got into a different lift from the one I'd come up in. It was a sort of superlift. The buttons were gold-coloured and the numbers were carved in a curly shape. It was wood-panelled. It was like an original eighteenth-century lift.

'We're going to meet our CEO,' she said.

'What?'

'Oh God, Mark. Where have you been? Don't you ever read *Vanity Fair*? It stands for Chief Executive Officer. It means the big boss. He's called Walter Broberg. He'll be very friendly, but call him Mr Broberg.'

We got out and were met at the lift door and led through

into an office that was about three times the size of Donna Kiely's. At the far end, close by the window, a man – Broberg – was standing silhouetted against the lights of the city outside. He was talking on a cordless phone, but I could only hear murmurs. The room was lit in zones, so whole areas seemed dark or blurred. Several small spotlights lit up a sculpture – it looked like a deformed hourglass carved out of rough granite and left unfinished. Other spotlights shone on paintings on the wall and on a bookcase, but a bookcase that had almost no books in it. And those few weren't like the insurance reference guides that Giles had down in his office. These looked more like the sort of expensive art books that an interior designer would get by the yard to furnish an executive's office. I felt ill at ease but then Donna Kiely didn't look entirely confident either. There was a bit of a feeling of a visit to the headmaster about it.

Broberg snapped his phone shut and moved towards us, into the light, so that I could see him properly for the first time. I was interested not just by his features, his milky blue eyes, greying hair drawn back quite casually over his head, his height – he was well over six feet tall. I was interested in the details. When you're at the top, what do you do to distinguish yourselves from those who are nearly at the top? I couldn't tell. His jacket was off. He wore a striped shirt and a blue satin tie, grey trousers, black shoes. Maybe it was the kind of outfit that was so expensive that it didn't need to try. Maybe it was just ordinary. I couldn't tell. As he came closer, I saw that his lined face was creased in mild amusement.

'Walt,' said Donna. 'This is Mark Foll.'

He held out his hand. It was one of those handshakes like a dry metal claw. Assertive.

'Good to make your acquaintance, Mark.'

The accent had a bit of mid-Atlantic about it. British, but probably spent some time in the States.

'Thank you, Mr Broberg.'

'Donna told me about that DDP thing yesterday. That was a good catch, Mark.'

'It wasn't such a big deal.'

'Gave me good a laugh, Mark. Jesus, those greedy bastards. You know I used to do deals on a handshake. Now it's every little sub-clause in the contract and let's try and squeeze a little more out of them. Did you smooth it out, Donna?'

'Yes, it was no problem.'

'Good.' Broberg walked over to his desk and picked up a piece of paper and looked at it suspiciously. 'Cleoford? That's where you went to?'

'That's right.'

'Never heard of it.'

'Yes, well, as I said . . .'

'I never went to university at all. I did all sorts of things. I worked on farms, then I trained as a chef. Hardest I ever worked in my life. Chopping the carrots at eight in the morning and I was still there at midnight scrubbing the stoves down. Then I worked as a salesman. In fact I sold stoves, funnily enough, door to door. I think if a few people in this firm had ever tried to sell a stove to a hatchet-faced housewife on a winter morning in Glasgow rather than poncing around at business school . . .'

'Then what?' said Donna, in a flirtatious tone. I assumed that she was one of the people who had been to business school. In fact I had as well, if you could call it that. He ignored her question. That's one of the things about being in charge. You don't have to answer questions, if you don't want to.

'So what do you think of Wortley, Mark?'

I looked across at Donna Kiely. I didn't know why I had been dragged up here to be asked the sort of stupid question that your uncle asks you when he can't think of anything to say.

'I don't know much about Wortley,' I said. 'I've been out of the office mainly. It's been interesting.'

'I sometimes think I should get out a bit more,' said Broberg. 'You know there's something you'll discover about the way companies work.' Oh, no, I won't, I said. Silently. 'I used to think I could sell anything to anybody. Now I go to meetings and talk to people on the phone. It's a funny thing. What do you make of Giles Buckland?'

Broberg had an unnerving technique. He would wander around the office, talking virtually at random, like some old man blabbering away about how wonderful it all was in the past. Then suddenly he would ask a question and look at you with a piercing expression and you'd feel you'd been put on the spot in a way you didn't quite understand. Now I thought of when I'd first met Giles and he'd been tiptoeing through the crap in his office and he'd told me that story of a Saxon that was betrayed by a bloody monk and he'd asked if I was going to be that monk. It had sounded paranoid, but he may have had this moment in mind. People talk about the key episodes in their life, the opportunity when you can take another step up the ladder. I thought of how to put it.

'Giles is not exactly like everybody else,' I said. 'But when I talked to Ms Kiely down in her office, she said how Giles had told her about that thing at DDP. He didn't have to do that. Lots of people would just have not got around to mentioning it and the credit for it would sort have stuck to them.'

'Hmm, interesting,' said Broberg, not sounding as if it was all that interesting. 'This DDP business. What did you think of it?'

'I don't know. Obviously it's not right to claim for things you've still got. A bit pathetic as well, this big rich company, all of them in their lovely suits, lugging a couple of computers downstairs. They could have been charged with fraud and for what? A couple of grand?'

'But we didn't call in the police. In the end we didn't even cancel the contract. What do you think of that?'

I shrugged.

'That's not my business.'

I felt that Broberg was jabbing at me, tempting me to say something. As if I particularly cared, one way or the other.

'You were the one who caught them out,' he said. 'You might be irritated that they weren't punished. Justice wasn't done.'

'It doesn't bother me,' I said. 'Ms Kiely said they rang up and grovelled over the phone. If they said they were sorry and promised not to do it again, I guess that's enough.'

'Are you married, Mark?'

That piercing look again. What the fuck was *that* about?

'No,' I said.

'Are you in a relationship?'

'I'm sorry,' I said. 'I don't really think . . .'

'I don't mean to be intrusive,' Broberg said. 'Well, I *do*, but it's for a reason. I was chatting to Donna. We were wondering if you'd be interested in doing some work for us. But it's not in London. You'd need to go away for a bit.'

'Just me?'

'You and Buckland.'

'What is it?'

Broberg put his hands in his pocket and wandered across the office, looking at the paintings on the wall. He was all casual and ruminative again.

'Nothing much,' he said. 'We've got a meeting tomorrow. What time is it, Donna?'

'Ten-thirty.'

'Ten-thirty. I'd like you to be there, Mark.'

'We've got some visits . . .'

'Put them off,' said Donna sharply.

'Sure,' I said.

'And you'll get Buckland,' Broberg said to Donna.

'Yes, Walt.'

'So we're done here.' We started to leave but then Broberg nodded at me. 'Can you stay for a moment, Mark?'

Donna left, a bit reluctantly. She probably thought Broberg was going to ask me what I thought of *her*. Broberg didn't look at me. His attention was apparently focused on one of his paintings.

'Donna told me that you said you wanted to do something fun. Something interesting. That right?'

'I said various things, I wasn't really . . .'

'It's not often that I hear people wanting to come into insurance for the fun. We should have you stuffed. We should have you stuffed and mounted and put on display in the foyer.'

An answer didn't seem called for. Broberg had the way of thinking aloud of someone who knew that people wouldn't interrupt him or tell him he was talking rubbish or just walk away from him.

'Like a whisky, Mark?'

'Yes, Mr Broberg.'

He walked over to a decanter stowed on one of the bookshelves and poured whisky into two glasses.

'How do you take it?'

'I don't know. I'm not really much of a whisky drinker.'

He handed me the glass as it was.

'Cheers,' he said. I sipped the drink carefully. 'What do you think of the painting?'

I took another sip. And looked at it. It was a huge canvas, mainly painted white. Pieces of wood and metal and barbed wire had been stuck to the surface and painted black.

'What's it called?' I said.

Broberg stepped forward and looked at a card propped up next to it.

'It's called: *To die is good. Better never to have been born.'*

'Interesting,' I said.

'We have a consultant,' Broberg said. 'He buys art for us. It used to be landscapes and winter scenes. But at the beginning of the nineties he started buying this modern stuff. He doesn't have half measures, this guy. He goes to the degree shows at Saint Martins and the Royal College of Art and if he likes someone he'll buy everything. He'll go to their studio and empty it. He's says if you're going to buy art, you've got to buy it aggressively. We've got a warehouse full of the stuff out in Staines. He ships a few in here every so often, for my office, for the lobby. If you want my opinion, most of this is a total con. But you've got to hand it to our consultant. He's a hell of an investor. A few years ago we were doing almost as well as art dealers as we were selling insurance. He'll pick the right moment and then he'll liquidate someone. Amazing.'

'I don't really know much about art,' I said.

' "Fun",' Broberg said. 'I was struck by that word. And intrigued. Because I think the exact opposite. Life used to be very interesting. Hundreds of years ago. If you took a thousand people. Let's call them merchants. In a particular few years, a few of them would be completely wiped out. Not by the market, but because their boat was wrecked or their warehouse burnt down. If you had a boat coming from Constantinople – or wherever the fuck these boats came from – full of silk and spices, you were tossing a coin. If it arrived you were rich, if it didn't you and your family were sitting in the mud with a begging bowl.'

'Yes,' I said. 'I sort of know this. I heard the pig story.'

'Fuck the pig story,' said Broberg. 'What I'm saying is that if you put your entire life on the line in that boat, then you'll do anything that's going. You'll pray, you'll give money to the Church, you'll throw bones, you'll talk about fate, you'll tell stories, you'll see patterns in the sky, whatever. Because if there's one boat out there on the sea, and it's your boat and your arse is tied to that boat, then all that matters is that boat. It's not as if there's a chance of seventy per cent of the boat arriving. It's a hundred per cent or nothing. It sinks or it arrives. Who the fuck knows why that one boat doesn't arrive? Maybe there was a freak typhoon. Maybe the captain was getting his end away in the cabin and it crashed into some rocks. Maybe the boatbuilder was pissed and forgot to bang a nail in. That's a story, that is. That's a fucking Shakespeare play.

'But with a thousand boats or ten thousand boats or a hundred thousand boats, now we've got something. Because then I don't care any more why people do things. If six per cent of boats sank two years ago and five per cent sank last year and seven per cent sank this year, then if you insure the merchant's cargo in return for ten per cent of what you'll pay him if it's lost, then his life stops being interesting. He knows where he'll be in six months' time. You hear what I'm saying? No God, no fate, no art. He doesn't have to slaughter a goat to stop a storm. Art and religion are things you do in the evening and at weekends. That's how we end up with this kind of shit on our walls.

'I'll tell you, Mark, I'm glad to have you aboard. But if you just remember that interesting is what you do in your own time, it'll go better with you. You hear what I'm saying?'

There was a long pause. I'd been trying to work out how the barbed wire was attached to the canvas. Was it just glued on, in which case it would eventually fall off? Maybe it was attached with small wires threaded through from the back.

'I don't know,' I said. 'I was happier with the pig story.'

He laughed, but the effect wasn't entirely one of warmth.

'Get the hell out of here, Mark. I'll see you in the morning.'

The phone rang in my flat at six-thirty the next morning. I picked the receiver up and groaned something.

'Mark? It's Giles. Are you up?'

'I am now.'

'What's happening?'

'Sorry?'

'Donna Kiely rang me late last night. There's a meeting. What the hell's going on? They went behind our backs on your DDP case. Are we out?'

'My DDP case?'

'It was a good call.'

'Giles, I'll ring you back in two minutes. Three minutes.'

I put the phone down. I felt unsteady on my feet. My skin was hot. Was I about to throw up? As I think I said, I didn't have much of a head for alcohol. I'd come back from the office and for some reason I'd felt in a panic and I'd drunk everything I could find in my room. There were three cans of lager and bottle of some ye olde traditional English ale and then something else. What was it? I thought it was brandy. I could easily find out. I'd thrown the bottle into the bin but I couldn't face looking at it. Bits of my tongue were stuck to the sides of my mouth. I went to the sink and swilled cold water until my tongue was freed and mobile again. I pulled some jeans on and made some instant coffee, which I drank hot and black.

I phoned Giles back and he picked up the phone after about a quarter of a ring. I told him about the previous evening, about what Broberg had said, everything. That just made things worse.

'He asked what you thought about me?'

'That's right.'

'What was that for?'

'I don't know,' I said. 'He was asking about this other job. Maybe he was sounding me out.'

'It's a trap,' said Giles. 'I don't trust them. Be careful what you say at this so-called meeting. When you go in there, look on the table. If there's a cheque lying there, that means you're being fired. That's your severance pay. There'll be a lawyer present. Admit nothing. If they can prove gross negligence, you won't even get the cheque.'

There wasn't a cheque on the table. There was coffee on it, in silver pots. There were two kinds of mineral water. The table was about twenty-five yards long and looked as if it was made out of slate. Something dark and heavy and expensive. When Donna Kiely brought Giles and me in, there were two people already sitting at the far end, a man and a woman. Donna had told us, or warned us, about them on the way up.

'They're Ross Cowan and Vicki Hargest. They're both vice-presidents,' she said. 'But these terms mean nothing. What you need to know is that Ross is an actuary. That's basically statistics and strategy. Vicki's risk management. They're big wheels in the company.'

'Fucking big wheels,' Giles murmured in my ear. He was still thinking about the cheque on the table. But he cheered up when he saw the coffee. Vicki made us go and sit at the end of the table with the others. She said it was going to be a small meeting. She introduced us all, and Ross and Vicki looked understandably puzzled. Who the fuck were we? Vicki Hargest was the most intelligent-looking woman, person, whatever, I'd ever seen. She had these round glasses with frames made out of what looked like thin copper wire. She even had intelligent-looking hair, fiercely curled. I tried to imagine her having sex. I wondered if she had sex intelligently, or maybe she was grossly sensual and uninhibited as a sort of counterpoint, and I was lost in this train of thought when I saw there were two more people in the room. Walter Broberg was murmuring to a man whose immaculately groomed hair and clothes and skin showed that he was even more senior. There was always someone grander, always somewhere with a better view.

Broberg introduced him as Fergus Nielsen from the Horton Group. I didn't dare ask what the Horton Group was, which was a good thing, because Giles told me afterwards that they were Wortley's parent company.

'It's good to be here,' Nielsen said in an affable tone. 'I

just came over to be a fly on the wall. You just go right
ahead.'

But when someone's flown over from the States in one of
the company's Gulfstreams just to be at your meeting, it's
like a ten-ton fly sitting in the middle of the table. Giles
started nervously lighting a cigarette and then Nielsen wondered aloud whether there wasn't a no-smoking policy in
the building and Giles virtually ate it in his rush to get it out
of sight. Broberg nodded at a woman in a black dress with
a white pinafore, and she poured us both coffee. Giles
spooned two sugars into his cup and started stirring it with
an irritating scraping sound.

'Giles, Mark,' said Broberg. 'We want you to go up to a
village called Marston Green for us. It's in Norfolk.'

For the first time Giles stopped looking nervous and
looked puzzled instead.

'In East Anglia?'

'Well, it's not Norfolk, Virginia.'

'What for?'

'Wouldn't you like a holiday in the country?' said Broberg
cheerfully. 'All expenses paid. It's a nice place, they say.'

'Yes, but why?'

'Vicki, can you give them the short version?'

Vicki Hargest took her glasses off and placed them on the
table. She rubbed the spot on her nose where they had rested.
She turned to us. Her brown eyes looked larger without her
glasses on.

'Marston Green is a medium-sized village near the south

Norfolk coast. But if you look at the map, it's really part of a network of small villages that stretch in all directions. Over the past few years there have been reports of illness scattered over the area. Some people, in the local press, in an action group, have described it as an epidemic. It has also been called a cluster.'

'What sort of illnesses?' asked Giles.

I took out a notebook from my jacket pocket.

'Put that away,' said Bromberg.

'I just wanted to make sure of the details.'

'Put it away.'

'I don't understand.'

'Mark, I promise you we have nothing to hide. But the purpose of this meeting is to kick some ideas around. In my experience, the only way for that to be done effectively is if people know they can make off-the-wall, crazy suggestions without them ending up in the *Guardian*. We're here to talk about options. So I wanted this to be an unminuted meeting. Vicki?'

Vicki gave a cough and carried on.

'The illnesses cover a whole range of conditions from respiratory illnesses, skin complaints and certain cancers. Note that I say "cancers". Cancer is not a single monolithic illness. Cancer is not a disease at all. It is a process that is shared in certain respects by more than two hundred different diseases. These are known as the cancers. There have been reported cases of forms of childhood leukaemia, of multiple myeloma, lymphoma, as well as breast cancer, sarcomas of the soft tissue and individual cases of others.

Obviously these illnesses occur across the country. The question is whether there is a concentration in the area of Marston Green. Whether there is a pattern.'

'What's our exposure?' asked Giles, sipping at his coffee. I didn't dare touch mine. I was feeling tense enough as it was. If any caffeine entered my system, I'd start babbling and shaking. Vicki Hargest leaned back in her chair. I was impressed. She was talking entirely without notes.

'Four miles north-west of Marston Green is an industrial site operated by a company called Marshco. In 1999, through our acquisition of Middleton Assurance, we took over the long-tailed public liability insurance contract with Marshco. There are many complicated issues involved here. But for the moment, suffice to say that they are a waste-management company and they operate an incinerator on the Marston Green site. There is also a landfill operation on an adjoining site.'

'And?' said Giles.

'There have been accusations about levels of dioxin emissions. There have also been claims about leakage into groundwater and into the River Teel, which flows beside the Marshco complex and through Marston Green. These have been denied by the company.'

'Truthfully?' asked Giles.

There was quite a long silence. Hargest looked around the table, seeming nervous for the first time.

'I'm choosing my words carefully,' she said. 'There is much about this situation that is complicated and unclear. We're here to talk about ways forward and there are a whole lot of variables. When we consider these, it would be realistic to assume that new information about Marshco's operating practices will emerge. There is nothing sinister about that. They are involved in a large-scale waste processing. They aren't just licking envelopes in there.'

'Has anything actually happened?' asked Giles. 'Are Marshco being sued?'

'No. There have been protests. A so-called action committee has been formed. The local Conservative MP, Sir Richard Coombes, asked a question in the House. There are rumours of a TV documentary.' There were some mutterings around the table. 'Only rumours. I should say that one possibility is that nothing will happen and it will all be forgotten.'

There was a pause. I started to feel a twitching in my stomach. I didn't dare look at Giles. This sounded big. Fergus Nielsen leaned forward.

'What is the very worst that could happen? Ballpark figure.'

Ross Cowan coughed.

'Obviously the worst that could happen is that lots of people are being made ill and dying, and that would be shocking.' There were murmurs and nods around the table to confirm how shocking that was. 'If what we mean is, what is worst for Wortley Insurance shareholders, and Horton Group and Horton Group's shareholders, the worst would be if this case came to court and it was established, one, that acts or omissions of Marshco had caused these illnesses and, two, that Marshco had behaved recklessly. If this were established it would be a question of hundreds of millions of pounds, possibly as much as a billion. But as we all know, Marshco, or other bodies owned by its parent company, Corton plc, have or have had operations in Lancashire, Yorkshire, and, well, across the country.'

'That's a lot to prove, though,' said Nielsen. 'You know, I'm thinking power lines, I'm thinking communities around nuclear power stations. Nobody's ever won a case.'

'I've been thinking asbestos,' said Cowan.

'But that was one fucking disease. What was it?'

'Mesothelioma,' said Giles.

'Right,' said Nielsen. 'And then Steve fucking McQueen died of it. This isn't asbestos.'

'There's Bhopal,' Cowan said.

'A Third World factory.'

'And Hiroshima.'

'I hear you, Ross. But these are different things.'

'Of course they're different,' said Cowan. 'Everything's as different from everything else as you want it to be. Especially catastrophes. The kind that wipe insurance companies out.'

Nielsen gave a dissatisfied grunt.

'One question,' he said. 'Marshco. They're big employers, right?'

'Pretty big,' said Vicki Hargest. 'They're not ICI but they are a medium-sized concern.'

'And they employ people from the Marston Green area?'

'Almost exclusively.'

'That's good to know. That's something for us all to

consider. But there's nobody to pay off, right?' he said. 'To make this go away?'

'There's no question of that,' said Vicki Hargest. 'What we've got are some ill people and some people making a fuss. And I should say that I'm a very long way away from being convinced that we've even got a case to answer. On the other hand, we're not sure how this case is going to develop. We don't know what these people have. Sorry, I don't mean the victims. The alleged victims. We know what *they've* got. I mean the campaigners.'

Now Broberg spoke: 'That's where you two clowns come in.' He meant me and Giles. 'We'd like you to go up there.'

Giles was pouring coffee into his cup, so vigorously that it splashed onto the table. Then he took a gulp.

'Sorry,' he said. 'And with all due respect, but what the fuck for?'

He took another aggressive mouthful of coffee. There was a terrible silence. Then there was a roar of laughter. It was not from me. It was from Fergus Nielsen.

'Point taken, Giles,' he said. 'What are our options? Ross, you do strategy. What do you say?'

Cowan thought for a moment.

'The best thing would be to prove that the contaminants . . .' He looked around the table. 'That Marshco's processes are not causing the illnesses. That's difficult. But I remember what my old maths professor used to tell me: if you can't solve a problem, find a related problem that you *can* solve. We could prove that something else is causing the illnesses, or is a factor. I assume we've noted the recent appeal court ruling that if an illness of an individual can be blamed on two separate persons or companies, then neither can be held liable.'

'Forget that one,' Vicki said. 'I was talking to legal about that one. It'll be reversed in the Lords.'

'That's a pity,' said Ross. 'I was excited about that. There's plenty else. We could demonstrate that another form of contamination was possible. If nothing else we – or you two – could kick a little dust around.'

'Another point,' Vicki Hargest said. 'This cluster idea might work for us. If we could show that one or a group of these illnesses had another probable cause, we'd be away. This is a weird area. You know, a group did research and they found that there was an increased incidence of cancer in areas where nuclear plants were planned but never built.'

'Why the hell was that?' asked Nielsen.

'I don't know,' said Hargest. 'Maybe something about what makes a place suitable for a nuclear plant is also associated with something carcinogenic. Who knows?'

'This is good,' said Nielsen. 'I like the sound of this.'

'The question is,' said Giles, 'whether this is a type-one error or a type-two error.'

This was a typical Giles pronouncement in that it resulted in an embarrassed silence with people looking at each other round the table.

'What the hell are they?' said Nielsen.

113

'Something I think about every day,' said Giles. 'A type-one error is seeing patterns that aren't there. A type-two error is not seeing patterns that are there.'

That cast a bit of a pall over the conversation. I think people were trying to work out in their minds which was which. And then, I don't know what made me do it, but I spoke for the first time since I'd said, yes, I wanted milk in my coffee.

'There is one other thing we might do, while we're up there. I mean one thing that Mr Cowan left out of his options.'

'Yes?' said Broberg. 'What's that?'

'We might find out that Marshco *were* responsible for the illnesses.'

Another long silence and I thought to myself: What did you say that for?

'That's true,' said Nielsen in a quiet voice. 'And if that is so, Mark, we would certainly like to be the first to know. So that we can make due reparation. But a thing like that is hard to prove.'

Suddenly it was like that awkward moment when you're having a drink with someone and you realize it's time to go but nobody can quite say it.

'Why us?' said Giles.

'What?' said Broberg.

'You've got loss adjusters. Ms Hargest has a whole department of risk assessors. We've got lawyers. We even use professional investigators from time to time. With all due respect to Mark and his fine qualities, why are you sending one and a half claims investigators?'

Broberg gave a shrug.

'Good question,' he said. 'We've thought about this a good deal. What we're not doing is sending down people to negotiate with the different parties on behalf of Wortley Insurance. In fact, what we feel at the moment is that there are no different parties at the moment. Nothing has crystallized. There's a few people sounding off. A couple of local journalists had space to fill when the vicarage fete got rained off. And we don't want to send in investigators or scientists, because, so far as we and Marshco are concerned, there's nothing to investigate. If a couple of City lawyers in their suits arrive in this excuse for a village, people will start smelling money.

'It'll all be nice and casual. We don't want you climbing over walls at midnight and listening behind walls. We just want you to go there, shake some hands, get to know people, get a feel for the place. Have fun. That's what you want, isn't it, Mark? But not too much fun. You hear what I'm saying? I'll tell you where you can start.'

Broberg had been fingering a piece of paper. Folding it, unfolding it, smoothing it out. Now he slid it along to Giles. Giles looked at it and then passed it to me.

'There we are,' he said. 'Document one for your file.'

I looked at it. It was the sort of handbill you might get for a school fete or a car-boot sale. 'The Marston Green Cluster' was written in large capital letters. 'The Marshco Incinerator has been poisoning our neighbourhood for years. People are dying and it is time to act. Residents interested in forming an action committee are asked to attend a meeting in the Village Hall.'

'All welcome,' I said, reading aloud from the bill.

'So there you are,' said Broberg. 'Go and get to know them.'

'How long do we go for?' asked Giles.

'You mean the meeting?'

'No. Marston Green. How long do we stay there?'

'Whatever it takes. A few weeks, whatever. You decide.'

'Weeks? I've got a family. I've got children.'

'Jesus, Giles, you're not going to Dubai. You can come back on the train. Bring them some rock or cheese or whatever they make up there.'

Giles was silent and glowering as we made our way back downwards to his office. He muttered a goodbye to Donna, who saw us down in the lift. We reached his office and he pushed the door shut behind us, roughly pushing piles of paper out of the way with his feet. I worried about his organic system.

'So what do you think?' he said.

'Can you get away?' I said. 'Is that all right with your wife?'

He gave a sarcastic, bitter laugh.

'That's the least of my problems. But what do you make of it? What do you think they're playing at?'

'I don't think they're playing at anything in particular.'

'They're setting us up.'

'How?'

'Don't trust them. If we achieve something, then they'll take it over, the way they always do. But this Marshco business, this gives us the chance to fuck up big time. If anything goes wrong, we'll be the ones who are hung out to dry. They don't care about us.'

'I don't think so, Giles. I think the main thing is that we're cheap and they can send us up there with nothing much to lose.'

'No,' said Giles. 'There's a plan. There's always a plan.'

'I don't know.'

'Oh, and there's something else.'

'What's that?'

'Can you come to supper? With me and Susan, my wife. Tomorrow. It would be good.'

Oh fuck, I thought.

'That would be great,' I said. 'Thanks.'

On the way to Giles's house, I'd bought a mangy bunch of flowers from a petrol station. I felt it was possibly worse than nothing. Petrol stations don't source their greenstuffs from the finest nurseries. I imagined them being chemically induced under aftificial light somewhere industrial and transported down motorways in chilled containers.

As I walked along the busy high street I saw what looked like a flower stall but on closer inspection turned out to be one of these strange modern shrines that are created at the spot where a child has been drowned or murdered or, I suppose in this case, run over. A photograph of a small boy had been taped to railings. Ornate golden plastic frame. He was wearing a school tie, his hair brushed so that it shone.

I remembered the 'kerb drill' we'd been taught when I was at school. 'Look right, look left, look right again and then cross.' They forget to add 'unless a car is coming'. Apparently some children thought they were magically protected by the act of looking and just set off regardless.

I looked left and right also, but I wasn't looking for cars. I was checking if I was being observed. I looked at the flowers. There was a particularly nice, fresh bunch. I looked at the raggedy flowers in my hand. I looked at the nice, fresh bunch. After all, it had done its job. The act of giving was the important thing. And it could be said that the needs of the living were more important than those of the dead. I unfastened the flowers. I didn't just steal them. I replaced them with my own bunch.

Susan, Giles and their two children lived in a small house in a terrace of small houses, joined all the way along the road. The internal walls had been knocked down so that the ground floor was one medium-sized room rather than about three mouse-sized rooms. There was no hallway. I stepped straight off the street and bumped into a sofa. While Susan was getting a jug for my rather fine bouquet, I saw that it had company. Around the room, on the mantelpiece and shelves and ledges, were small vases and glasses and pots with feeble stalks projecting out of them. I knew that one of the signs of being grown up was to have indoor plants, the sort you have in offices, out in reception; they had huge creepy plasticky dark-green leaves. These were just shoots, dotted around.

'You're puzzled,' said Giles, appearing in the doorway. He had come from the kitchen, which was in an extension built out into the small garden. He was in his off-duty dress of a T-shirt and very faded jeans with a hole in one knee that was so large and wide that the lower part of the trouser leg was almost falling away. 'You're wondering what it is, all this horticulture.'

'I don't really know much about it,' I said, meaning I didn't care much about it.

'Guess what they are, though,' he insisted. 'You want a beer?'

He had two bottles in his hand and he handed me one.

'I couldn't possibly,' I said.

'Don't you drink?'

'I mean the things. The plants.'

'Look more closely.'

I bent down and made the effort.

'They look like pips,' I said. 'Pips and stones. Is that a peach stone?'

Giles took a gulp from his beer.

'Probably. There are peach plants, grapes, nectarines, apples, pears, avocados, almost anything you can think of.'

'I'm amazed you can get all this to grow.'

'It's not me, it's Susan. It's a Darwinian process. Every single grape pip, every avocado stone that enters these premises is put in water, and some of them sprout and some of them don't. The ones that don't go into the bin. They are replaced by the stones or pips from whatever plums or apples we've eaten that day.'

Susan came back into the room with my flowers in a plastic measuring jug. She put them on the table. It had been laid with three places, so I realized that nobody else was coming and also that I would have to look at them for the entire evening. She noticed that I was looking at her plants.

'The ones that do well,' she said, 'I'll take outside and put in pots.'

'Will you get peaches and avocados?' I said. 'I mean eventually.'

'No,' said Giles, so firmly that there didn't seem anything else to say.

There was a silence and I looked at Susan. I tried to decide whether she was a female version of Giles. Whenever I meet a couple, I compare them, see which one is better looking. At first glance, I thought that he had done a bit better than she had. She had a face that was all angles, cheekbones and chin, but it looked softer because of her curly dark hair and her large brown eyes. She wore black trousers and a floppy purple sweater. Those eyes were shiny, dark-ringed, the aftermath of something. I wondered if there had been an argument before I arrived. She said she had to finish putting the children to bed and that I could come and say goodnight to them. For just a second I thought of saying, no, I was happy where I was, but I chickened out and followed her upstairs. There was a three-year-old girl called Jude and a boy called Roland who was one. Roland immediately went for me and started hugging my knee. I was more interested in Susan as she did her dizzying performance act of getting her children ready for bed. Items of clothing, toys, books, shoes, children were tossed in different directions, and at the end of the process there was a pile of clothes by the door, Roland and Jude were in bed and things were arranged in neat piles. I thought of the slanted picture on my wall. When we got out of the room she became aware of my gaze and looked at me suspiciously.

'What?' she said.

'Looking at you,' I said. 'Doing all that clearing up. It reminded me of something.'

'What?'

'I don't know. I think it might be *Mary Poppins*. It's so long since I saw it. Didn't she clear up a room?'

'I don't know.'

'Except I think she did it just by twitching her nose.'

She gave me a funny look. I mean a really odd one, as if she was a bit worried about the man who was spending time with her husband. It didn't matter. It was a quarter to eight. I'd got to the house too early by mistake because there'd been no delays on the Underground. But even so, I reckoned two and a half hours would be enough. Even that sounded quite a long time with just the two of them.

When we came back down, Giles was looking distracted. He was staring at a big fat fly which was buzzing and buzzing around the room. Sometimes it swept past his head and he flinched each time as if it was hurting him.

'Why is it so irritating?' he said. 'Do you ever feel that the fly is inside your head?'

'No,' I said.

'I sometimes think of inventions. While you were upstairs, I was thinking of a good one for people like me. It would be a miniature vacuum cleaner, the size of a spray can, just for sucking up flies.'

Susan looked dubious.

'Aren't there flyswatters for that?'

'That's the point,' said Giles. 'People are disgusted by flyswatters. They mash the fly. You end up with fly viscera smeared on your window and on the swatter itself. Then you have to pick up the fly itself and dispose of it. With my invention it would just be sucked into the vacuum cleaner.'

'Couldn't you just use a real vacuum cleaner?' I said. Giles looked puzzled, so I explained. 'You could just take the attachment off at the end and use the nozzle. You can probably generate more suction with a large cleaner.'

Giles shrugged.

'Obviously I wasn't literally saying I would invent a miniature vacuum cleaner. It was just an idea.'

He glanced over at Susan. I thought she was going to give one of those shared winks that couples exchange but Susan looked unresponsive. She left the table and while Giles and I were talking she came back and forth from the kitchen with dishes, bottles, glasses. She opened two bottles of Bulgarian wine, which reminded me that I should have brought a bottle myself. She ladled soup with stuff in it into three bowls. Giles just started eating without apparently noticing it, as if it was something that had always been there in front of him. Susan poured about a third as much for her as for me and just dipped her spoon in an exploratory way as if she just wanted to get a sense of the texture. I tried to think of something to say.

'Do you work?'

'I'm a social worker.'

'Nice,' I said.

'What do you mean?' she said with a frown.

I was fully aware that it had been an inane comment, but I thought it was mean of her to make a big deal of it. I was tempted to say that 'nice' was what you say when somebody tells you what they do. Instead I just mumbled something about helping people. Susan didn't reply. At least time was passing.

'How are you feeling?' Giles asked.

'You mean me?' I said.

'Yes.'

'You mean here, now, at this exact moment?'

'I was thinking about work. And about going up to sniff around in this village.'

'I'm rather looking forward to it. What about you?'

Giles took a couple of spoonfuls of soup and then scraped the remainder out of the bowl. He took a sip of wine. I made a gesture of starting to collect the bowls up but Susan shook her head. She took them off to the kitchen.

'When I want to know how I feel,' Giles said, 'I observe my own behaviour, just in the way I would look at someone else's behaviour. Does that sound strange?'

'I don't see the point.'

'So what do *you* do?'

'If someone asks how I feel, I look at how I feel and tell them.'

'What do you look at?'

'I don't mean look,' I said. 'As it happens, I don't spend much of my time talking about how I feel. But when you asked me how I felt, I thought for about one second and then told you.'

'But what did you think *about*?'

'About how I felt.'

'You mean, you noted some sensations in your brain and then decided what sort of feelings they were.'

'I know how I feel, Giles. It's not a difficult thing to find out.'

Giles looked dissatisfied, as if he had an itch down at that awkward spot in the lower part of your back, and he knew that he couldn't reach it and so he was just sitting there thinking about the itch.

'You see,' he said. 'Imagine a frozen pond. You ask a woman if the ice is safe to skate on and she says yes. But then you notice that she's keeping her own children away from the ice.'

'She's just lying about what she really thinks.'

'Lying?' said Giles. 'If she was a politician, she would say it was matter of privacy and personal choice. "Why should I sacrifice my children to my personal views?"'

'You've lost me a bit,' I said.

Susan returned with a large piece of fish in a yellowy sauce on a platter.

'Why is it a woman?' she said.

'What?'

'Why does the villain in your little parable happen to be a woman?'

'That's irrelevant.'

Susan cut the fish deftly and arranged it onto three plates. She gave herself hardly more than a spoonful. Then she heaped broccoli, green beans and potatoes around the fish. I took a bite of the fish.

'You might make the same observation of yourself,' Giles

said. 'Someone might ask you how you are, and you say, "Fine," which is the compulsory answer to that question. You might even think you really are happy. Then you look at your own behaviour. On examination you discover that you find it hard to get out of bed in the morning, you get into trivial arguments, you leave your food unfinished, and you realize that you're depressed.'

'The reason that you leave your food unfinished,' said Susan, 'is that you talk all the time.'

'I was giving an example.'

I noticed that Susan wasn't eating her food at all, just rearranging it on the plate in a way that mimicked all the processes of eating except for the bit where the food is put in the mouth and swallowed. She looked at me and we held each other's gaze for just a beat too long.

'Do you know why Giles went into insurance?' she said.

'No,' I said.

There was something wrong with the evening. It was like having dinner in some primitive pagan hut. I was thinking of the sort of Viking household where there's a man of the household and a guest comes to dinner and the two of them talk and the wife stands in the corner and only comes forward to pour a jug of mead or whatever it is that Vikings drank with their food.

Susan was sitting at the table but she might as well not have been. She might as well have been in the corner with the mead. It was all about Giles and me. Even when Susan spoke, it was to get Giles to say something to me or me to ask Giles something. None of it was about her. If she was trying to prompt a reminiscence it didn't work. He spoke dismissively.

'The story of why I came to work for Wortley is not why we're here this evening.'

Susan took a deep drink of wine. I wondered if they had been drinking, as well as arguing, before I arrived.

'Giles was an evolutionary geneticist,' she said. 'Doing research in a laboratory outside Cambridge. And now he's going door to door checking stains in carpets. Surely that's worth a story.'

'It's not much of a story,' Giles said.

'It's a great story,' said Susan.

'It's not a great story,' said Giles. 'It's not a story at all.'

'I bet that Mark would like to hear it,' said Susan, looking at me. Some kind of answer was called for.

'There'll be plenty of time for that,' I said. 'In the long evenings up in East Anglia.' Susan shot a look over at Giles. Maybe this was not a good area to stray into. 'I'm still thinking about that skating rink.'

'It was ice on a pond.'

'You know,' I said, 'I'm not at all clear what you were on about. But if what you're saying is that you don't want to go, you don't have to. Or you could come later and just be there part of the time. You've got a family. I don't care where I am. And Wortley's paying, so I guess it'll be some-where better than my place in Camden.'

'So what are your thoughts, Mark?' said Giles.

That was the problem. Giles's answers to me never quite seemed to follow on from what I'd said.

127

'You mean going to Marston Green?'

'I mean the whole thing. Marshco. The cancer. The cluster.'

'I'm not sure why they're sending us. I mean, why they're sending *us*.'

'That's the whole point,' said Giles. He emptied the last of the wine bottle into his glass. He was becoming expansive. 'Want some more?'

'Well . . .'

He nodded at Susan, who went off to get another bottle.

'So?'

'It's going to be interesting,' I said.

'Thinking of making a name for yourself?'

'What?'

'That DDP thing might have gone to your head.' Another sip of wine. 'You'll do something brilliant. Spot something no one else has spotted.'

'I've got no plans,' I said.

'You haven't thought about it?' he said. 'You might find the smoking gun. Become a hero.'

'Giles,' I said, 'I've been trying to get some clothes together. I've been looking for Marston Green on the map. I haven't thought about what we're going to do when we get there. You're the one in charge.'

Susan returned with another opened bottle of wine. She filled the three glasses. Giles saw her coming and quickly emptied his, so that he would get the full amount.

'With this cancer stuff,' he said. 'Who's going to prove that there is a connection? And who's going to prove that there isn't?'

'You're the biologist,' I said.

He snorted into his wine.

'It's not my field,' he said. 'Look. The point is ... The point is ...' His brow was furrowed as if the point was eluding him. 'It's like gambling. You don't play poker, do you, Mark?'

'I think we've had this conversation, Giles.'

'The point about gambling is not who plays beautifully. It's about who walks away with the most money at the end. That's all that Wortley give a fuck about. I don't know what the hell we're going to get up to in that backwater. We can look into the mouths of dying children and take soil samples and collate statistics and argue with Green activists, but Wortley want to get out of there having maximized their shareholder value. They'll want a deal, and they haven't sent us up there as deal-makers.'

'Why not?' I said. 'If we happened – for example – to find something else that could have caused the cancer.'

'That'll be a matter of opinion,' he said. 'It's all seeing patterns. If there's any science there it will get shouted down. We've got no kind of brief, so we've got to make our own and I'll tell you what it is.' He waggled a trembly finger at me. 'We'll go there, compile a brief report, get out.'

I took a small sip of my wine. I was taking about a quarter of a sip for each eight sips he took.

'Giles,' I said. 'If you want, I could go ahead, get things ready, find somewhere to stay.'

Giles shook his head.

'No, not at all.'

129

'That's a good idea,' Susan said.

'I'll just do the routine stuff,' I said. 'I'll find out who's who and make some basic arrangements. Then after a couple of days you can come up and we can get to work.'

There was a silence. I wondered if the argument had been about Giles going away.

'We could talk about that,' Susan said.

'It's fine by me,' I said. 'Just let me know.'

'Giles said he thought you were a good thing,' said Susan.

'Thanks,' I said.

'You know why it was that he gave up research?'

'Susan . . .' He made an attempt to stop her.

'He got depressed by it.'

'That's not true,' said Giles.

'Not true?'

'Not true. That's what you said at the time. And I said then, as I'm saying now: not true.'

'I'm sorry, Giles,' she said. 'I'm just following the example of your pond story. I know that when asked if you were depressed, you said no, you were fine. But for me that was just another one of your symptoms. I was thinking of things like, that you were unable to get out of bed in the morning, that you couldn't sleep.'

'I didn't want to get up because I hadn't slept.'

'You didn't eat. You started drinking more heavily. You stopped looking after your appearance.'

'I could argue with these points one by one, except it would start to bore Mark.' He turned to me. 'It generally needs to be explained to people who blunder into our little psychodrama that my wife has a theory not only that I need therapy but that it ought to be conducted in public.

'As it happens, the reason that I went into insurance was not because of depression. It was because of my aunt.'

'Your aunt?' said Susan, looking baffled.

'She's sort of an aunt. At least, I used to call her Auntie Frankie. But her real name is Frances McDonald.'

'What's this got to do with anything?' asked Susan.

'It was before your time.'

'Before my time? I've never even heard of this woman.' Susan turned to me. 'Giles has the strangest family.'

Giles paid her no attention.

'She was the cleverest person I've ever met. When I was a kid she'd play games with us but it was all about numbers: magic squares, triangular numbers.'

'You're losing me,' I said.

'She was a real mathematician. She did secret stuff in the war, codes or something, but her real work was with an insurance company. She was an actuary, like Ross Cowan, who you met yesterday. I was amazed by that, using figures and formulas to tell you how many people were going to die in car crashes next year.'

'She could do that?' I asked.

'More or less,' he said. 'I liked that. She was applying mathematics to people falling off ladders and going through windscreens. So when I wanted a change, insurance seemed a good idea.'

'Which is why you now spend your time checking up on broken washing machines.' Susan gave Giles a sarcastic look.

'What's the problem?' he asked.

'It's just that I don't remember you talking about Aunt Frankie at the time.'

I wondered if Susan would dare to carry on. Susan was looking at me, as if she expected me to prompt her by asking questions about Giles's psychological condition. I sort of wanted to, but then I thought I'd better not use up all the intriguing stuff on our first evening together.

'It's late,' I said, making that strange sort of symbolic preliminary movement out of my chair signalling that I'm not actually making a run for the door as if the fire bell has gone, but departure is imminent. 'I've got to get across London.'

'Make your escape while you can, Mark,' said Giles. 'The laser beam of my wife's analytic attention hasn't moved on to you yet. Soon it'll be your turn to be interrogated about your parents and your childhood.'

'It's not very interesting,' I said.

'Ah,' said Giles. 'That'll be Susan's starting point, your strange evasiveness.'

'We'll do it next time,' said Susan, standing up. That meant that my symbolic movement out of the chair had to turn into a real one. Sometimes you have to fight your way out of people's houses. Oh, please, have some coffee. Have a third portion of cake. But Susan seemed happy for me to go. At the door I kissed her on both cheeks and said thank you and how wonderful the food was.

'You could have brought someone,' she said. 'If you wanted.'

I shrugged.

'I was in a relationship,' I said. 'But, you know . . .'

'Oh, I'm sorry,' she said, as if somebody had died. She may have wanted a heart to heart on the subject but I already had one foot through the door. A minute later I was walking towards Kilburn High Road feeling relieved and wondering which way the tube station was. It was a weirdly warm spring night. I would like to have walked home. I thought about it for a moment. I had an idea that the canal went near Kilburn and that I could walk beside it all the way to King's Cross. I thought of the moon reflected in the waters and walking along by the trees. I also thought of being set upon and gang raped and thrown into the water unconscious. So I went home by tube.

Marston Green's website invited tourists to visit the village and see the tenth-century church with its unusual rood screen. There was the Guildhall and there was a cross in the High Street which marked the spot where the Catholic martyr John Cornysshe was burned at the stake. I wondered what Cornysshe would have thought, as his skin started to bubble, about his execution being used to entice people to Marston Green to eat cream teas. I'd sat in the office at Wortley and read about the bus service (four a day, fewer at weekends) and felt a little gloomier.

It was all so simple. The site gave the phone number of a tourist office that was attached to the town hall. I rang and spoke to a very nice woman called Jo and told her I was looking for somewhere to stay that wasn't a hotel. The thought of spending weeks scraping butter out of little foil wrappers and making coffee with a kettle in the room gave me acute suicidal impulses.

That wasn't a problem, said Jo. She knew of some holiday cottages, well, chalets, really, that had been refurbished over the previous couple of years. It had cost a fortune, she told me, and then there had been the foot-and-mouth outbreak and they were hardly ever occupied. Those were just off the High Street. If I wanted something more rural and remote, she had a list she could fax me of cottages further out. I said the chalets sounded fine. Within two minutes I was talking to Geoff Otley, landlord of the Four Feathers Tavern and owner of the chalets, and within five I had made a deposit on my new Wortley credit card and made an open-ended booking of two of them. Two. That was very important. If I was going to be spending days in the countryside, I didn't want to see Giles's face over the breakfast table. Or wait for him to get off the toilet.

It was the right idea, anyway, because then Giles could have Susan and the kids up whenever they wanted. I would go up ahead and get some basic information. Giles would follow a couple of days later and we would cobble together a report and get the hell back to London. We had a brief meeting with Donna Kiely before we left, and that seemed to be what she wanted as well.

'No heroics,' she said. 'Mr Broberg has been very clear about your brief. This is a preliminary fact-finding visit. Don't provoke anything. Don't try and solve the problem on our behalf. You have no authority to speak on behalf of Wortley or Marshco, or to enter into any agreement of any kind.'

'And if we're caught,' I said, 'you'll deny all knowledge of us.'

'What?' said Donna.

'It sounds like a spy film,' I said. 'We're being sent on a hopeless mission.'

'I think it's more like one of those science-fiction stories,' said Giles. 'We're being sent in a time machine into the distant past. I mean, going into the English countryside *is* like travelling to the distant past. And our prime directive is that we mustn't interfere with history while we're there or else we'll come back to London and discover that electricity hasn't been invented.'

Donna left a long pause.

'Are we done?' she said finally.

'No,' I said. Giles looked at me and mouthed an urgent no at me but it was too late. 'Donna, what is it that you *really* want?'

Donna looked thoughtful.

'We want a resolution we can all feel good about,' she said finally. 'But what we want mostly is for nothing to happen. That's how insurance companies earn their money. From nothing happening.'

I wanted to ask who 'we' was. The three of us in the room? The Wortley board? Marshco? All of us, including the ailing citizens of Marston Green? God? But Giles must have noticed a dangerous gleam in my eye because he hurriedly told Donna that we would report to her and then he hustled me out of the door.

I had arrived at the station in Worsham, a town dominated by the huge silos of a sugar-beet factory. A taxi took me through a council estate, along country lanes to Marston Green and the Four Feathers. I found Geoff Otley in an office round the back. He was tapping numbers into a computer. He didn't look like the host of a country pub. In

136

fact he soon told me that he was an ex-social-worker from Dudley. He was tall and pale with curly dark hair. He took me through to the empty bar to collect the keys. I looked around the saloon bar. On the walls were cartwheels and bridles and horse brasses. There was an engraving of a horse pulling a plough. 'All fake,' said Geoff. 'There's a company in Malaysia that makes the whole range.'

We walked out to the chalets. They had been made from an old stable yard and each chalet was given a horse-type name – Blackie, Dobbin and so forth. I was put in Clover. Giles would get Dobbin when he arrived. The chalet was neat and simple inside. I had a bedroom, decorated with a picture of a windmill above the dressing table. ('Malaysia,' said Geoff. 'They're incredible. As long as you don't want anything Malaysian.') The living room had a sofa, a little kitchen in the corner, a dining table, everything.

'If you want to do your shopping,' said Geoff, 'there's a superstore the other side of Worsham.'

'I don't have a car,' I said.

'Got a computer?'

'Yes.'

'Just go to their website. They'll deliver.'

I met Geoff for a drink as soon as the pub opened that evening. Wortley bought us both a pint of Suffolk bitter. It was a meal in a glass. I thought that Geoff could fill me in on the anti-Marshco campaign. He'd never heard of it.

'I know about the Marshco plant,' he said. 'A lot of the employees drink here. Now if you want to hear about a campaign, I'll tell you about the one to stop the airfield.

There was a farmer up the road wanted to turn his farm into an air club. They were up in arms. When I arrived, it had already been going on for years. There were lawyers, a public inquiry. Total failure. Later in the summer you won't be able to move for parachutists landing on your head. Gets me a lot of custom. Anyway, they've got to do something with the countryside. It's not worth growing anything on it. I'm surprised they've got the stomach for another fight.'

I've always disliked the countryside but previously I'd only disliked it from a distance. My reasons were vague and underinformed. What I disliked mainly about it was that it wasn't London. There wasn't enough in it and what there was was too scattered. Sometimes I'd switch on the radio and hear someone from the countryside moaning because the one shop in their village was closing down and my main response would be: shut up or move to London. One shop. In London you can think of the weirdest thing you can imagine and you can choose between ten shops devoted to it.

But you have to spend a lot of time in the countryside to hate it properly. My authentic loathing only began after I found myself with a spare hour before the meeting in the village hall, the inaugural gathering of the Marston Green Cluster Action Group, or whatever it was going to be called. I couldn't think of anything else, so I decided to do that thing that people do in the country: go for a walk.

The previous day I'd stood with Geoff and looked up at the fields that sloped up and away to one side of the town. I'd thought there was mainly wheat and corn and sheep in the countryside, but the two giant fields were beautiful. One of them was full of yellow flowers so bright that it was hard to look at them. They merged into a golden dazzle. The other field was a much more delicate blue, like a blue cloud hovering just above the ground.

'Is that lavender?' I said.

Geoff shook his head.

'That's linseed, that is.'

'What's that for? I used to get it in cans when I was a boy and rub it into my cricket bat.'

'Dunno,' said Geoff. 'The other's rape.'

'That's a really terrible name,' I said.

'You wait till you cop a whiff of it.'

So on this May afternoon I walked along the lane that led up and between the two fields and I couldn't believe that a couple of hours would get me back to Camden Town.

I saw a ripple of wind across the rape field and then the smell hit me in waves. At first it was just the basic nice smell you get from a bunch of flowers, but there was more to it than that. First there was something abrasive about it. I don't go to the dentist very often. I've got good teeth. But once or twice I've had some drilling done. The dentist had done his injection with that insanely oversized needle that looks like it was invented for a mad scientist. Then he started drilling and the funny thing was that I knew the pain was still there but I didn't feel it. It's like being drunk and you know you're behaving embarrassingly, you know there's embarrassment in the air, but you're not feeling any of it. It was like that with the rape. Rape. Rape. Rape. Rape. Rape, rape, rape, rape. I had to say it lots of times to try

140

and get over the ridiculousness of the name. I thought of some scientist developing this new plant and saying to the people in the lab, 'I think I'll call it rape,' and them all going, 'Yeah, right.' And then in six months they look at the seed packet and they see that, fuck, he wasn't joking. Or maybe he did it while pissed, and it was too late to change. He probably made some pathetic explanation: 'Its real name is oil-seed rape. Nobody will ever get them confused.' You think of them at their scientific conferences, talking about rape this and rape that. The potential for misunderstanding is enormous.

I've never suffered from hay fever at all, but when I felt that breath of the rape flowers in my nostrils and my throat, I knew what hay fever must be about. There was a miniature, almost undetectable scratchiness, like tiny razor-sharp hairs being dragged through everywhere I breathed.

And there was the smell. You really had to be there, but it made me think of this time when I was sixteen and one of my friends called Aidan had a party. His parents had gone away for the weekend and they said he could have a party, that he was mature enough. The fools.

To put it very briefly, everybody came. Psychotic friends of friends. People who had been expelled from school for being too scary. By they end it was just anybody. The worst time of all was had by Aidan, who spent the entire party trawling around trying to establish if people lying unconscious were actually dead and trying to stop people from pushing bits of furniture out of upper windows. Aren't there people who say that if God doesn't exist, then everything is allowed? It's not something I particularly understand. The last time I looked at the world, everything was already allowed. But in any case, that certainly applies for lots of people in parties in other people's houses when the parents are away. That's when people start testing boundaries.

A few of us had agreed to meet on the Sunday morning to help clear up. It was a scene of amazing destruction, but the really funny thing was how, once you turned stuff the right way up and back in its place, how much of it turned out not to be broken. There was a window with a crack in it that was only visible from a particular angle. There were a few smashed glasses and a shelf had fallen off the wall taking some plaster down with it. A bed upstairs had collapsed. But we were able to take remedial action of various kinds of dubiousness with all of those.

The real problem was in Aidan's parents' bedroom, where some unidentified person had copiously puked up. With much holding of breath, we cleared up the actual vomit and then scrubbed the entire area with some carpet cleaner we'd found in a kitchen cupboard. We opened all the windows. An hour later, when everything else was proceeding merrily, a couple of us did a major second scrub of the affected area.

Then we did a third scrub with some water to which we added some bleach because someone thought they'd read something in a household advice column somewhere. We could still smell puke but tried to tell ourselves that maybe puke molecules had got caught in our nose hairs, or we knew what to smell for so we were more sensitive. So an hour after that when another friend came round we took him up to the bedroom and didn't tell him anything. His face crinkled up immediately and he asked who had thrown up.

So one of us went round to a corner shop and bought a spray can of rose-scented air freshener and we emptied virtually the entire can into the air of Aidan's parents' bedroom. We tried to kid ourselves that we had succeeded. Certainly there was a rich collection of smells in the bedroom. There was the sickly sweet imitation rose, there was washing-up liquid, the sharp tang of carpet cleaner, the bleach fumes that made your eyes water. But stubbornly beneath it all there was puke, pungent and unmistakeable. And somehow all the other smells, especially the air freshener, made it worse. It was like trying to make dirt easier to eat by mixing it up with chocolate. If you're going to eat dirt, just eat the fucking dirt and get it over with.

The smell of the rape was like that. Under the smell of the flowers, there was something that was a bit difficult to place, but it wasn't nice. It was a little bit like puke, but there was also just a whiff of dog shit, but sort of dog shit in the next room. And once I'd noticed the under-smell, the flowery over-smell started to seem sickly and made me want to gag.

I decided that when I next went to the supermarket, I would find the rapeseed oil and take a surreptitious sniff to see if even the oil had a touch of dog crap about it. It couldn't, could it? But then there was goat. I'd been taken to the children's zoo when I was a child and I'd stroked a goat. There was that unforgettable sharp goaty smell and the first time I ever had some goat cheese I recognized that same smell and it put me right off. I've never been able to eat anything connected with goat ever since: goat's milk, goat's cheese. I saw leg of goat in the supermarket once. There didn't seem to be much of a rush for it.

I wended my way along the road and left the rape seed behind me. There was a field of grass, then a pair of semi-detached houses that looked as if they had been lifted by helicopter out of a street in Croydon and dropped here. I heard a moo and saw that there was a farm ahead. I don't want to go on about smells too much, but the smell from this farm was staggering. There were some cows in the field on the far side, with matted muddy coats and snotty noses. In the main yard, there was a line of pigsties. I couldn't be exactly sure which one the smell came from, but I would have bet on the pigs.

I guess you don't have particularly high expectations of a place where pigs live. Hence the saying, this looks like a pigsty. But this pigsty really did look like a pigsty, even for a pigsty. It looked like the pigs had built and maintained it themselves. Except on closer examination I wondered if they were really to blame.

I didn't want to get too close. The smell was so rank I thought it might be toxic, it might be dissolving my interior tissues. But this yard really was worth looking at. Take the stalls themselves that the pigs lived in. There were six of them in a line perpendicular to the gate I was leaning on. There was a breeze-block construction that the pig or pigs could retreat into and then there was an open area sur-rounded by fences, and at the front, a gate that covered the entire width of the stall. This was the only way in or out for the pig. You would have expected that when choosing the gates for your pig stalls, you would go to the gate shop and buy half a dozen. But this was the clever thing: no two of the gates were alike. I checked carefully and they weren't.

Also, I'm not an expert, but it didn't look to me as if any of them were designed for the purpose. If they had, they would have been on hinges and not fastened on with bits of clothesline and rope and electric cable. There were a couple of rusty farm gates. One of them was too big and overlapped the next stall entrance as well. There was a wooden gate that looked as if it had come from a horse paddock. There were some bits of fencing, a sheet of corrugated iron, and for the furthest stall, the farmer seemed to have given up altogether and just leaned an old door sideways and propped it in place with a couple of oil drums.

I thought of the sort of books you'd read as a toddler with pictures of Things You Find in a Farmyard. This muddy smelly yard was full of things you wouldn't expect to find in a farmyard. There were piles of wooden pallets. Some of them had been broken up and I could see that here and there they had been used for reconstructing parts of the wall in the wooden shelter, where I could glimpse various tools. There were piles of bricks and breeze blocks, a stack of railway sleepers. There were a couple of plastic buckets, heavily stained with white paint. Many sheets of corrugated iron were leaning against walls, but they weren't even the same sort of corrugated iron. They were different shapes and widths and in different states of decay. There were blue plastic barrels that had been jaggedly cut in half. There were also various mysterious parts of machines, dark red with rust.

If you were tempted to wonder why the owner had rescued all this rubbish from tips and skips and the sides of roads, you only had to look around. The strangest things, torn bits of plastic sheeting, lengths of inner tubing, half-door frames, had been incorporated into various structures. It was almost an advertisement for recycling, except that it was the best advertisement in the whole history of the world for throwing things away, for burying them, or, best of all, for burning them, in places like the Marshco incinerator just a few miles up the road.

The pigs were giving snuffling, phlegmy grunts, rooting in the rancid mud for fuck knows what. I heard a yelping and a dog skidded round the corner of an entrance I hadn't seen, further along the road. It ran towards me, all teeth and dripping tongue. I had an impulse to make a run for it but even in a panic I realized that I wouldn't get more than a few feet. I stood still and stared at the mutt and hoped he would mistake me for someone who wasn't crapping himself. Look them in the eyes, I remembered from somewhere. Why? But the dog did stop, and flapped around as if there was an invisible barrier about a yard away, and barked at me.

I heard an angry muttering and a man followed the dog out from the gateway. He was wearing rubber boots, green canvas trousers, a ribbed grey sweater and, oddly, a white shirt and tie.

'Oy, Stiff,' he said, or something like it. It could have been almost anything. 'What yer doing?'

That last bit was addressed to me, not the dog. What did he think? Did he seriously think I wanted to trespass into that incredibly disgusting pile of mud? More insanely still, did he think I wanted to steal something? There was, for example, that battered metal watering can without a spout. Did he think I had my eye on that? I was a little bit tempted to say something sarcastic, but I was wary of what he might say to Stiff, if that really was his name.

'I'm going for a walk,' I said. 'And I was just taking a look into your farmyard. Er . . .' I tried to think of something sane I could say about it to him. 'It's interesting.'

'What do you mean, interesting?'

I realized that it wasn't burglars this man was frightened of. He might think I was from the public health department. That really would be a frightening prospect for both sides. Where the hell would an inspector start? Where would he put his feet?'

'I'm from London,' I said. 'Up for a few days. I don't often see a farm.'

The man relaxed visibly.

'Never been to London,' the man said. 'Couldn't stand all the crowds.'

'It *is* crowded,' I said.

'It's not natural.'

I felt that that man belonged in London. In the middle of the city he could have walked along the street with strange parcels, he could have talked to himself on park benches, he could have rummaged in litter bins and stolen supermarket trolleys. Out here in East Anglia he was leading the same sort

147

of life. But in London people wouldn't have to eat his parcel or his scroungings. I started to think that if those materials were what he built with, what did he give his pigs for food?

'I was going for a walk,' I said, again. 'I was wondering if there was circular walk.' He looked blank. 'So that I could carry on and go in a curve that would bring me back into the village. That's where I'm staying.'

He looked blank and said nothing.

'I need to get back to Marston Green and I know what you're going to say,' I said. 'You're going to say, if I were you, I wouldn't start from here. Because that's what people say when you ask them the way. But obviously I've got to start from here. Because here is where I am.'

If I had been anywhere but there – and at that moment I would genuinely like to have been anywhere but there – I would have started a conversation about how this was the story of my life. You've got to take responsibility, you take the decisions, but you don't take them in circumstances of your own making. I would like someone to explain this contradiction, but it was typical that the thought had entered my mind as I was talking to a man who didn't seem to be able to direct me to a village that he lived next to.

'So anyway,' I said, 'I'll carry on to try and find that circular route. If that's all right with your dog.'

The man nodded and then grunted something at his dog, only this time the name sounded something like 'Runce', if there is such a name. Or maybe it was something else, or nothing. Maybe the dog didn't have a name. Why should things have names?

I set off again. Just around the corner there was a wooden footpath sign pointing across a field. But here, the earth didn't feel like the earth I'm used to. It was a matter of texture. I've spent most of my life separated from the soil by layers of concrete and tarmac, but I have occasionally walked in parks and back gardens. Earth is either firm or muddy. The texture of this field was more like powdered chocolate with not enough water added. My feet kept sinking into it and after a few minutes my shoes were coated in a brown paste. Maybe this is just the problem with England. You spend thousands of years growing things out of the same thin layers of soil and eventually the soil just gives up and turns into a sort of residue.

However, I was now walking across the slope to the west of Marston Green and it gave me a nice view of the village, freakishly clear on this late spring evening. I could see all the bits of the village almost as if I was flying over in a balloon. It was easy to identify the core, the bits that had basically been there for centuries, almost all the way back to where it had been mentioned in the Domesday Book. (I'd read that on the village website.) There was the church, of course, and a patch of green in front of it, and there was a line of half-timbered houses along the main street. There were a couple of pubs, a small hotel and some shops. I could see the tiny school with its playground, which was a field with a fence around it. Next to the field was the village hall, where the meeting was due to start – I looked at my watch – in just over twenty minutes' time. Looking slightly away from the centre of the village there were other fairly large houses, a farmhouse, a manor house, groups of cottages with thatched roofs, a few handsome converted barns, a mill that now had a Range Rover parked next to it and so, I guessed, wasn't grinding stuff into flour any more.

At either end of the village, a couple of factories had come and gone, leaving rusting hulks of warehouses and tanks and pipes. I had no idea what either of them had manufactured or processed. In fact, come to think of it, that was something that should be checked out. What if one of them was an asbestos factory? Could life be so simple and lucky? It didn't seem very likely.

Those were in the past but there were also three new housing estates, and to the right of one of the defunct factories a fourth one was clearly marked out. There were even a few yellow trucks there in readiness. Clearly there were still a few people willing to move into this contaminated area. In the clear afternoon light, the completed estates had the look of models. I could see the curves of the streets, the cul-de-sacs, the driveways, many of them with two cars in them (one of them had a boat), the neatly clipped lawns and hedges. It was all so neat and correct, you would hardly have known you were in the countryside. The newest estate, on the eastern edge of the town, was the most obviously prosperous. These people didn't work at Marshco. They drove to work in Bury St Edmunds or even up to Norwich. If it wasn't for them, the village would have died.

Geoff Otley had told me that there were fifty-two children in the village school. Before the last estate had been built, it had been forty-two. Admittedly not all of the families in the new estate sent their children to the village school. There was a natty little private school down towards the coast, St Jude's. My taxi had driven past it on the way from the station. I didn't see much of it but I saw acres of playing fields and a driveway leading up to the school's main entrance that must have been half a mile long, with beautifully maintained hedges all the way. Still, there were a few families who had stuck with the village school and one of them had twins. I wondered if any of them had cancer.

It was time to get to the meeting. I walked more quickly across the field, my feet popping as I pulled them out of the sticky soil. At the end of the field I found myself with relief in a lane that led back down into the village. On the far side of the lane was a field with five medium-sized horses. I stopped for a moment and leaned on the wooden fence, looking at them. Three of them were feeding while rubbing up against each other in a clump. For a moment it looked to me as if one of them had a fifth leg, or maybe it was the leg of a horse behind it, and then I saw it was the horse's cock. This will sound pathetically naive, but I really had no idea. You probably know all this, so excuse me for a moment, but it was like a very long floppy sausage dangling out of what was already a rather long leather sock. I thought that the horse must be about to have sex, but no. The cock was rather deftly withdrawn back into the sock and you would never have known. It was just as if the horse, without making too much of a fuss about it, was just saying: There, that's what I've got, what do you think? They never show you this stuff on TV, and it's what you really want to know.

151

The good thing about lying in the dark thinking about how I got here – or there, from your point of view, because I'm here and you're there – is that it's like watching my life on video. Sometimes I freeze frame on one bit, play it over and over again, trying to work it out. Other times I just fast forward until I get to the bit I'm interested in.

The problem with real life, with things like the second meeting of the Marston Green Cluster Campaign, is that it proceeds at the same pace as the parts of your life that you're interested in. I suppose that most meetings are the same the whole world over. You get fantastically excited about something and you believe you can change history and then someone says, Yes, I agree, let's form a committee. And before you know where you are, you're appointing auditors and arguing about whether you've got a quorum. There's always someone, and as some people started to make their way out onto the stage at the front of the Marston Green village hall, I could guess which one it was. It was the florid-faced bald middle-aged man, wearing a blazer and a striped tie.

He introduced himself as Charles Deane, the chairman of

the campaign group, he said he just had a few things to say and then there was about forty-five minutes of procedure. That's another problem. The fact that almost all meetings are boring doesn't necessarily mean they aren't important. You fall asleep in the wrong meeting and suddenly Stalin has been elected chairman of the party and there are people banging at your door. But I couldn't see any immediate threat to Wortley as they proceeded to 'we must appoint auditors and committee members'. I looked around at the audience, who almost filled the hall. They didn't seem different from what you'd expect at any event that offered tea and biscuits afterwards. It was starting to look as if this would be a short visit.

While the discussions about secondings and shows of hands droned on, I distracted myself by looking at the other two people on the platform. The first was a man who must have been in his mid-thirties. He was more casually dressed than Charles Deane. He wore red canvas shoes, grey chinos, a faded blue shirt and a brown jacket. He had close-cropped hair, which was receding drastically.

Beside him was a woman who may have been a touch younger, around thirty. She was tall, very slim and the effect of that was emphasized by her hair, cut spikily short and tufted up. She was wearing a blue velvet suit with a white T-shirt underneath, and white tennis shoes.

The man was looking at Charles Deane, paying close attention to what he was saying. The woman looked lost in thought, glancing round the audience, as if searching for someone she knew or checking the attendance. She caught my eye and looked puzzled. Someone she didn't recognize. It was all right. I was in my countryman's disguise of jeans, topped with a heavy-duty brown jacket. In fact, her noticing it made me self-conscious and wonder what the fuck I was wearing something like that indoors for. I quickly took it off.

After about nine hours, Charles Deane said that without further ado he would ask for brief reports from Mr Kevin Seeger and Miss Hannah Mahoney.

'Kevin and Hannah have been busy on the ground, on our behalf. As you all know, they've both been very instrumental in bringing matters to our attention. They've been continuing their activities and I've asked them to give us a brief summary of how things stand. Kevin?'

Kevin stood up. He was holding a single sheet of paper. That was a good sign.

'Hi,' he said. 'Glad to see so many of you here. Obviously, the big question we face is how to go forward. In the face of so much suffering, it all should be very simple. But what we urgently need is good-quality data. As you know, I'm dealing more with the environmental aspect. What I've been doing is hunting up the health and safety issues, and I've requested information both from Marshco themselves and from various local and central government bodies. It's a bloody bureaucratic nightmare, I can tell you. Marshco, needless to say, have not been very forthcoming.' There was a murmur of laughter. 'Their reply basically deflected all my enquiries, and referred me to the inspectors. I'll show the letter to anyone who wants to see it afterwards, but what it mainly talks about is the proposed substantial expansion of the whole incineration and landfill operation. We've all known about these plans for a long time because of the coverage in the local press. But let everybody be very clear: we're not facing a company that's on the defensive here. They are planning an aggressive expansion in the Marston Green area. Yes?'

A hand had been raised in the audience. A man stood up.

'Kevin,' he said. 'I just wanted to ask whether that might help us. We might embarrass them into meeting our demands.'

Kevin frowned and shook his head.

'I don't think we're in that area yet,' he said. 'In their letter, it's all about economic opportunities. Employment opportunities, especially. They talk about a hundred new jobs in the expanded facility.'

'Do jobs come before people's lives?' the man asked, and there was even a ripple of applause.

'That's what we're here to find out,' said Kevin. 'It's my view that we're not really going to get very far approaching Marshco directly just at the moment. We need more ammunition. So, as many of you know, I've been making feelers in different directions. Most notably the physical science department down the road at the university in Warsham. All that's very much at an early stage.'

Feelers. Early stage. That meant he hadn't achieved anything. He looked at his piece of paper with a furrowed brow, as if there should have been more on it. 'I think that's about it. As I've always said, if any of you can think of any other lines of enquiry, doors I should be knocking on, well, you've all got my number. So I'll pass you on to the, uh, capable hands of Hannah. Thanks very much.'

His speech had petered out into a mutter and he shuffled awkwardly back towards his chair. There were a few scattered handclaps which quickly died away.

Hannah Mahoney stood up and walked to the far right of the stage. There was what looked like a painter's easel with a large blank card on it. She dragged it out so it was almost in the centre of the stage. She started talking without any of the preliminary flourishes of the other speakers. Nor did she give any of the ingratiating half smiles that the other speakers had used to punctuate what they said. Her style was passionate, earnest, humourless. Not that a talk about an epidemic of cancer should be mixed with jokes, but still. She talked about the difficulties in defining clusters. This wasn't going to have them storming the barricades. I kept looking at that easel. What was she going to do? Draw something on it?

'Our situation is like smoking and cancer fifty years ago, but even that was simpler. Smoking causes a whole range of cancers, but the convenient fact for researchers was that lung cancer is almost entirely caused by smoking.

'This is crucial. Kevin has been doing some good work but what the companies are always going to argue is that we have no proof of how the Marshco waste plant causes these cancers. When the first research was being done into smoking and cancer, the researchers had no knowledge of the mechanisms involved, and no imminent prospect of knowing. Instead they just looked at the figures. There was this cancer, there was no doubt about that, but it wasn't clear at all that it was caused by smoking. As far as I know the first hypothesis was that car fumes were responsible. But they collected the figures, they put them together and just through the power of statistics, they showed without a shadow of a doubt that tobacco was responsible. Which brings things back to me.'

There was something about Hannah Mahoney that alarmed me. It wasn't so much what she was saying, which seemed routine enough. It was difficult to feel neutral about her. You'd either become a disciple or be irritated beyond belief. Maybe it was the fervency of her tone. In the earlier part of the meeting, the audience had been bustling and fidgeting and murmuring among themselves. But now there was a stillness and a concentration across the hall. The audience had stopped being a collection of people who might as well have been waiting for the results of the tombola. They felt like a group. A congregation, maybe. It struck me that it was like it would have been sitting in a country church, a hundred and fifty years earlier, and listening to a persuasive preacher recount her spiritual awakening.

'There's a possibility that this will sound impersonal,' she continued. But she had a husky insistence in her voice that made everything sound personal. 'This is about you and me. About us, about our children. One of our ways forward is to collect the figures and make them compelling, just as the researchers into tobacco and cancer did in the 1940s and 1950s.'

Tobacco and cancer. It was all about connecting. If they

157

could associate their cluster in people's minds with tobacco and asbestosis rather than, well, I don't know, crop circles and alien abductions, then their battle would be won. The strategy of Marshco and Wortley would be to break the connection and make them seem like cranks and fanatics. Then I caught myself. What was I doing? I wasn't a Wortley shareholder. Anyway, so far as I could see, there wasn't even a real campaign underway. And if there ever did turn out to be a campaign, what chance would it stand against the companies lined up against them? Hannah Mahoney had talked about cigarettes and cancer. Had the tobacco industry ever admitted responsibility? I wasn't sure. They'd certainly fought it in court all the way.

I was a long way down the feeding chain. I was even below Giles. I was the one who had been sent ahead of the person who was being sent ahead. I put my feet up on the empty chair in front of me and settled back to enjoy the show.

'What I've been concentrating on,' said Hannah Mahoney, 'is building up a picture of the people who are affected. This isn't the easiest business. I can't just walk in to the medical centre and read through the medical records. I'm afraid to say it's been quite a crude process. I started just by asking everybody I knew, including parents of my pupils.'

Parents of my pupils. Did she teach at the village school? Or was it at the high school over in Hyland?

'As we've progressed, we've got a bit more professional, developing a questionnaire we can circulate.

'Then there is the question of what we are actually looking for. As I said, we're not going to find any compelling one-to-one correspondence here. We're not going to find that sort of smoking gun. Instead, what we're going to be interested in is the sort of pattern that emerges. There won't be a single killer detail. It doesn't work like that. Imagine dots on a piece of paper. Individually they mean nothing. But as more and more are put on the paper, a picture takes shape, like a body appearing out of a mist. That's what we're doing.

'You've probably been wondering what I've got on my easel here. What I've done is to take the significant illnesses I've found in this area and mark them on a map. I should say that there are immediate problems here. People have an awkward habit of not staying in the same place for us to examine them. Just to be safe, I've eliminated any illness suffered by anyone resident in the area for less than five years. As you know, that includes a significant proportion of the population of Marston Green. We're a growing village, I'm glad to say. There's been plenty of new housing in the village and there's more to come. Good. We need it. In my view everybody in Marston Green is at risk. But the effects on these new arrivals will only show up in ten, fifteen, twenty years.

'All I've been able to do, in my limited way, is to deal with the people I know about, whose histories I'm fairly secure about. I want you to bear in mind that the markers on the map I'm going to show you represent, in many cases, unusual forms of cancer. Apart from more familiar kinds, breast cancer, maybe, we have liver cancer, various forms of leukaemia, myeloma, sarcomas of the soft tissues, thyroid cancer, lymphomas and a few very rare examples. So here it is.'

She stepped forward and lifted the card. There was a gasp in the room.

'Fuck,' I said under my breath.

Even on my small acquaintance with the area, I could make it out from the river through the middle, the church, the school, the Old Rectory at the other end, the busy road that arrived from the east, became the High Street and left to the west. Two small lanes crossed the road north to south, forming a large capital H. I had walked up one of them this afternoon and come back on the other. But the map looked as if it had measles. There were clumps of different round stickers, black, red and yellow.

I tried to make a rough count but it was difficult to identify the individual blobs, even from where I sat in the third row. It was clear that there was a large number. Maybe forty. In this village. Suddenly I felt nervous about being here alone. Giles should be here. Maybe he would have some scientific comment to make. But I was just imagining that diagram being unveiled in front of a jury. Of course, a coloured sticker doesn't mean anything in itself. The question is what it stands for. And whether it really stands for what it's meant to stand for. Who knew?

I'd just arrived in the village. Hannah Mahoney could be a fantasist who concocted her map in the privacy of her bedroom. Not likely. Then there was going to be the question of what diseases the stickers represented. It depended on how wide she had spread her net. Presumably the stickers showing people dead or dying in a village like Marston Green would be pretty grim. We don't like to think of us all dying.

There were so many what-ifs. One of them kept coming into my kind: What if Hannah Mahoney and Kevin Seeger were right? What then? I didn't mean, what would it be like when we went back to the boardroom at Wortley. That was never going to be a problem. Because there was one thing I'd been clear about five minutes into that meeting by the London Wall. These people in Marston Green would never make this thing stick. There were too many links in the chain. All the way from Marshco and their incinerator to the people lying ill in bed. And only one link had to break. Not even break. Be brought into question. I wanted to see how Giles would react to it, what questions he would ask. After all, it was just a map made by someone from a pressure group.

Hannah Mahoney now thanked everybody and sat down. Immediately there was a babble of questions and comments from the audience. People stood up and raised their hands. This was Charles Deane's moment. He stepped forward, holding his hands up, calming people down, hushing them. He looked at his watch and said that a lot had been got through this evening and that there was a lot for everybody to digest. He fully appreciated that there were many issues to discuss, that almost everybody in the hall had questions. Rather than continue the meeting any further, he was going to propose that another meeting be held again a week today.

Was that generally agreed? There were shouts of agreement. Passed *nem. con.*, he said. Another meeting. And so soon. He was a happy man.

Mainly people drifted away, still in animated conversation. But some others drifted to the front and I followed them. It was like a party where everybody knew each other, and I caught snatches of conversation referring to people and places I didn't know. In particular I saw people talking to Hannah Mahoney. At least a couple of them seemed to know the names of other sick people. She leaned close to their faces as if they could whisper their grief to her. More stickers for her chart. And it was the chart I was looking at. I quickly tried to tot up the number of stickers, without looking too much like the man from the ministry. Suddenly I became aware of a presence behind me, looking over my shoulder. I looked round. It was Hannah Mahoney herself. I felt unnerved to have her full attention.

'This is amazing,' I said.

'We haven't met,' she said.

'My name's Mark. Mark Foll.'

'Do you live here?'

I took a deep breath. I'd decided all this in advance but it didn't make it any easier. I'd talked to Giles and we'd agreed, or he'd told me, that there was going to be no cloak and dagger about our presence in Marston Green. We had nothing to hide, he said. We weren't going in as a dirty tricks squad. We weren't attempting to sabotage the campaign. In fact, as far as he could see, we had no particular authority of any kind. We were checking things out. So there was to be no deception. We were to be completely open.

'I live in London,' I said. 'I work in a very junior capacity for Wortley Insurance. It's a bit complicated but they're Marshco's insurance company. More or less.'

Before my eyes Hannah Mahoney's friendliness and interest drained from her face and was replaced by suspicion. When she spoke it was in a guarded, sour tone.

'You're a spy from Marshco.'

'I've never had any dealings with anyone from Marshco.'

'So what are you doing here?'

'I just came up to have a look.'

'You're here for the day?'

'I'm going to be here for a while. I'm staying in one of the holiday cottages by the pub.'

'Marshco should approach us directly.'

'Miss Mahoney . . .'

'Hannah will do.'

'Hannah, to be honest, I'm basically the office teaboy and I've been sent to look around Marston Green and see what's happening.'

Hannah's expression hardened still further.

'To see what's happening, eh? You were examining my map. What's your particular field of expertise? Epidemiology?'

'No.'

'Statistical analysis?'

'No.'

Sean French

'Ecology?'

'No.'

'Industrial chemistry?'

'You know, you can keep on asking these questions and I'll keep saying no. I'm a claims investigator. A pretty low-grade one.'

'That's interesting. Is a claim imminent? Are Marshco trying to assess how much they can pay us off with?'

We were getting into very dodgy territory.

'It's nothing like that,' I said. 'The people at Wortley heard about your campaign and they sent me down to have a look.'

'And we're supposed to be grateful for the attention, are we? Are you here as part of your work experience? People are dead and people are dying, horribly.'

'I know. I'd like to find out more about them, meet them.'

'I bet you would,' Hannah said, angry now. 'Would you like their medical files so you can get some paid medical expert to tear it apart? Or would you like to meet the dying people and con them into signing some sort of release?'

There was an awkward pause. I was going to say in some sort of high dudgeon that I didn't do that sort of thing, but then I remembered that I did do that sort of thing. And then I couldn't think of anything to say at all. Hannah's expression softened very slightly.

'Put yourself in my position,' she said. 'What can you do us except harm?'

'They just want to know what's going on.'

She looked at me with what I took to be pity, or contempt.

'They? Don't you work for them? I'll tell you, I'm not going to let you anywhere near any of the victims. What you should do is talk to Kevin. He's the walking encyclopaedia on what Marshco have been up to. Hey, Kevin.'

Kevin was much friendlier. He seemed eager to do anything for me that he could. I almost felt like telling him not to be so trusting. He suggested a proper meeting.

'I teach at the comp over in Melwarth. Tomorrow I'll be back around five. That sound all right?'

I thought for about a second and it seemed that I didn't have alternative arrangements for the following day. Kevin tore a piece of paper out of a notebook and wrote his address on it, then added his name and his phone number. He handed it to me and started to give me quite involved instructions about getting there. I knew after about five seconds that I would never be able to remember them, but I kept on nodding. This was a pretty small village. Someone would be able to direct me.

He gathered a couple of files together and we walked out of the hall together. I asked him if he'd like a drink, but he shook his head and looked glum.

'No, Mark, thanks for that. But my wife's at home. I've been working a lot on the Marshco stuff in my spare time, so Pam has been bearing a lot of the brunt in, you know, domestic matters. She's very good about it, though, on the whole. But I'd better be on my way.'

For a time we walked in the same direction. In Marston Green there weren't all that many directions to walk in. We didn't talk for a couple of minutes. Then, for no obvious reason, Kevin told me that until a few years earlier he had lived in Colchester.

'But I had to move out of the town,' he said. 'I had this bad feeling that the town was built on top of the country-side.'

'And what's the countryside built on top of?' I said.

'Good point,' said Kevin. 'I'm not sure what it means, but it's a good point.'

We parted outside the Four Feathers. Kevin went home and I went inside and bought a pint of Suffolk ale. I talked for a minute or two with my landlord and new friend, Geoff Otley, but then I made an excuse and stepped outside with my drink. I had noticed while walking with Kevin that although it was now almost ten, the sky in the west was still yellow and orange and red behind the trees on the hill. I stood in the car park and watched it fade and sipped my beer.

I didn't just want to be the guy who had booked the room for Giles. I wanted to be able to tell him something useful. Kevin Seeger seemed perfect for this. The campaign was his hobby, he knew the science of it and also he was a teacher at the local high school, so he was used to dealing with the ignorant.

He lived in one of the new developments I'd seen from up on the hill. It was an enclave called 'Hawthorns' that twisted and curved off the High Street on top of what, ten years ago, must have been a green field. So, contrary to what he had said to me earlier, his house was as much built over the countryside as anywhere else, as much as any house must be, unless it's built on stilts or underground or in a cave. But from Kevin's study there was a view over fields, fields of blue and yellow and purple. Or linseed and rape, and the purple was a scrubby, abandoned field full of thistles with purple flowers, like the sort you see on tins of shortbread biscuits.

The upstairs consisted of the bedroom he shared with his wife, the small bedroom that was almost filled by the bunk beds that the two children slept in and the slightly larger room at the back that he used as his study. When his wife, Pam, opened the front door to me, she said that Kevin was in his study. She said the word 'study' in a tone that, with incredible skill, managed to be at the same time a bit amused, slightly contemptuous, a touch resentful, while also conveying that the study ought to be used as a second bedroom for one of the children and in any case Kevin ought to get his arse out of it occasionally and help her with the housework, since she had a job as well. That's the wonderful thing about marriage. You can convey so much in shorthand. When you're single, everything takes so long. So much of your communication is misunderstood.

I liked Pam, though. She was pretty and tired and slightly sarcastic, and was wearing a red T-shirt that didn't quite reach the waistband of her jeans. I could see the pinched pink of her tummy. I didn't go straight up to Kevin. There didn't seem to be any rush. Maybe I was adjusting to their slower country ways. I went through to the kitchen and she made us some tea and I rummaged in the cupboard and found some flapjacks she'd made earlier in the day. They were really meant for the children but I only had one. Pam talked about how she worked in an old people's home but that she was training to be a dental hygienist. It was a growing profession, she said. There was going to be a big demand for dental hygienists. While I sipped her tea and she talked, I noticed that the tea made her lips glossy and that every now and then she licked it off with a dab of her tongue.

There was a rumble and thumping from the stairs and Kevin appeared in the doorway.

'Mark,' he said. 'I didn't know you were here.'

'I was on my way up.'

We waited while Pam made another pot of tea and I took another half of a flapjack and then Kevin led me upstairs. In Kevin's study there was no sign whatever of his work at school. The room was crammed, stuffed to the ceiling, with material to do with Marshco and environmental cancer and waste management and incineration. There were three filing cabinets and bundles of material on every surface but it wasn't at all like Giles's office back at Wortley. Everything was ordered and filed. Kevin pulled open a succession of drawers in the cabinet and showed me the identifying tabs, sometimes arranged by date, sometimes by area of concern, sometimes by disease. An idea seemed to occur to him and he stopped and looked at me.

'Why are you here?' he asked.

'You mean in this room?' I said.

'In Marston Green.'

'There's nothing complicated,' I said. 'I work for Marshco's insurance company, Wortley. My boss is coming in a day or two. They sent us up to see what's happening.'

He grinned.

'Are you going to sabotage the campaign?'

'Nothing interesting like that. We'll probably just write a report.'

He gestured around the room.

'The whole story is in here,' he said. 'It's just a matter of knowing how to find it.' He tapped one of the filing cabinets gently, as if it was the bonnet of a classic car or the head of one of his children. 'You know, I like being a teacher well enough. But at the level I teach it, I'm just passing on a pre-packaged body of pretty basic knowledge. What I've always wanted is to do some really startling original research. You know, like in those science stories you read as a child, where everybody tells the scientist that something can't be done, and he goes ahead and does it anyway. Or maybe there's a bit of me that wants to be a journalist. So anyway, what do you want to know?'

'I want the story,' I said.

'It's long.'

'I'm in the middle of the countryside,' I said. 'I've got nothing but time.'

Kevin sat me down on his chair, while he paced up and down, apparently collecting his thoughts. I felt sure I'd come to the right place. He was a teacher. Also, it would give me an unfair advantage over Giles. That was another bonus.

'People have always been concerned about the Marshco complex,' he said. 'We – I mean all of us – produce tons of rubbish but we don't like to think of how it's got rid of. A lot of people have vaguely Green ideas about recycling. As far as I'm concerned, recycling is largely bullshit. You know all those bottles you take to the bottle bank? All those newspapers you bundle up and shove into that huge metal container?'

'I don't generally get around to it,' I said. 'But I know what you mean.'

'In terms of resource management, whatever you choose to call it, you'd be better off burying it in a big hole.'

This was my kind of Green activist. The one who didn't believe in doing anything.

'But whatever our point of view,' he continued, 'none of us likes having a rubbish dump in our backyard. Landfill sites occupy a lot of space and incinerators spew out fumes. I've looked into the history of it and Marshco was sprung on Marston Green back in the fifties, without any real consultation. It all happened in stages. Marshco bought it as a small dump and they gradually expanded it, buying land whenever they could. Over the years there have been rumours and reports of shoddy practice. There was a prosecution in the early eighties for dumping unauthorized waste on site. When I arrived here a few years ago, I knew about the facility and didn't think much about it. Then I started to hear about the cluster of illnesses in the area. There was a woman called Fiona Jopling. She was the Green candidate for this area for years. She was the first to make the connection between Marshco and the sickness. Trouble was she made lots of other connections as well. You name it, global warming, crop spraying, acid rain, capitalism, hormones in meat, water pollution, salmonella – have I left anything out? They were all to blame. She was a lovely woman, Fiona, mad as a hatter, but lovely. She'd done a bit of work on dioxins, in an amateurish sort of way. She showed it to me and I had a look at it to humour her and then I suddenly realized that she had something. A group of us in Marston Green became interested. Some of them have looked at it more from the illness end, like Hannah Mahoney, who you heard at the meeting. Me, I'm a scientist and I've done the industrial chemistry.' He gestured around the room once more. 'It's not a small job. Now, you really want to hear all this?'

'If it's all right with you.'

'Are you kidding? I spend my life looking for people to tell this to. I should start by making a very simple point. Industrialists and politicians love incinerators. They take large bulky messy rubbish and make it small and neat. But it's not magic. All the process does is to effect a chemical transformation. Sometimes a technician at an incinerator will go to a public meeting and produce a plastic box containing, say, eight pounds of rather sanitary looking ash. He'll say that this is the product of a hundred pounds of garbage. The ash can be buried in a tiny landfill and that's that. To which the simple answer is that this means that ninety-two pounds has been pumped into the air.'

'Yuck,' I said.

'Exactly. From what I've said so far, you'd think of it mainly as a physical problem and it certainly is a problem. The rearranged molecules of the rubbish can cause all sorts of problems. The buried ash can contaminate the groundwater. And obviously the fumes can do all sorts of harm.'

'Can't they filter the smoke?' I asked.

'Sure,' said Kevin. 'But this doesn't solve the problem.

It just rearranges it. The better the filters in the incinerator, the more toxic the ash that remains. There's no way around the law of conservation of matter. But, as I was saying, this is a physical question. My main concern has been the chemical transformations involved. I'm afraid that at this point I'm going to have to give you a very basic chemistry lesson. During the incineration process, which necessarily involves both heating and cooling, carbon and chlorine atoms rearrange themselves to create molecules of dioxins, and the relatively similar molecules of furans. There are many types of dioxin and furans molecules, but they share some crucial characteristics.'

Before I left London for Marston Green, I promised myself that I would make the effort to understand everything that it was necessary to understand about this case. I wasn't like Giles. I didn't know things the way he knew them. But I had found over the months I'd been working with him that I could learn just about what I needed for every case, given the occasional late night. It might be about building construction or car mechanics. I didn't need to know how to fix the car. Just as long as I could make sense of what was or wasn't relevant to the insurance policy and apply it, that was enough. Sometimes it took an effort that made my head hurt but I could manage it.

When Kevin started to talk about his dioxins and his furans, it was something different. He started with what he said was a 'very simplified' account of one of the most poisonous dioxin molecules. He mentioned benzene, which I thought was some kind of petrol, and by the time I realized

173

it couldn't be, it was too late. By then he was talking about enzymes and the nucleus of human cells.

I was starting to feel lost. Worse than that, or was it better than that, I wondered if he was lost as well, in a way. I knew too little. He knew too much. While saying something, he was always aware of something else that needed mentioning in order to explain it and something else to explain that and sometimes he never got back to the thing he'd started with. He would wander into another area, such as the problems of tracing dioxins in soil or in human tissue. He went on an extended excursion on what he described as a 'very complicated, and in some ways confused, and very technical' report that someone from Greenpeace had done on incinerator dioxins a few years earlier. This then led on to a further mini-excursion to explain that the incinerators dealt with in that report were actually a different generation, and yet the bulk of the findings were applicable – to a certain extent.

Every so often he would rifle through a filing cabinet in search of a particular figure. The narrative was disrupted even further because it was slightly but inconsistently recast in the order in which he had discovered certain pieces of information. Because, although he never actually said it, this wasn't just the story of a polluting company or of people with cancer. It was the story of a schoolteacher making something of his life.

At first I felt as I had on our previous meeting when he had given me elaborate directions to his house and I had gradually realized that I had no chance of remembering it all, and so I had just stood and nodded. At one point, early on, I did make an attempt at keeping up by asking a question.

'An enzyme?' I said. I said it in a slightly non-questioning way, as if it had only just slipped my mind and I just needed prompting. He paused and, I thought, looked very slightly alarmed. It was as if Einstein had been giving someone a highly advanced description of the theory of relativity and had been suddenly interrupted by the question: 'By the way, that word "multiplied", what exactly does it mean?' Kevin thought for a moment.

'An enzyme is a complex protein,' he said, 'produced by living cells. It promotes specific biochemical reactions without undergoing change itself. The point in this context is that the dioxin molecules are exceptionally stable and can't be broken down by the enzymes.'

'Right,' I said, nodding.

That hadn't helped at all, and anyway I had chosen the word 'enzyme' almost at random. As his dioxin narrative washed over me, with little whirlpools and flurries and rapids and tributaries here and there, I began to think about what it must be like to drown. You'd struggle and struggle for breath, with the waves lapping over your face and it would get more and more tiring. Maybe you would decide to give up, or maybe the effort would suddenly be too much, but then there would be the relief as you slipped under the water, let the water fill your lungs and descended into darkness and death. That's what it was like, me and Kevin in his study full of papers and documents and filing cabinets. With a feeling of calm I gave up any attempt to follow what he was saying.

He must have noticed something wrong, the way people notice that people are dead in movies. They push up the eyelids and look at the eyeball. I was never quite sure what they were looking for. When I was younger someone once told me – in the playground I think – that when you die your eyeballs point backwards. When I was about twenty, I suddenly decided that this couldn't be true. There are muscles that hold the eye in place. There must be, though I'm still not sure. I suspect there are similar signs, concerning a deadness of the eyes, that enable experienced teachers to recognize when they are losing a class.

'Is this too technical?' he said.

For about a quarter of a second, I thought of saying, no, please go on, we're just getting to the good bit. Then I thought: what the fuck for?

'Kevin,' I said, 'I'm sorry but I've done my best. You've lost me.'

'At what point?'

'I'm too lost even to know.'

He looked crestfallen.

'Should I go over it again?'

'It's not you,' I said. 'It's me. I should have explained in advance that I'm an ignoramus. I'll just say two things: the first is that my colleague, more specifically my boss, is arriving tomorrow and apart from being generally more intelligent than I am, he's also a trained scientist. I'll put you two together and you'll be talking the same language. The only thing I'd say in my defence is that at some point in the future, you're going to have to tell your story to an idiot like me. It'll be a lawyer or someone from an insurance company or chairing an inquiry, and those sorts of people didn't study anything except Latin at school. When all this is over, you can write a book about the case and explain it all properly, but until then you're going to have to come up with a remedial version of your story.'

He walked me down to the door. We shook hands.

'You're probably right,' he said. 'It's probably too complicated. I sometimes wonder if you can reduce real science to the sort of evidence you can present in a courtroom. You probably think I've wasted my time. It probably seems crazy, all those files.'

'I don't know about that,' I said.

His expression turned serious.

'Maybe we'll lose,' he said. 'But the fact will remain that I will be on the right side and you'll be on the wrong side.'

'I'm not on any side,' I said. 'I'm too low grade.'

'You can't hide behind that,' he said.

When he said that, I was sure he was wrong. The way I saw it, I wanted to be there in Marston Green, I wanted to observe the different sides, see Giles at work, but I had the idea I could somehow remain invisible while doing it.

It was such a relief to get outside again. He lived about four twists along in the snaky road of Hawthorns, so it took five minutes' walk to feel that you were really in the village again. It was a warm, bright evening, with only streaks of cloud in the sky and birds circling, far, far up. There was a

177

light wind blowing that must – if I had understood at least part of Kevin's talk correctly – have contained an unhealthy dose of dioxins, and furans as well, no doubt, downwind from the Marshco plant.

As I entered the High Street I saw coming towards me, from a long way off, Hannah Mahoney accompanied by a small boy. She didn't recognize me at first because I was walking from the west end of the High Street with the evening sun behind me. So I could watch her in conversation with the boy, who had a small ball that he was throwing up and catching. Not very expertly, because he dropped it twice while I was watching. Once it bobbled out into the road and she gestured the boy away from the road, while she ventured out into the dangerous flow of traffic to retrieve it. That was what they really should have protested about. All day and all night heavy lorries drove along the narrow High Street, travelling to and from the container ports further down south. They should have started a campaign to get a bypass. Except that people like Hannah Mahoney are generally against bypasses as well, aren't they?

She recognized me when there was still an awkwardly long distance between us. Awkward for her, I mean. It didn't bother me. She caught sight of me and then, I think, pretended she hadn't seen me and busied herself talking to the boy, leaning over him. She was wearing tight jeans that came halfway down her calves and a white sweater with green and blue hoops. When we were just a few yards apart, she pretended to recognize me for the first time.

'Oh?' she said. 'It's er . . .'

'Mark,' I said. 'Mark Foll. We talked at the meeting.'

Then I realized that actually I felt a bit awkward too. I hadn't made the most brilliant impression when we met. She was the most impressive person involved in the campaign and she was someone that I or Giles or we would have to deal with in some way.

'I remember.'

'Is that your little brother?'

She looked puzzled.

'Are you joking? He's my son.'

'I was just being nice.'

A sarcastic expression came over her face.

'Oh, I get it. You must be too young to have a child of your own. That's a really suave line.'

'It's not a line,' I said.

'This is Bruce.'

'Hello,' I said. Bruce didn't seem aware of my existence. He was trying to pull a thread out of his tennis ball. I turned back to Hannah. 'I've just been at Kevin's.'

'And?'

'I got the talk. Well, some of it.'

'And?'

'It was a bit tricky to follow.'

'Just a bit?'

'I was completely lost.'

She was already looking over my shoulder, thinking, should she just get away.

'So what did you expect?' she said. 'Did you think you could just breeze in and learn everything you needed to know about this complicated and controversial subject in an evening?'

'Do *you* understand all the science?'

'I know what I need to know.'

'All right,' I said, thinking desperately. 'What's the difference between a dioxin and a, er, furans?'

She gave a sour laugh.

'I'm not going to stand in the street and answer a half-arsed pub quiz by someone from an insurance company.'

'I'm not "from an insurance company".'

'Aren't you?'

'As it happens I am, sure, but you make it sound as if that's all I am.'

Bruce was tugging at her sleeve.

'I'd better go.'

'Hannah, do you think Kevin is going to convince anybody?'

'It's not a question of convincing anybody. Kevin is assembling data. It's technical. It has to be. But it needs to be scientifically robust.'

'He's certainly got the data,' I said. 'I wonder if anyone apart from Kevin will ever look at it.'

'There's a lot of it, admittedly,' said Hannah.

'From your point of view it needs to be simple,' I said. 'Are these dioxins or whatever they are dangerous? Are they causing the illness? Those are simple questions. I assume it will be Marshco's job to drown everybody in data, not yours.'

Hannah looked at me more keenly.

'Whose side are you on, Mark?'

'I'm just having fun in the country.'

Her face hardened again.

'There are people dying in this village.'

Fuck. Wrong direction.

'Sorry, I didn't mean that. Anyway, don't judge anything by me. My boss is coming tomorrow. He's clever. He's a scientist.'

The sarcastic expression appeared again.

'So you're just the pretty face of the company,' she said, and then stopped herself, looking embarrassed. 'I mean the *public* face of the company.' Bruce's tugging was now impossible to resist. 'See you. On the High Street, if nowhere else.'

I was left thinking if there was anyone I'd met in Marston Green that I hadn't made a fool of myself with. Geoff Otley, maybe, and there was that pig farmer.

The next evening, Giles's BMW purred into the parking bay outside the Four Feathers. He had phoned me just before I arrived so that I could be standing waiting for him like a butler. When he got out of the car, I saw he was wearing jeans, a checked shirt and scuffed brown shoes.

'You'll see that I'm dressed for the country,' he said. 'No gentleman wears brown shoes in London. That's what they always used to say.'

He opened the rear door and took out a leather hold-all and a bright new pair of Wellington boots.

'I should probably have brought a tweed jacket and a cravat,' he said. 'For sherry with the vicar.'

'I'm not sure if there is a vicar,' I said.

I took him over to Dobbin, his chalet, and he seemed moderately satisfied. I filled him in on what I'd seen at the meeting and then I walked him over to Kevin Seeger's house. Out of guilt, I had arranged with Kevin that I would bring someone over who was capable of understanding his research. I had intended to escape but Pam made tea for me and I stood and talked to her while she did the ironing in a corner of the kitchen. I asked her what she thought about the cluster campaign and she just looked tired.

'I don't know,' she said.

I asked her if she knew Hannah Mahoney.

'She's Daniel's teacher.'

'Daniel?'

'Our nine-year-old.'

'She seemed like a good teacher,' I said. 'I mean, at the meeting.'

'She's been away, but people think she's very good.'

'What does her husband do?'

'She's not married,' said Pam. 'I've never seen her with anyone.'

I'd got through a couple of mugs of tea before Kevin and Giles came down the stairs. It felt like the adults coming down to join the children. Giles had a grimly polite smile as he said goodbye and I led him back to the Four Feathers. I promised that I would do a supermarket shop but in the meantime we could try Geoff and Jan's food.

Giles ordered cod and chips and I ordered a steak and kidney pie and a salad and two pints of beer. When Giles's fish arrived, he cheered up very slightly.

'Like being a bachelor again,' he said.

'That's good, isn't it?' I said. 'I mean, for a bit.'

He just muttered something. I don't think all had gone well with Sue after I'd seen them. He picked at his food with his fork and took a taste.

'I was about to do my rant about shameful food in English pubs,' he said. 'But this isn't bad.'

Sean French

'It's all right,' I said. 'I talked to Geoff about it. A van comes from the coast every morning. His wife, Jan, does the fish in a Thai style.'

Giles prodded the fish again.

'I knew there was something odd about it,' he said. 'At least it's fresh. A few years ago, I went for a walk with Sue, in the days when I still went for walks with Sue, and . . .'

'Giles,' I said. 'I don't want to intrude, and tell me to fuck off if you want, but is everything all right? With you. With you and Sue. Generally.'

Giles looked puzzled, as if the thought had never occurred to him before.

'I'll give you the short answer,' he said. 'I'll give you the really short version, the haiku of my marriage. You know how when you buy a suit that doesn't quite fit and you tell yourself you'll get it altered and it'll be fine. Then about a year later you trip over it because the trouser legs keep dragging over your heel and you think, oh fuck, I never got around to it, and at that point you can either decide to put up with the trouser legs dragging along the ground, or you can get rid of the suit. But you have to choose.'

'Why not get it altered?'

'It's too late. By that time the fabric has faded and you can't get the creases out any more.'

'I'm not sure about that. I found this suit a few months ago that I hadn't worn for over a year. I took it to this little guy round the corner and he did the most amazing job on it.'

'This isn't a conversation about tailoring, Mark,' Giles

184

said. 'I'm the suit in this story and Sue is the man who owns the suit.'

'I know that,' I said. 'I was just trying to say that there are different ways of looking at the story. There are different options.'

'To get away from the fucking suit for a moment,' said Giles, 'we did this walk on the coast the other side of London from here, in Kent. It's real Dickens country, lobster pots and barges and old oyster beds. It was a very cold, very sunny winter afternoon. We walked along the edge of the stony sand and talked and we arrived at an old pub on the edge of a promontory. It was old and weatherworn and it was called something like the Smuggler's Arms or the Fisher's Ketch. The guidebook said it had been a spot hundreds of years ago where boats dropped their illegal consignments of brandy. It makes you wonder if in a couple of hundred years' time families will be sitting at picturesque beauty spots on the south coast with plaques and leaflets telling that this is the place where boats came and dropped bundles of heroin that had been brought all the way from Afghanistan.

'We sat on the decking outside and we ordered fish. We could almost have leant over from our table and lifted the fish out of the water. And I saw the woman behind the bar open a fridge, tear open two plastic bags and put them in the microwave and that was our fish and chips. I was going to give them the full rant about how they had betrayed their culture, but Sue tugged at my sleeve and told me not to spoil things, so I didn't.'

'It probably wasn't their fault,' I said. 'Lots of pubs are part of groups. The individual tenants don't have much choice.'

'There's always a reason,' said Giles. 'Nobody ever seems to have a choice. So, the point of that is it was a formative, symbolic moment in creating my attitude to England and the English countryside. Unfair and irrelevant, of course, since this is really quite good. On the other hand, I don't know what it is with this Thai thing. They ought to rediscover their heritage. Beef and oyster pie, chitterlings. How's your pie?'

'Great,' I said. 'Very traditional. Please don't complain. We're going to depend on Geoff heavily in the next few days. So how was Kevin? I know that you're both scientists, so I guess you speak the same language.'

'I'm a biologist, if I'm anything at all, so it wasn't exactly my field.'

'But you know what an enzyme is,' I said.

'Yeah, I heard about you and enzymes,' said Giles. 'I think Kevin was quite touched by the effort you made to understand the subject, in the face of your various disabilities. By the way, what did you think of Mrs Seeger?'

'You mean Pam?'

'It's Pam now, already, is it?'

'That's her name.'

'I could see she had her eye on you.'

'Don't be daft, Giles,' I said. 'She's married with two children.'

'What does that matter? Meeting someone like Mrs Seeger

plays a bit to the fantasies I have about provincial life. People think that it's all very respectable and prim out here, but it's the opposite. All wife-swapping and adultery.'

'Wife-swapping?'

'You know, the men throw the car keys into the centre of the room and then the women . . .'

'Yeah, I know what wife-swapping is. But where do you get this information from?'

'You hear,' he said. 'You read about it. Hasn't it occurred to you that here we are, two men, away from home, in a strange place, amusing, intelligent, not unattractive. For example, look at those two young women over there.' Two admittedly good-looking women, around twenty, one blonde, one brown-haired, were indeed sitting at the far end of the bar. 'If we were real men, we'd be wandering over there and buying them a drink.'

This was becoming ridiculous.

'Giles, I don't want to cramp your style but I reckon that Mrs Seeger just saw me as this lonely, slightly pathetic person stuck out on his own in a new place. And thought I'd like a cup of tea.'

'That's one way of putting it,' he said.

Giles seemed like a man who didn't spend very much of his life in pubs and now that he was in one he was going to talk in the way he assumed that men are supposed to.

'You were going to tell me about your meeting with Kevin,' I said.

'Oh, that,' he said reluctantly. 'It's funny about men, isn't it? Some of them build conservatories and some of them go to the moon and some of them construct cathedrals out of matches and Kevin has spent two and half years of evenings and weekends doing an unofficial doctorate in solid-waste incineration. And you know the funny thing? He's never actually seen an incinerator. You'd think he might have wandered around at an open day and had a look, but they probably don't have open days at incinerators. Kevin reminds me a bit of those medieval popes who wrote about sex, even between married people, how it was befouled by the stench of lust and besmirched by the heat of passion and the itch of flesh. I mean, if only. If they'd had some sex, they'd have realized that there wasn't all that much to it. If Marshco had any sense at all, they'd give old Kev a ring and invite him for a wander around the plant with their technical director. Kevin would finally meet someone who would understand what the hell he was going on about. He'd also see these strange furnaces that he's been fantasizing about at night and see that it's a pretty ordinary industrial complex which could probably do with a tweak here and there. And he'd go away satisfied and stop bothering them.'

'You think so?'

'Shall we get some coffee now? I'm not sure about poor old Kevin. Is he happy at his job as chemistry teacher at Melwarth High? I don't think so. Is he someone who wants recognition, who wants attention to be paid? I think so.'

'Yes, but is he right? Are these dioxins in the air giving people cancer?'

Giles pushed his plate aside.

'I haven't got a clue.'

'They're pretty fucking unpleasant, aren't they?'

He pulled a dismissive face.

'I'm not sure. I haven't spent the entire time that you've been away crying into my coffee. I rooted around a bit and there is at least argument about the harmfulness. There seems to be general agreement that if you take a lump of it and shove it up a guinea pig's arse then the outlook isn't too good, but beyond that, there's been a debate.'

'Did you mention that to Kevin?'

'I assumed he must already know about it. If he doesn't, then it's not my job to do his research for him.'

'So he can be ambushed in court?'

'The one thing I'm sure about, Mark, is that whichever way this goes, it's never going to end up in court.'

'So was it a waste of time seeing Kevin?'

'Not at all. I learned quite a lot of the basics from him and it's good to be on friendly terms with him.'

'You mean for him to think that you're on friendly terms with him.'

'No, Mark. I like the guy. We're not going to double-cross him. In any case, his work isn't finished. Poor old Pam isn't going to see much of him for a long time to come. He's started talking to some geographers about soil tests and emission levels. That's going to be complicated. Marshco won't allow him access to the site. And as for the soil tests, everybody accepts that the dioxin levels are very low, even in affected areas. Ever since the industrial revolution, at least, we've all been riddled with it. We'll see.'

'So what way is there of knowing, one way or the other?'

'What do you mean, "know" it?'

'I mean prove the connection. Or prove that there isn't a connection.'

'Oh, I see. You've got this confused with pure mathematics. Almost every other kind of science is basically a mess. What you have is a whole lot of different data, some of it contradictory, some of it dodgy or untrustworthy, most of it controversial. Also you've got different *kinds* of data, some of which are more relevant than others. Some may be positively misleading. What you try to do is to put it together in a way that makes some kind of sense and that we can live with.'

'So what are we actually going to do?'

We had our coffee now and Giles drained his cup. He wiped his mouth with the paper napkin.

'In the medium term,' he said, 'my plan is that we do almost nothing. We prepare an interim report. "Interim" means that we do it very quickly and we don't come to any conclusions. We hand it over to Donna and then we get back to what we are good at, which is looking at carpets which people have spilled things on.'

I finished my coffee.

'I'm still surprised that you don't see this as an amazing opportunity for you to make your name.'

'You're right,' said Giles. 'I've never thought that. And the reason I've never thought it is because what it really is is an amazing opportunity for us both to fuck up and get fired. The real task is for us both to get back to London without anybody properly realizing we've been away.'

'So what are we actually going to do?'

'The one thing Donna told us we really have to do is to look at the Marshco site. You know, due diligence and all that. But we're not going to be climbing the perimeter fence at night and stealing illicit soil samples. Kevin Seeger may not be able to get through the gate but we can. We're going there at noon tomorrow and we're getting the full tour. Are you up for that?'

'Great,' I said. 'Not that I think I'm going to be able to look at an incinerator and spot a dodgy valve or whatever's relevant.'

Giles laughed, which was a welcome change.

'It's never like that,' he said. 'What was it somebody said about scientific theories? The way a new theory gets accepted is not by proving it. It's by the old scientists dying and being replaced by young ones. We're not going to change anybody's mind here. And now I'm going to bed, and we're going to leave those lovely young women over there without talking to them.'

'What's the big deal?' I said. 'If you want to talk to them, let's go over and talk to them.'

'Are you serious?'

'Sure.'

'No, it would be gross. Don't women have a right to sit and talk in a public place without being hit on by two predatory men?'

'You make them sound like bits of dead meat. They might want us to come over.'

'No, absolutely not. I'm physically and psychologically incapable. I've got a wife back in Kilburn. Anyway, I've had girlfriends and relationships of different kinds and not a single one of them came about because I walked up to someone I didn't know and started talking. I've never done it.'

'You must have done it some time.'

'Never.'

'How did you meet them, then?'

'I worked with them. Or I was in the same class at college. They were friends of friends. There was always a way I got to know them that had nothing sexual about it, and then that came as a bonus. I've always felt sorry for women, especially attractive women, being looked at and bothered all the time, whistled at, hassled. I thought they could do without me on their back as well.'

'Rubbish,' I said. 'That's just an excuse. Have I told you about my sister?'

'No,' said Giles. 'I thought you were an orphan left on a doorstep.'

'My sister works in a bank now. It's funny, when I look back at us as teenagers. I thought she'd be a film star or an artist. Now she works in a bank and I'm in insurance. She's a year older than me and the thing I most remember her saying to me is when she was fifteen and I was fourteen and she said I should ask some girl out. Some girl. She was called Fiona Seaton and she had hair that was so blonde you could almost see it in the dark. I reacted the way you just did. I said absolutely no way, she'll just laugh, she's not interested in me. Val said something like, she's not a different species from you. She's just a girl, she's a bit shy, she doesn't have a boyfriend but she'd like one and she's keen on you, and it's not a big deal. When she said that, it was like a window opened.'

'So did you ask her out?'

'Yes. It turned out that she already had a boyfriend. But it didn't matter. I'd done the difficult bit. Then I asked Samantha Mitton out and she said yes. And so, in about thirty seconds, I'm going to go over to those women at the bar and talk to them.'

Giles held up his arm, almost as if he was going to stop me physically from leaving our table.

'And then there's point two,' he said. He looked embarrassed now. 'I don't want to seem like the Reverend Buckland at this late stage of the evening but I'm married. I suppose I could put a sticking plaster over my wedding ring, but instead I'm now going to my bed in a place that I can't quite believe is called "Dobbin".' He took a final attempt at a sip of his cup of coffee, but it was empty. 'I'll see you at breakfast. Or thereabouts,' he said and then he left the room.

I looked across the room at the two young women sitting at the bar. One of them – the blonde one – caught my eye and then said something to her companion and laughed. It was either do something or go to bed, or sit there looking like an idiot. I stood up and walked over to them without the faintest idea of what I was going to say. They turned round and looked at me with an expression of surprise.

'Hi,' I said. 'This is going to sound pretty stupid. But I'm in Marston Green for my work. I'm doing some research. I need to talk to some typical residents of the village. Would it be all right if I asked you some questions?'

'Like what?' said the blonde one.

'Is it all right if I sit down?' I said. They shrugged. 'Can I get you a drink? Don't worry. It all goes on expenses. It's part of my research.'

'Really?' said the brown-haired one.

'Completely,' I said. 'It's important that you feel relaxed while you answer my questions.'

They both ordered Bacardi Breezers and I had a bottle of cold beer that I could see in the fridge.

'Do you feel relaxed?' I said. They looked at each other and giggled. 'Is that a yes?' They giggled again. 'Right. For the purposes of my investigation, I need to know your names and your professions.'

The blonde one was called Sandy Yates and the brown-haired one was called Linda Perry. They were both catering students over at Worsham but they lived in Marston Green with their parents. They had been friends all their lives. They had both gone to school at the church school in Marston Green and the High School in Worsham.

'Perfect,' I said.

I explained that I was in Marston Green doing research about the Marshco incinerator.

'My dad works there,' said Sandy.

'That's interesting,' I said. 'What does he do?'

She shrugged.

'I don't know,' she said. 'He's worked there for years. He just works there, with the furnaces. He's an engineer.'

'What I really want to know is what *you* think about it.'

It turned out they didn't think all that much about it, really. They hadn't heard about the protest movement. Come to think about it, Linda had heard something, but she wasn't sure exactly what it was about. I asked if they had heard about people getting ill in the village. They looked at each other.

'There's always people getting ill,' said Sandy. 'But it doesn't have to do with anything.'

Did they like living in Marston Green? That made them laugh.

'It's a right old dump,' said Linda. 'There's sod all to do. You should see it on a Saturday night in the summer. The kids just hang about the bus shelter. You come here late on Saturday night by the car park and they come up from Hyland and Worsham to deal.'

'Really?'

'You know, drugs.'

'Yeah,' I said. 'I knew what you were talking about.' I'm only bloody twenty-six. They were talking to me as if I was their geography teacher.

They looked at each other. Linda said she had to go. She said she had to meet her boyfriend. I think she may have expected Sandy to go with her, but she stayed where she was and said she'd phone Linda tomorrow. I told her that was good because I had more things I wanted to ask her. She said fine. Linda raised an eyebrow, suspiciously, and left us.

I bought Sandy another Bacardi Breezer and a beer for myself. Now that Linda had gone, she turned and looked me directly in the eyes. She smiled. She was wearing more make-up than her very pretty rounded pink face needed. Her blonde hair was streaked. She was wearing a red T-shirt with puffed-up very short sleeves. The shirt was tight so that the pattern on her bra showed through clearly. I asked her why she was living at home with her parents. She must be eighteen. Nineteen, she said. She said that if she left home and organized a flat then she'd probably get settled and she didn't want to get settled around Marston Green. Her plan was to finish her course and then she could get a job in London. The pretence that I was meant to be asking her questions had been quickly dropped.

'So what is it you're doing up here?'

'I told you,' I said. 'There are people getting ill in Marston Green. Some people say it's because of the incinerator plant. We're here to see if there's anything in it.'

'Are you going to close it down?'

'We're just the insurance company.'

She took a sip from her drink and looked mischievous.

'I've always thought that insurance was boring. It's just stuff you don't want to know about filling in forms and people knocking at the door trying to sell you life policies. This man would come and sit with my mum and dad for hours. Is that you? Would you like to sell me life insurance?'

'I don't do that sort of thing. I'm a claims investigator.'

'What's that?'

I was deeply, deeply grateful that Giles had gone to bed and wasn't going to hear what I was about to say.

'It's hard to say,' I said. 'It's a bit like a private detective. There's a lot of money involved in insurance, and some people fake fires or burglaries or accidents. If there's a claim that looks suspicious, then we go in and investigate it.'

Her eyes widened.

'Is that ever dangerous?' she said.

I gave a shrug.

'You need to develop a feel for situations,' I said. 'An instinct.'

'What do you feel about Marston Green?'

'We've only just got started.'

'My dad thinks the protests are stupid.'

'Really?'

'Maybe you should talk to him.'

'Maybe I will. We're going up to the plant tomorrow.'

'He's called Steven Yates. Steve, people call him.'

'I'll look out for him.'

It was eleven o'clock and Geoff was starting to clear up. Everybody else had gone.

'So where are you staying?' she said.

'I haven't far to go,' I said. 'I'm staying in one of the chalets. The ones that have been converted from the stables out the back.'

'Those stables? I heard about that. Can I come and have a look?'

'Sure,' I said.

We walked out the back way of the pub. There was someone doing something with a rattling sound. It may have been Jan, putting out some used bottles. I opened the door of Clover and we stepped inside.

'There we are,' I said, as I put the light on and closed the door behind us. 'A beautiful work of conversion.'

Often at this moment there is an awkward moment in which I lean forward and stroke her hair with my fingers, then touch her neck and move closer. Or touch her shoulder or just take a step and kiss her. But Sandy moved herself against me and looked up so it was really only giving in to gravity when I let my face down on hers and kissed her. She put her arms round me and I first held her face, then moved my hands round her head, onto her neck, which was cool to the touch. I ran my right hand down the centre of her back, down her spine, and I felt her shiver. I thought: how good not to be married, like Giles. How good to be out here in the country away from everything.

Later we dozed. I hadn't closed the curtain and we were both woken by the sun through the window, hot on us on the bed, before five. She was lying against me. Her skin felt sticky, or maybe it was mine.

'Mark,' she said.

'Yes?'

'Have you got a girlfriend? In London.'

'No,' I said.

'Are you looking for one?'

Everything had seemed simple the previous night, and in the bright morning light it seemed even clearer and more hard-edged.

'No, I'm not,' I said.

'Oh,' she said. 'Right.'

She put her hand on my chest, leaning on it to raise herself up. She got out of the bed. She walked naked across the room into the toilet and I heard her piss and then the sound of water from the tap. She came back into the bedroom and she started to pick up her clothes. For some reason this made me feel sad, the sight of her looking around on the floor for where her socks and knickers had fallen to the floor. She pulled her clothes on, standing sideways to me, not looking at me. She looked lovelier than she had the night before, the sun coming in from an angle, making her features look sculpted. When she was done, she came and sat on the bed by me. She put her hand on my shoulder.

'We could have done stuff,' she said. 'While you were here.'

'I'm going to be busy,' I said.

'Yeah,' she said.

Before she left, I saw her picking things off the window sill.

'What are you doing?'

'Dead flies,' she said. 'There are swallows outside. They

199

live in the old stable roof. They're walking around outside in the yard. I'll leave the flies out for them. They'll like that.'

'That's nice.'

'What do you care?'

And with that she was gone.

Giles smiled cheerfully, as I got into the car.

'So did you go over and talk to those two girls?'

'Yes, I did.'

'How did it go?'

'Fine.'

'How long did you talk for?'

'Quite a long time. One of them, Linda, the brown-haired one, had to go.'

'So you talked to the blonde.'

'That's right.'

'What about?'

'Just stuff. She wants to move to London. She asked a bit about what I did in London, where I lived. I talked about what we were doing in Marston Green. Her dad works at the incinerator.'

'Really?' said Giles. He didn't sound particularly interested. 'But what I want to know is what you actually did. When did she leave?'

I gave a casual jerk of my shoulders that was meant to show how none of this really mattered and that we ought to get on with our work.

'Oh, no,' he said. 'You didn't?' He looked across at me. 'You did. You bloody did. With the blonde one? Oh, no. While I was lying miserably in bed counting sheep and thinking about dioxins. What was it like?'

'Giles, I'm not going to say anything.'

'You've got to tell me. I exist in a state of sexual deprivation. Even hearing about it would be something.'

'You're married.'

'Yes.' He banged the steering wheel with his hands. 'All right. No questions about sex. Just one question. Completely harmless. I just want to know, just in case – God forbid – Susan should be run over by a truck and I should find myself a single man again. I'll need everything I can get to survive, like Robinson Crusoe. Just tell me what was the very first thing you said. I heard somewhere or saw on TV that psychologists have said that the most important part of any relationship is the first thirty seconds when you first meet. So what did you say to them that got that blonde girl to come back with you and get into your bed? You may notice that I can hardly say the words. It causes me physical pain to utter them. But what was it? What was the magic first sentence?'

'Is this a good idea?' I said.

'Is that what you said?'

'I'm saying it now.'

'I need to know,' said Giles. 'You have to tell me. In fact, until you tell me, we're not going anywhere.'

'We talked about this yesterday evening,' I said. 'I thought it was obvious that they wanted to meet us. So I just went over and said something stupid like, I was working in the area and wanted to ask them some questions about it.'

'Is that it?' said Giles. 'I could have thought of that. There's nothing clever about that. I could have managed that. So you think that's a good line. Does that one always work for you?'

'I don't have a line. They wanted to talk. I talked to them.'

'So you're saying that the best line is the line that doesn't seem like a line.'

'No. I'm saying that there's no such thing as a line.'

'That's quite Zen. The only line is not to have a line.'

'Maybe the line is not to want to have sex with women. It's wanting to talk to them.'

'You mean as a way of having sex with them?'

I looked at my watch.

'I think we've reached a dead end,' I said.

'An interesting dead end, though,' said Giles. 'To be resumed. I suppose we'd better get going.'

We drove a few miles out of Marston Green and turned off down a side road. We drove along a perimeter fence for more than half a mile before we got to the main gate. In fact, there were two sets of gates, one for cars and the other for the trucks that were driving in and out. I told Giles that I'd never seen such security at a rubbish dump before.

'How many rubbish dumps have you been to before?'

'A few.'

'This is a major waste-management facility. This isn't just a pile of stuffed binbags with a bulldozer pushing them into holes. There's toxic waste of different kinds here, industrial, medical. You don't want people wandering in here with their picnic baskets.'

We gave our name in at the gate and we were given a chit and told to go to the car park at Block D. It was a complicated drive, following signs and twisting and turning past a series of grimy buildings. As we arrived at the car park, two men were waiting for us, both in shirt and tie with no jacket. Paul Creek was the technical services manager – basically the manager of the operation: a tall, broad-shouldered man with greying hair, neatly parted. Graham Bittles was the operational manager, heavy set, with large, rough hands. Creek did most of the talking. He welcomed us and said how pleased they were to meet us and what good things they had heard about us. He said that we could go in for a coffee and then we could get the tour.

They led us up the stairs of the modern office block to an empty room. There was a Thermos flask of coffee, a jug of milk and a tin of biscuits on the table. Creek collected cups from a sideboard and served us all. I chose a chair at the table that looked out of the window over what was unquestionably a rubbish dump. It looked from this distance as if the pile of rubbish had dandruff but then the dandruff rose into the air and I saw there was a flock of seagulls across the heaps of rubbish that scattered whenever a lorry came near.

'That's the biggest rubbish dump I've ever seen,' I said.

Paul Creek smiled.

'That's only part of it,' he said. 'We've got seventy acres

of landfill operative on this site at the moment. And as you know, we hope that that's only the beginning.' He took a gulp of coffee. 'Now, gents, I just wanted to say, as I said before, that we're delighted to have you here. You have completely open access. We'd say you could wander off where you want, but frankly we've got some nasty stuff around here and most of it won't make sense to you without having someone like Graham here with you. Is that all right?'

'That's fine,' said Giles. I could already see out of the corner of my eye that his manner was completely different from what it had been in the car, with his ridiculous, slightly creepy questions about me and Sandy. 'I know you've talked to our head office. Was it to Donna Kiely?'

'That's right,' said Creek. 'Nice woman.'

'Yes,' said Giles. 'I'm sure she's told you that this should all be routine. We're down here to get a feeling for what's going on and we'll report back to Donna. I hope we'll be back in London in a few days. But what I want to say is that I don't want you to see us as inspectors. We're more like your doctors or your priests. What I mean by that is that we're on your side and what we don't want is any surprises. If there is any problem you know of, something dodgy, some problem you had that is now solved, then please let us know.'

Creek and Bittles looked puzzled.

'I don't know what to say, Giles,' said Creek. 'We're in waste management. We deal with hazardous materials and there are constant technical challenges. That's what we do.

But what I brought you in here to say, in all sincerity, is that we're all genuinely baffled by these protests in Marston Green. You talk about being on the same side. We should be on the same side as the protesters. I hope that when Graham takes you round, he'll show you how refined our incinerating process has become. One of the major problems the world faces is what to do with rubbish, and I think we're dealing with it in a more responsible way – dare I say a greener way – than almost anyone else in western Europe.'

It was very unfair, but I was becoming very slightly irritated by Paul Creek. I felt he was trying to sell me something. He was like the voiceover in one of those films about industry we used to be shown in chemistry lessons that made me want to give up chemistry.

'Furthermore,' he continued, 'there is the small matter of employment. We're a people-heavy business and we're already one of the most significant employers in the region. When we push through the next stages of the expansion programme, we'll be employing almost two hundred more people. More if you count ancillary services.'

'I'm sold,' said Giles. 'But it's not me and Mark that you need to convince. So why don't we have the guided tour?'

'Lovely,' said Creek, looking a little dissatisfied. We probably hadn't reached the end of the talk he had prepared. 'We'll go down. It'll be a short drive. But first.'

On the way down, we were taken into a changing room. We were given pristine orange overalls, which we put on over our clothes, and yellow hardhats.

'You look lovely,' said Paul Creek. It sounded like a joke he had made before.

In the car park a minibus with a driver was waiting. We got in and set off, driving along past the stinking, rotting remains of the last few weeks' leftovers and chuck-outs from quite a slab of south-east England. Paul Creek was looking at it with a sort of fascination.

'It sounds stupid,' he said. 'But I love rubbish. I always have. Does that make me sound crazy? So be it. I like making fires at home. We spend weeks at home piling up branches and old cardboard boxes at the end of the garden. I pretend it's for the children but really it's for me. I love it when the first crackles turn into an inferno.'

I couldn't resist it.

'Does your bonfire produce dioxins?' I said.

Creek shook his head.

'The temperatures are too low. That needs furnace temperatures. I love setting fire to things, but even more I love reusing anything that can possibly be reused. I regard it as a personal defeat to throw a household item away. It drives my wife up the wall. I think she throws everything away whenever she sees my back turned. But my real hobby is composting. Do you compost?' I said no. Giles didn't speak. He was looking out of the window like a tourist. 'It's one of the great pleasures of life. A good compost heap is a living organism. It's warm to the touch and within a few months you can turn your old teabags and grass and egg shells into a loamy chocolaty compost that you almost want to eat. Here we are.'

207

We pulled up at an industrial building that I would have guessed was a blast furnace. It was huge, like an ocean liner. The outside was in brick and ridged metal, but from the top rose a huge metal container and to the right of it a tall chimney, also of metal. At the far end, away from the chimney, the building was open. Forklift trucks and lorries and vans were driving in and out. Fifty feet above there was a crane moving on rails.

'Hats on,' said Graham Bittles.

He was different from his colleague. Paul Creek seemed like the sort of person you'd find running a stall at a trade fair. He'd give you a T-shirt and a pen and you'd try and swat him off like a fly. Graham Bittles was more like a man doing a job. He looked rather as if he wished he was still doing it and wasn't having to deal with guests. I quite liked that about him. He pointed at the building.

'This is the basic incinerator facility.'

Giles leaned against me and whispered in my ear.

'Do you ever notice that everything in the world has become a facility. It can't just be a plain old incinerator.'

Graham didn't hear him and continued with his explanation.

'That there at the end is the storage. We can keep three days' supply of solid waste there. You see the bridge crane. That lifts the waste into the feed hopper. We'll go inside in a minute. Hang on a second.'

He walked across to say something to a man operating a hoist. Just a few yards away two men were struggling with the hydraulic lift behind the cab of a lorry. I wandered over.

'How you doing?' I said. They looked round and nodded at me. 'I'm just getting the guided tour. We're doing some enquiries into pollution.'

One of them laughed.

'Pollution?' he said. 'In this place? It's all fucking pollution, mate.'

'Yeah, that's right,' I said. 'You live in Marston Green.'

'No, I live down the coast,' the man said.

'I live there,' the other man said.

'Maybe I'll see you around,' I said. 'You ever go in the Four Feathers?'

'Sometimes.'

'I pretty much live there. Either of you know someone called Steve Yates?'

They looked at each other.

'Steve,' said the Marston Green man. 'He works the cabs. You want to see him?'

'No, I'll see him sooner or later,' I said. 'He's sort of a friend. Friend of a friend.' I noticed that Bittles was back. 'I'll see you.'

Bittles took us up some steel steps and through a door. We were in a large corridor. There was nothing there except for the ceiling. It looked as if railway transport cars were suspended upside down for the full length of this very long room. I looked over at Bittles.

'Right above these,' he said, 'is the combustion chamber

and these are the ash-removal containers. It's just a simple process. You saw the beginning outside. The solid waste is fed in at one end and it's inclined down into the combustion chambers. Then into the subsidence chamber, the dust collector and then finally into the stacks.'

Paul Creek was hovering eagerly.

'But, Graham, tell them how the process has been improved. We've got to make it clear that it's not just a bonfire we're talking about.'

'Right,' said Graham. He thought for a moment, no doubt working out how to make it simple-minded enough for us. 'People might think that an incinerator is like a furnace in a crematorium.' Giles pulled a face. 'You shove whatever it is in the furnace and it burns and the smoke goes up the chimney and you shovel out the ash. But if you do that with these quantities of solid waste, then the ash clogs up the machine and the chimney fills up and then there's the pollution and whatnot. So a new model like the one we have here removes the ash, it burns the exit gases and at the same time there's the wet scrubbers that remove the fly ash from the exit gases. So what goes up the stack is almost nothing.'

'When was this new model built?'

'About ten years ago, something like 1990.'

Giles got intently in conversation with Bittles about a piece of machinery called an inclined rotary kiln that Bittles was very excited about and so I drifted away. I walked along the corridor and out of an open door that led back out into the sunshine. The smell was appalling, like a barbecue that had gone tragically wrong. After a few minutes the others followed. Creek was talking urgently, jabbing with his finger.

'But the really good thing is that we're taking this further. The next stage – and this is part of the proposed expansion – is to use the exit gases to generate electricity. We'll be less and less polluting, we'll be creating energy out of what just went up the chimney and there's jobs as well. Who could possibly object to that?'

'It all sounds so nice,' said Giles.

'It's nothing more than the truth,' said Creek.

'Have you never thought of reaching out a bit to the local community?'

'What do you mean?'

'Open days. Parties of schoolchildren. Inviting your critics over to discuss their concerns.'

Creek shook his head.

'There are health and safety issues,' he said. 'You're an insurance man. Could we get insurance for a party of toddlers running around here?'

'You can get insurance for anything,' Giles said.

Suddenly Creek looked serious.

'Giles. We've got a business to run. Waste management is one of the fastest-growing businesses in the Western world and we're at the cutting edge. We're not a theme park. This protest is crap. It's a few people with a grievance. What we need – what the people of Marston Green need – is for them to go away. As you said, you're on our side. Can't you make that happen?'

As we drove away, Giles was looking cheerful again.

'What did you think?' I asked. 'Do you think they're polluting?'

'Who cares?' he said. 'I like that Graham Bittles. He's my sort of man. Miserable sod. But happy, if you know what I mean.'

'No, I don't.'

'I should have been an engineer. It's always about making the mousetrap just that little better. The process can always be done to a finer tolerance, just a bit faster.'

'Cheaper,' I said.

Giles didn't seem to have heard me.

'Interesting problem, incineration. They've made some imaginative advances. You know, Mark, there's a true story of an American engineer at the end of the First World War who wanted to show a German engineer how far America had now progressed. So he sent him a microscopically fine thread. And the German sent the thread back to the American engineer with a perfect, beautiful hole drilled through it. Isn't that a happy story? Didn't you like Marshco? Didn't you like all those machines, that activity?'

'I had a problem with the smell.'

'That's not them,' said Giles. 'They're not manufacturing the rubbish. We are. What else should we do with it?'

'Recycle it?'

'When did you last even go to the bottle bank?'

'So are you letting them off the hook?'

'I don't know if they're even on a hook. But that's not our business. We'll sniff around a bit and then head back to London. Nice place, though.'

'Marston Green?'

'Marston Green's a real dump. I mean a metaphorical dump. I was talking about the waste facility.'

And so we drove back to Marston Green, with the smell following us downwind and Giles talking about it with more enthusiasm than I'd ever heard from him.

I tried to look up Hannah Mahoney's phone number but it wasn't in the book. It's probably a necessary protection, even if you're a primary-school teacher, to protect you from insane parents coming round and killing you. But this is one of the good things about being in such a small village. I walked out into the High Street. There'd be someone who could tell me. The post van was parked outside the village shop and I walked in to find Dave the postman drinking a mug of tea with the woman behind the counter. See that? Dave the postman. In my entire life before, I'd never known the name of a postman, and no postman had ever known my name. Now I used to talk to Dave in the morning, and I'd only had two letters while I'd been in Marston Green, and they were both packages from Wortley. They weren't exactly the sort of letters that arrive with a whiff of perfume.

I told Dave that I had something I wanted to drop off at Hannah Mahoney's. Could he tell me where she lived?

'No problem,' he said. 'I'll drop it off on my way home.'

'I wanted to talk to her as well.'

Dave shrugged. That was no problem either. He even took an old envelope from his pocket and drew me a map.

214

It was half-past four, school was finished, so I walked along the High Street and turned right up a narrow lane. There was a line of cottages, on a raised bank along the edge of the line, and the third was where Hannah Mahoney lived. It was whitewashed stone with a thatched roof, and so narrow that you could see through the front window to the back garden, apparently just a few steps further away. I could see and hear movement inside, so I knocked at the door. She opened the door and looked puzzled, and not especially pleased. I was getting used to this slightly sarcastic, slightly amused expression that she reserved especially for me. She was wearing jeans and a man's shirt that was way too big for her, with the sleeves rolled up to just below her elbow.

'Sorry for just appearing on your doorstep,' I said. 'Your number isn't in the book.'

'That's to stop people calling around like this,' she said.

'I just want to ask you something very quickly and then I'll go. I won't be more than a minute.'

She gave a sigh.

'What?'

'My boss, Giles Buckland, has arrived.'

'Yes, I heard.'

'How?'

'This is a small village.'

'Doesn't that bother you?' I said. 'Everyone knowing what you're up to and commenting on it.'

'Sometimes,' she said. 'And sometimes it's nice. People help each other.'

'Anyway, we went up to the site and looked around.'

'What did you think?'

'I don't know,' I said. 'I don't think I could tell a good rubbish dump from a bad one. In any case, it only gives us a partial view of what's happening. I was wondering if I could come here with Giles and we could have a proper talk. He's not like me. He's a real scientist. Well, he was.'

There was a wailing inside and then Bruce wandered out. He looked up at me and fell silent. She reached down and took his hand without looking. She just knew where he was.

'You know what I'd like to know?' she said.

'What?'

'How can I do my cause anything but harm by talking to you and your boss about it? What your company wants is for this campaign to go away. Why should I clue you in on what I'm up to? I don't see why you can't just come to our meetings. We've got another one next week.'

'I've been here just a couple of days,' I said. 'I've talked to Kevin and I've looked at the incinerator and I've heard their spiel, and the only really impressive thing I've seen so far is your map. My bosses have made it very clear to me that I've got no authority here at all. I don't know much about your campaign. All I can say is that if there's anybody who can lean on Marshco, it's Wortley.'

She looked undecided, which was better.

'I can send Giles on his own,' I said. 'If you prefer.'

'I can look after myself,' she said. 'Even if I'm outnumbered.' A smile appeared slowly on her face. 'I gather that Sandy's pissed off with you.'

For a moment I was completely baffled. I could hardly even speak.

'What?' I said.

'Her sister works part time at the school. So what is this? A sort of Club Med holiday. You think you're in Ibiza?'

I took a deep breath, conscious that my face had gone a deep crimson colour.

'Sandy seemed very nice,' I said. 'I don't want to say anything.'

'There aren't many young women in Marston Green. You should be careful with them. I don't mind you both coming. When did you have in mind?'

'In about half an hour?'

'No. Come at seven. Bruce will have eaten and be pretty much ready for bed.'

'I don't want to stop you, if you're going out.'

She looked suspicious.

'Are you being sarcastic?' she said.

'Not at all.'

'Do you think I'm not likely to have somewhere to go? Are you being rude about me or are you being rude about Marston Green?'

'You'll have to run that by me again,' I said. 'I'm not following you.'

'It's just that I don't happen to be going out tonight.'

'Which is great,' I said. 'For us.'

She shook her head.

'I'll see you later.'

When we came back at seven, Bruce had only just finished his supper and was running around the living room. This was a perilous thing to do because the whole ground floor was polished boards with rugs dotted around. Whenever Bruce's feet hit a rug, the rug followed him. Giles and I sat awkwardly clutching mugs of coffee. Hannah was clearing the supper things away and wiping surfaces and occasionally swooped past us. Suddenly Bruce halted in front of us, wiped his nose with his sleeve and said:

'How many ears does Davy Crockett have?'

'Two?' said Giles in mock puzzlement.

'Three,' said Bruce. 'A left ear, a right ear and a wild frontier. Wassa wild frontier?'

'That's a hard one,' said Giles. 'A frontier is a border between two countries. There was a frontier between the cowboy country and the Indian country. Davy Crockett used to fight against the Indians a lot. So there's a song that calls him "King of the Wild Frontier".' Giles could see that he was losing Bruce's attention. Bruce seemed to have an itch at some weird remote spot on his back. He had pushed his hand up inside his pyjama jacket and was trying to reach it, which involved twisting around. 'I know another question about Davy Crockett. What was Davy Crockett's favourite meal?'

Hannah was back in the room by now.

'Is that a riddle?' she said. 'Let me see. Is it something to do with the Wild Frontier?' She started to hum the tune of the song to remind her of the words.

'No,' said Giles. 'It's not a riddle. It's true. What was his actual favourite meal?'

'How could we possibly know that? What did they eat on the range? It's probably pork and beans or something like that.'

'Snake,' said Bruce.

'No.'

'We give up,' said Bruce.

'Davy Crockett once said that his finest meal was potatoes, from the basement of a burned-down building, roasted in the fat of Indians that he had burned alive there.'

'What?' said Bruce. 'Did he eat them?'

'He ate the potatoes,' said Giles.

Hannah pulled a face that looked as if she might be about to be sick, or to throw us out.

'And now it's time for bed,' she said. 'Say good night, Bruce.'

'That was so yucky,' said Bruce.

Hannah took him by the hand and led him up the narrow staircase. He was chattering all the way up, but I could only make out the word 'potatoes'.

'Is it all right telling that to a little boy?' I said. 'That'll give me a nightmare.'

'That sort of thing doesn't bother children,' said Giles confidently. 'They find it funny.'

'He's probably up there weeping into his pillow,' I said.

219

Giles didn't look concerned. I felt agitated, so I stood up and looked around the room. There weren't many things in it, apart from quite a lot of paperbacks in a shelf. I was hoping there would be some photographs but there was just one, Hannah with longer hair and a much younger Bruce on a beach in bright sunshine. She was holding him on her knee and smiling at the camera, dazzled, her eyes narrowed in the bright sunshine. There was a fairly shapeless shadow cast on the sand by the photographer. I wondered who it was. I picked it up and looked more closely.

'She's not married,' I said. 'No sign of a man anywhere around in the house, that I can see. I wonder if she's gay.'

'Why don't you ask me?' Hannah said.

I put the picture back on the shelf with amazing control. It would have been quite possible for me to have dropped it on the floor and then the situation would have been just a little bit worse.

'That's all right,' I said.

'Maybe you can tell from the decoration of my house,' Hannah said. 'Is it basically heterosexual, or is there a touch of dyke-ishness about it?'

'I'm trying to think of something to say,' I said.

'Mark is normally good at thinking of things to say,' Giles said. 'With women.'

'Thanks, Giles.'

'I've heard,' said Hannah. 'Now that you've traumatized my child, I may need to go and tell him another story quite soon, so maybe we should get a move on.'

'Giles says that children aren't frightened by that sort of

thing,' I said. That was me getting my own back for Giles saying I was good at thinking of things to say to women.

'We'll see,' she said. 'Or rather, I'll see. Probably at about three in the morning.' Giles and I were sitting on the sofa. She pulled a hard-backed chair over and sat on it. 'You'll understand that I'm going to be a bit cautious talking to you. There's a bit of me that feels I have should have nothing to do with you. Anything I show will either show a strength or a weakness in our case, and either way that will help you and harm our campaign.'

'But do you want your campaign to work if it's based on false information?'

'Come off it,' she said. 'You know that the real world doesn't work like that. All cases have weaknesses. Opponents can seize on them and use them to defeat a decent case.'

Giles rubbed his face. He looked as if he was tired and rather bored. I could recognize his expressions by now. This one was a sign that he was enjoying himself.

'I can see that,' said Giles. 'Obviously what I'm interested in is the data you've collected and we can talk about that in a moment. But I'm just curious: in an ideal world, what is it you want?'

'We're not in an ideal world,' said Hannah. 'We're in a messy, contradictory world. What do we want? We're trying to formulate that at the moment. I don't speak for the campaign and I don't speak for the victims. But I suppose it will include a proper inquiry into the damage caused by that incinerator, a discovery of where the responsibility lies, reform so it can't happen again, and in the end some kind of compensation for the victims. But nobody believes that this compensation will come in time for the majority of them. I think what most of them want is for someone to stand up and say: "It was our fault and we're sorry."'

There was a silence. Hannah's face had gone very pale, with just pricks of red around her cheekbones. Her dark eyes showed fiercely against her pale skin. I could only think that if I had been anybody from Marshco or from Wortley – well, I was from Wortley, but I meant someone important from Wortley – I would have been glad that she had said this in her own front room, and not in a court or in front of an inquiry. And yet, what had she really said?

'More coffee?' she asked.

'Yes, thanks, that would be good,' said Giles and I just nodded. Giles asked where the lavatory was and Hannah pointed to a door at the far end of the house from the kitchen. They returned at the same moment, Giles looking ill at ease and sombre.

'I can't do much to dispel your worries about us,' he said. 'Obviously we haven't come to town to help your campaign. All I can say is that we're not here to campaign against you. We're not here to have any influence of any kind, excepting what Mark gets up to out of office hours. Could you tell us what you've been doing?'

She filled our coffee mugs and her own. Mine had the face of a Teletubby on it. She took a sip of coffee.

'There's nothing complicated about it,' she said. 'Mark must have told you. I've been gathering the information about illnesses in this area, deciding which seem relevant. Then I've put them on a map to see if there is a pattern.'

'There's a problem with that . . .' Giles began.

'There are lots of problems,' she said. 'One is that it's hard to see a pattern if it's only in one place. If the dioxins emitted from the incinerator are causing the cancers, then it's crucial that we are downwind of the plant. So what I've been doing is extending my search into similar-sized communities that are further away from the site and in the other direction.'

'That's excellent,' said Giles. 'What I don't understand is how you're getting your information. You can't just walk into GPs' surgeries and examine their records.'

'We've sent out questionnaires, not just in Marston Green but, as I say, in five other communities, in what is basically a continuous strip running north-east from here.'

'What's your response rate?' asked Giles.

'We only sent them out a few weeks ago, but it seems to be quite high. And it seems to be about the same level in each community, so it should be a fair representation.'

'I suppose,' said Giles slowly, 'that the responses will be weighted more in favour of those with cancer.'

'Almost certainly,' said Hannah. 'But that doesn't matter. If anything, it will only work against our case. We're not interested in the percentage of respondents with cancer. We just want to know the numbers, their types of illness and where they actually live.'

'And then?'

'We take it stage by stage. The plan is to plot it on the

map, the way I did for Marston Green, and then maybe a compelling pattern will emerge. There's so much argument about this or that chemical process and this or that alleged effect. I'd like something that people could just look at. Something that would be as clear as the hand in front of their face.'

'Could I have a copy of the chart you made of the Marston Green illness?'

'Sorry,' said Hannah. 'One of the promises I've made to people who've responded to me is that their anonymity will be protected. In the end, I would like to make the information public. But I've got to think of how best to do it.'

'You showed it at a public meeting.'

'I know. I worried about that. But I thought it was important for people to have a look at what we were talking about. I was careful to keep it anonymous.'

'Can I at least have a look?'

She paused and looked thoughtful.

'Why not?' she said.

She got up and left the room and returned with her large piece of card. She propped it up on the edge of the sofa. Giles looked at it in silence, his eyes screwed up, his right hand under his chin. He tilted his head sideways. He looked like an art expert valuing an abstract painting: thirty blobs on an English village.

'And these are . . . what?' he asked.

'Leukaemias, multiple myeloma, lymphomas, lung cancer, breast cancer, bone cancer, bowel cancer. A range.'

'Mark was right,' Giles said. 'For once. That's startling.

You've done a remarkable job, Hannah. That's something for us all to consider. It's the most interesting thing I've seen since I got here. Maybe the only interesting thing, apart from Mark's extracurricular activities . . .'

'Giles . . .' I said.

'What about Kevin?' said Hannah. 'What about that mass of information he's gathered?'

'I don't know,' said Giles. 'I don't know what it means. I don't mean I don't understand it. I don't know what that mass of information says about incineration and ill people in Marston Green.' He rubbed his face with his hands again as if it was all too much for him. 'I think that Mark told you that I was a sort of scientist, years ago. One of the many reasons I gave it up . . . Well, the main reason was that I stopped being able to get out of bed in the morning. That was the final obstacle. But when I started out I used to think that when we did science we were finding out about reality. More and more of it. What I came to see is that it was nothing like that. What we were doing, in effect, was building bridges and sometimes the bridges stay up, and you can use them, and sometimes the bridge falls over and you assume something must have been wrong so you build the next bridge in a different way. That's why I got more interested in probability and worked for an insurance company. It's a funny sort of science. I can't tell you whether a coin will fall heads or tails. But if I toss a coin a hundred million times I can predict with absolute certainty the range within which the numbers will fall.

'That's what I like about your map. It's not like Kevin

Seeger's room full of files. He's trying to find out how the world works. Maybe he's right, maybe he's wrong. But you've given us figures we can work with.' He rubbed his eyes again, like a small child past his bedtime. Then he looked directly at Hannah. 'Would it be possible to meet any of the cancer victims?'

Hannah looked startled by this.

'What for?' she said. 'That goes against everything you've been saying. What could meeting one or two or three suffering people tell you?'

'We'd like to know about people's mood,' said Giles. 'I'm interested in figures, of course. We also want to gauge the feeling of people in the village.'

Hannah looked uncomfortable.

'I'll have to think about that. These people are in a very vulnerable state.'

'We're aware of that.'

'And I'm worried about them being picked off individually.'

'Hannah, I can promise you that we're not empowered in any way to negotiate with anybody on behalf of Marshco or the insurers.'

She stared at him.

'Then what is the point of you being here at all?' she said. 'You come in here and you're being all sensitive and, "I couldn't get out of bed in the morning", and I feel your pain ...'

'I didn't say that,' said Giles.

'What you're doing is flirting with us. You pop into our

lives, and Mark here thinks he's in Ibiza or somewhere, and as soon as anything actually arises, then you're sorry but you're not empowered.'

There was a pause. I certainly wasn't going to say anything. Hannah scared me. I'd never met a woman who scared me like that before. I looked at the ground.

'I'd never say anything as crass as "I feel your pain". If you think about it, how could we possibly arrive and start negotiating? What meaning would that have for anybody?'

Hannah was panting slightly, as if shouting at Giles had been a physical effort.

'You're probably right,' she said. 'I'm oversensitive on the subject.'

'We'll go,' said Giles, and she ushered us over to the door. Opening it and showing another golden evening outside.

'So you think I'm gay, do you?'

'I hope not,' I said.

'What?' she said. 'What do you mean?'

My mind went horribly blank. Worse than blank. It was a black hole which sucked up words and thoughts obliterated them.

'Er, well, you've got a child.'

That was a stupid start.

'A child? Oh, I see.'

'But obviously,' I added, 'I hope you're happy whatever you are.'

'Oh, fuck off,' she said.

That was her very crude way of dismissing us because she closed the door without saying anything more.

Giles and I sat in the garden behind the Four Feathers with our beer and our sandwiches. I hadn't got to the supermarket yet, so we were still depending on Geoff Otley. I decided to wait until it rained. On an evening like this it would have been waste of time for me to be indoors, struggling with the stove. The garden was just a few seconds from the old stable yard. Picnic tables were dotted around and we chose one away from anybody else. The garden looked out on a scrubby piece of field behind. Bunches of gnats, blurred like smoke, were caught in the evening sun. Swallows were swooping and circling, feeding on the insects. For me it wasn't at all a peaceful, rural scene. The swallows were like fighters, F16s coming in low, hovering over the contours of the ground, twisting to wheel and bank in steep turns. It wasn't just insects. A magpie sat on a fence pole and then I saw that the swallows were attacking it at high speed, diving and then curving away, missing it by a couple of inches. The magpie seemed to ignore them for several minutes, then flapped noisily away, the swallows still harassing him.

Giles took a sip of his beer.

'You know the saying, "this isn't a bear garden"?'

'No,' I said.

'Teachers say it at school. Or used to. The pupils are messing around and then the teacher shouts: "What do you think this is? A bear garden?"'

'I've never heard that.'

'Maybe they meant a *beer* garden. I saw the sign out front. This is a beer garden.'

'What's a bear garden?'

'You know, in Elizabethan England where they'd tie a bear to a post and then set dogs on him.'

'That sounds rowdy.'

'Rowdy?'

'I mean rowdier than a beer garden. I mean, this beer garden seems fairly peaceful.'

'It was just a thought,' said Giles. He took another sip of beer. 'Your lines are getting worse.'

'What do you mean?'

'With Hannah Mahoney. "Is she gay?" "I hope you're happy, whatever you are." Even I could do better than that.'

I took a bite of my sandwich. Good, strong cheese with pickle, a doorstop-size hunk of fresh white bread. Jan had her own bread-making machine out back. Why should I ever go to the supermarket?

'For a start, Giles, it's not a line. I don't have lines. I don't believe there's any such thing as a line. And secondly we were there interviewing her about people dying of cancer.'

'It's the best way of meeting women,' Giles said. 'When your mind is meant to be on other things. That's good for romance. What do you think of her?'

This wasn't the conversation I'd thought we were going to be having.

'What do I think of her? I don't think that our meeting went particularly well.'

'I think she's wonderful,' said Giles. 'She's really my type. Or would be, if I weren't married. Intelligent, forceful, beautiful.'

'She's not *that* beautiful,' I said.

'Not beautiful?' said Giles. 'Who's beautiful? Oh, you mean your floozy, Sandy?'

'Will you stop it with Sandy, for fuck's sake? But yes, Sandy is more obviously pretty, I guess.'

Giles took a gulp of beer and gave a little burp.

'This is what I like,' he said. 'We're sitting in a pub sizing up women. This is what men ought to be doing. It's almost like being single again. It's like Michael Caine and Terence Stamp in the sixties.'

'Terence Stamp?'

'Don't you think there's something particularly attractive about a woman with a child?'

'Not really.'

'Research has demonstrated that we're attracted to the breasts and rounded hips of women because they suggest fertility. And having a child is just another version of that.'

'I don't think it's the same thing.'

'I wasn't lying to her. I'm genuinely impressed by what she's doing, by that map.'

'It looks amazing.'

'It's not just that. Information like that is hard to get.

I hope it's as reliable as she says it is, but that can be checked in due course.'

'That sounds very businesslike,' I said.

'She's got breast cancer, you know.'

I almost felt as if I were going to tip over and fall. I had to grip the table.

'What?'

'Or at least she's being treated for it.'

'How do you know?'

'There were bottles of tamoxifen in her bathroom. You have to take it for several years after certain forms of cancer treatment.'

'Giles, you've got to stop doing this. You can't keep rooting around in people's bathrooms. It's not right.'

He took another sip of beer.

'I wasn't rooting around. I asked if I could use the lavatory. She pointed me to the only bathroom in the house. I saw the bottles which were in the open. I can't force myself not to see what's in front of my eyes. I can't make myself unknow what I know. In any case, our knowing it doesn't do her any harm, unless we go around blabbing about it.'

'That's not true.'

'Why not?'

'Because now you'll judge her in a certain way.'

'I won't.'

'You will. Now you'll see her campaign differently. Before, we thought she was campaigning on behalf of other people, now we know that she's doing it on her own behalf.'

'You want another beer, Mark?'

'Fuck, yes,' I said. 'I'd like to stick my head in one.'

Giles went into the pub and I went over our meeting with Hannah again in my head. It was basically a matter of remembering one bad thing after another. Such as, is she a lesbian? I thought of the bad-tempered end to the meeting. Her telling me to fuck off and shutting the door. Then I tried to remember our exact words when we'd talked about wanting to meet some victims. Had either of us made any light-hearted comments about them? I couldn't remember, but I couldn't be sure. If we didn't, it was only a matter of luck. He came back with his two large glasses, and two packets of crisps held in his teeth. He leaned forward and deposited them on the table, like a trained bird. The beer had tipped over the rim of his glasses and run over his fingers. He took a paper napkin from his pocket and wiped them. I took a deep drink.

'Do you never feel guilty about spying on people?'

Giles calmly opened a bag of salt and vinegar crisps and put a couple of them in his mouth, crunching them obnoxiously loudly.

'I thought we could have these for pudding,' he said. 'We should take advantage of not having anyone around to tell us what to do.' He sounded like a six-year-old whose mother had left the room. 'You mean, do I feel guilty about looking at people, thinking about them, making judgements about them? What else is one meant to do with people?'

'Just be with them. Let them get on with their lives.'

'It so happens that you're wrong. I don't think worse of Hannah Mahoney. I think better of her. *Even* better of her.

You felt that we might think that she was just in it because she's had cancer herself. What impresses me is that she doesn't talk about herself. It would have been so easy for her to take on the moral authority of the victim. She didn't say a word about it. Amazing.'

'We know now.'

'If it were me,' said Giles, 'I'd be talking about it all the time. I would be obsessed with it every second of the day. I'm almost obsessed with it already and I'm just thinking about it. I don't know which would be the worst bit. First hearing that you've got it. I would be thinking all the time of these cells in your body, doubling and growing. I studied cellular oncology briefly at university and I used to sit there and I could almost feel, I could almost *hear*, the tumours growing in different parts of my body. You know, Mark, that a cancer cell, any cell, is so small that you can hardly see it under a microscope. If you had a single cancer cell and it grew by dividing in half once a month, how long would it be before you had a two-kilogram tumour which your body couldn't tolerate and you would die?'

'I don't know.'

'Guess. I mean, estimate.'

'Once a month?'

'That's right.'

'I don't know,' I said. 'Twenty-five years?'

'When we get back to London, if we ever do, I'm going to get Wortley to send you on a maths course. People like you, Mark, walk around in a fog of bemusement. The world acts in strange ways. You are amazed by coincidence. All because you don't understand the way large numbers work. A French mathematician once said that the most important questions of life are, for the most part, really only problems of probability, and I agree with him. The answer is less than three and a half years.'

'Oh.'

'Where was I?' said Giles. 'Oh, yes. Then I'd be obsessed with death. Again, I'm obsessed already. Some people lie awake at night and worry about dying. I don't do that, I go through the clever reasons why one shouldn't worry about dying. Do you want to hear them?'

'Well . . .'

'Are you frightened of not having existed before you were born?'

'I've never thought about it.'

'You're not, are you? If you hear about the Battle of Hastings or see *The Wizard of Oz* on TV, you don't start weeping because you weren't alive at the time.'

'No.'

'So why be frightened of not existing after you die?' Giles took a sip from his beer and looked gloomy. 'The problem is that I *am* frightened of not having existed before I died. Sometimes I look at photographs that were taken before I was born and I get a little jab of horror because that's a hint of what being dead will be like. Not being there. Not being everywhere. And in fact, being dead after you die is very slightly worse than being dead before you are born. Do you want to know why?'

'Well . . .'

'Before you were born you were dead for a finite amount of time, which must have had a beginning as well as an end.'

'What beginning?'

'If the universe has existed for ever, then it could never reach the moment of your birth because an infinite amount of time would have to have elapsed to get to it. So it must have had a beginning.'

'I'm not sure I follow that.'

'Doesn't matter. The point is that when you die, you really could be dead for ever. And then there'd be the treatment for the cancer. Knowing you are damaging your body as much as possible in the hope it will kill your cancer before it kills you. Feeling nauseous all the time. If I had cancer, I would certainly be tempted to start a campaign to blame it all on somebody else.'

'Is that what you think? I thought you liked her.'

'I don't know what to think,' said Giles. 'But I do adore her.'

'And you're married, of course.'

'You know one of the problems with growing old?'

'Is this to do with dying?' I said.

'No, I'm talking about marriage. One of the problems is not growing old but being married to an old woman. Does that sound cruel?'

'I don't know.' Of course it did.

'I don't particularly think of Susan as old. Or I don't *see* her as old. But sometimes I'll see a woman who I think of as middle-aged and I'll think, she's the same age as Sue. What do you think?'

I was lost in thought.

'I don't think you're really frightened of cancer,' I said.

'Why not?'

'You talk about it. You spin ideas about it. But if you actually got cancer it would be completely different.'

'You think I'd suddenly turn out to be brave?'

'I just mean it would be completely different,' I said. 'It would have nothing at all to do with what you've said or thought about it. And I think it's wrong of you to say that she would have started this campaign because of her cancer. We don't know about her attitude to cancer. We don't know how the campaign started. You just saw some bottle in her bathroom. Maybe she's got a lodger with breast cancer.'

'They had her name on.'

'Oh, for fuck's sake. So you picked them up and looked at them.'

'Isn't this great?' he said.

'What do you mean?'

'It's pastoral.'

'What?' I said.

'You were talking about this as a way of helping our careers. Fuck that. There's no chance of that. But we've escaped from the noise and the dirt and the intrigue of the city and we're here in nature and we can talk and relax and examine our lives.'

'Dirt?' I said. 'We've just visited a rubbish dump.'

It was almost as if I had fallen asleep and suddenly woken up because I looked around and saw that the garden had now filled up with people. Giles looked around and smiled.

'It looks like everybody who is anybody in Marston Green is here,' he said.

'I think that's right,' I said. I wondered if Sandy would be here. Was she really bitter at me? I noticed a familiar face. 'That's a guy from Marshco.'

'Where?'

I pointed him out.

'I had a chat with him where the lorries were loading up the incinerator. He told me he lived in Marston Green, so I guess it was only to be expected.'

'Let's go and say hello,' said Giles.

'Oh, no,' I said. 'We can't just do that. Let's give the poor sod a break.'

'Grab your beer, Foll. This is an order. We're working. Come on, introduce me.'

The man was leaning on the fence talking to a friend. He saw us approaching and gave a sign of vague, half recognition.

'Hi,' I said. 'We met up by the incinerator.'

'Yeah, that's right.'

I introduced Giles and me and the man told us he was called Tony Thorn and introduced the other man as his brother-in-law, Ewan. He seemed reluctant, waiting for us to go, but the two of them perked up when Giles asked them what they were having. They looked into their glasses, which were almost empty.

'A pint each of County, cheers very much,' said Tony.

Giles went off to get it and in the meantime we had that ritualistic conversation I'd got so used to in my very short time in Marston Green. I said that we came from London and they went into an elaborate expression of horror as if it was some combination of Sodom and the Western Front. They couldn't live there. The traffic. The crowds. The crime. A friend of a friend of Ewan's had had his mobile phone pinched in Oxford Street. He was just walking along talking on it and it was whipped off of his ear. Would you believe it?

Giles returned with the beers and the mood became very affable. It turned out that Tony and Ewan were both fishermen in their spare time and, weirdly, it turned out that Giles knew quite a lot about fishing. They had an almost entirely incomprehensible conversation about rudd and chubb and pike and perch and different ways of catching them. Early on, Tony turned to me and asked if I ever fished. I said no. If there had been the tiniest temptation to lie and say, well, occasionally, when I get the chance, that was killed off by a single horrible thought: I imagined saying that and then being invited out for a day's fishing with Tony and Ewan. Even from what I could hear, it was grimly clear that they left with their anoraks and tackle very early each Saturday morning and returned very late.

'By the way,' Tony said. 'The bloke you mentioned, Steve Yates. He'll be in later.'

'That right?' I said.

'Who's that?' Giles asked.

'Someone Tony knows.'

'Yeah,' said Tony. 'And Mark here knows him as well.'

'How's that, Mark?'

'I've never met him,' I said. 'I just heard about him. He's the father of . . . you know.'

'Oh, really?' said Giles, interested now. 'Well, when he comes in, we must have him over. I'd like to meet him.'

'Great,' I said.

'You all work at Marshco?' said Giles.

'That's right,' said Tony.

'You too?' he said, nodding at Ewan.

239

'Five years,' said Ewan.

'You make it sound like a prison sentence,' said Giles and we all laughed, mates together.

'No, it's a good job,' said Ewan. 'I work on maintenance.'

'It's good to get together,' said Giles. 'We work for Marshco as well, in a way.'

'You work in the office?' Tony asked.

'No, we work for their main insurance company. We heard about the problems with illness in the area and that people say it's connected to the plant. Have you heard about that?'

The two men exchanged glances. Tony gave a shrug as if it didn't matter much.

'What do you reckon?' asked Giles, as if it didn't matter much to him either.

'Bloody troublemakers,' said Tony. He took a deep gulp of his ale, like he was trying to cool himself down and failing. 'I mean, what do they want? Do they want Marshco to shut up shop and go somewhere else with their money and their expansion and their jobs? Then this place'll go straight down the toilet.'

'Too right,' said Giles. Giles had the curious, almost sinister, ability to start echoing whoever he was with. He'd done it at least three times today. Up at the Marshco plant, when he'd been with that systems engineer, it had all been two engineers together, talking about gaskets or whatever it was, off on their own. Then with Hannah he'd been confessional and vulnerable, about how he couldn't get out of bed in the morning. Now, with these rubbish shifters from

Marshco, even his accent had shifted slightly. He was now one of the blokes, railing against the know-nothing bleeding-heart activists. Was that what he did with me, with all that crappy pub talk about women? If that's what he was trying, he wasn't very good at it.

Giles nodded at me and I went off and returned with a tray of four more pints of beer and a selection of crisps and peanuts and pork scratchings. We all settled down around one of the tables, which was a relief because I was becoming slightly unsteady.

'Now,' said Giles. 'If you want to find a really toxic substance that is a major threat to the health of humanity, then I offer you the pork scratching.' He tried to open the packet but it resisted his attempts and he had to bite it violently until it split open and scattered on the table. We all helped ourselves and there was a contented crunching sound around the table.

'The pork scratching,' continued Giles, 'has been banned around the world. It is well known that its basic ingredients are the bits left on the floor of slaughterhouses after the rest of the bits have been taken away to make cat food. These bits are left to harden in the sun, then they are deep fried in oil recycled from fish and chip shops in the north of England. They are then salted with salt retrieved from popcorn containers under cinema seats.'

There were groans from around the table and then another pint of beer appeared in front of me as if by magic. It didn't seem long enough since the previous glass. I thought I might have drifted drunkenly off to sleep, but then I remembered I'd been telling them in detail about my comparison between swallows and fighter aircraft, which had taken quite a long time, as I described the different manoeuvres. Tony and Ewan were quite impressed and actually began to cheer the low-level attack of one particular swallow, which featured a spectacular bank and twist as it grabbed a mosquito and then went on its way. 'Send it out to Iraq,' someone shouted. It might have been me, and there were shushing sounds from surrounding tables. Then there were shouts of 'Steve, Steve, over here, mate' and a tall, solid man with freckles and very light brown hair sat down at the table.

'These gents were asking after you,' Tony said.

'We met your daughter,' Giles said from the other end of the table.

I took a gulp of beer.

'That right?'

'We're working up at Marshco,' I said.

'They're not on the trucks,' Ewan said. 'They're insurance salesmen.'

'Not exactly . . .' I started to say. My surroundings were becoming hazy and I was concentrating on keeping my thought processes very precise and logical so that nobody would think I was drunk and so that I wouldn't say anything stupid. I was also thinking about Steve Yates, who was sitting opposite me, and I was making a very carefully constructed plan on how to deal with him. It all depended on what he knew. For all I knew East Anglia might be like Sicily and he would turn up at Clover chalet with a sawn-off shotgun and two huge brothers. I would be led off and have to marry Sandy. I'd settle down in Marston Green and get a job here. Probably at Marshco. I could be the person who feeds rubbish into the incinerator. That would be a simple, good job. Then maybe I would get cancer from the dioxins and Hannah could use me as an example at meetings. She could lead me out onto the stage with a blanket over my head and then at the crucial moment she would whip it off and I would be standing there like the Elephant Man. That would all be neat and fitting.

Maybe he didn't know, however. Everybody else in the village seemed to, but maybe he didn't. Therefore my immediate plan would be not to drink any more, except for the occasional sip to give the impression that I was joining in with the guys. And the second plan, or rather, the second part of the first plan, was to stay almost entirely silent. I could then give an impression of great thoughtfulness and deep pondering. I could imagine people around the table glancing my way and murmuring to each other: 'That's a shrewd 'un, all right.' New glasses of beer occasionally appeared on the table but I kept a firm hold on my own half-full glass. Nobody would be allowed to get hold of it and swap it for a full one. I felt mellow and in control. I sat quietly and listened to the conversation going on around me, although I found some of it hard to follow, like Kevin's lecture about dioxins. There was a slight lull in the conversation and people were staring reflectively into their beers. It was one of those moments when somebody needs to break the silence and start a new topic of conversation. But it wasn't going to be me. They couldn't catch me out. The first to speak was Giles.

'I work for insurance now but the reason I'm on this job is that I've got a bit of a background in waste management.'

There was a slightly surprised murmur around the table. I was completely stunned but on the other hand I was deeply grateful that Giles hadn't, as he was quite capable of, started a discussion about sex, about young women, about sexual behaviour in Marston Green. Also I was quite interested to hear what Giles would say about his non-existent experience in waste management.

'I was right at the bottom, mind you. It was after I left college and I spent some time just trying to earn money. I got a job with a guy called Don Kiely in the Black Country. He was a right old cowboy. He had a few lorries and some contracts and he also had – what shall we say? – cash-flow problems. It was a laugh what those guys got up to. We'd clear out a site, and then we'd strip off anything you could trace, and then we'd dump the stuff any old place. In people's skips, on other building sites – you'd have to watch that one, because you make some serious enemies that way. We'd tip loads over bridges into canals, onto other loads of rubbish that were ready for collection.'

There were chuckles around the table.

'It's part of the skill of the job, isn't it?' Giles continued.

'I know what you mean,' said Tony. 'We've all been there and done that. Sometimes there's so many bloody rules and regulations sent from Brussels that in the end you think, just fuck it and you tip it off the side of the road.'

'I guess that Marshco aren't like that?'

'You'd be bloody surprised,' said Ewan. 'Bloody surprised.'

'But they've got all that space,' said Giles.

'Yeah,' said Ewan. 'The question is: what do you take and where do you shove it? I can tell you that if you're starting up a new waste-disposal operation, you're not going to grow like Marshco if you start saying, oh, I'm not sure if we can take that, and, oh dear, have you separated that one out. They talk about people in the village who may or may not have got ill. They should talk to the poor sods who were handling the stuff back in the eighties.'

'That's when they were done for it, wasn't it?'

'That's right,' said Tony. 'A lot of that was sorted out. It had to be or it would have been closed down. It's different stuff now. It's all about speed, growth, throughput, so and so money per cube. Us lot round the table, we work for the company, but a load of the driving is contracted out and the managers are on their backs every second one end and their own bosses are on their backs at the other. Who bloody knows where half their stuff comes from? Then there was the bloody foot and mouth.'

This roused me briefly from my torpid state.

'I saw that on TV,' I said. 'They weren't put in rubbish dumps. They dug big pits and burned them.'

'I wasn't talking about the pits,' said Tony. 'I was talking about the lorries. The ministry were hiring hundreds of them, any they could find, paying anything the companies asked. They were faxing open invoices to the depots. Bloody unbelievable, it was. Bloody Christmas Day every day. So there was a knock-on effect up at Marshco. We were working double shifts. We'd have worked triple shifts if we'd have the transport. It was absolute bloody chaos up there. I'm surprised they didn't shut it down. One manager totally lost it. What was his name?'

'Preece,' said Steve.

'He was under so much pressure that he'd been sending everything, industrial, medical, contaminates, other stuff all with the general waste. By the time they discovered, it was all bloody mixed up like a Christmas pudding. What a shambles.'

There was a pause. More beer staring.

'Preece,' said Giles.

He was smiling, blokeish, one of the gang, but suddenly there was a chill in the atmosphere. People seemed to have sobered up, except for me.

'It wasn't that big a deal,' said Ewan. 'He was booted out, end of story. I think they got most of it sorted anyway.'

Tony and Steve nodded agreement.

'There's always one, isn't there?' said Giles, and sounding drunk once more, he told a long, involved and entirely untrue story about his time in the Black Country, about a pile of garbage and how his name was found in it and he was almost arrested. I looked at Steve. He looked quite like his daughter, which was a bit strange. I tried not to think about it. He was running his finger around the rim of his glass, very gently. When the story was finished, they all laughed, but the spark had gone. They muttered their thanks and talked of work and home and they drifted away.

Giles was staring at his current pint of beer, which was more than half full. He pushed it away.

'Sometimes I'm not sure I like beer,' he said.

We were sitting in Paul Creek's office at ten past ten the following morning. Creek stirred and stirred his coffee.

'You haven't put sugar in yet,' said Giles.

Creek looked down at the spoon.

'I don't take sugar,' he said.

I gulped my coffee while it was still too hot. It stung my mouth but that was deliberate. I was well below my best and I needed anything that could jerk me into full consciousness. The caffeine wouldn't be enough. Creek gave a sniff.

'His name was James Preece. He was dismissed fourteen months ago because he wasn't up to the job and this has absolutely nothing to do with what you're here to deal with.'

Giles took a sip of coffee and flinched. He wasn't completely at his best either.

'Nothing?'

'This is an issue of environmental cancer. Cancer that must have developed over ten, fifteen or more years. This was a dumping incident that happened last year.'

'That's why you didn't tell me about it, when I asked?'

Creek took a deep huffy breath.

'I didn't decide not to tell you about it. Mr Buckland,

we're a large operation and part of an even larger international concern, and the fact is that we're a company like other companies. We have good employees and bad employees, good practices and bad practices. When you asked me about problems, I'm afraid I didn't come up with every single example of incompetence in our history.'

'Maybe you should, Mr Creek. I should say straight away that if, God forbid, this issue comes in front of a jury and you're in the witness box, I wouldn't put too much stress on your argument that you're just another company with good and bad employees. In fact, I wouldn't recommend any company to mention that in a liability case. You're handling dangerous materials. The claim that you have some incompetent employees and bad practices would, for a jury, be an explanation of *how* you poisoned the good people of Marston Green rather than a defence.

'Secondly, Mr Creek, if we were having a university seminar about dioxin contamination, then your statement about the irrelevance of this man Preece's dismissal might possibly be worth making. But let me give you an example. And bear in mind that I'm speaking as someone who spends his time paying out money to claimants. Imagine you've gone for a restaurant meal and been up all night with food poisoning. You return to the restaurant next morning to complain. You go into the kitchen and find a piece of beef crawling with maggots. You point this out to the manager who waves you away. That's not relevant, he says. That meat only arrived this morning. And anyway, you ate fish, not meat, so there's no connection.'

249

Paul Creek had gone very pale, and he was pale enough
to start with. He had stopped stirring his coffee, which was
something, but he was now holding his pen in his left hand,
flicking the cap off and clicking it on, again and again. That
was even worse.

'Where did you hear about Preece?' he said.

'What?' said Giles.

Giles had a very good way of saying one-syllabled words
like 'what' when he was angry.

'I just wanted to say that there are some disaffected
people in this company. You shouldn't play games with my
words, Mr Buckland. Let me be clear. Four years ago, when
I arrived here, in my view this was not a well-run operation.
What I've done, bit by bit, is to introduce a modern management structure, to invest, to upgrade the machinery and
processes and also, with no apology, I've imported new
flexibility. If it's cheaper to buy in a service than to provide
it ourselves, that's what I've done. If it's more effective to
employ people on short-term contracts than to have them as
full-time employees, I've altered their terms of employment.
I've had to bang heads together sometimes. There are a
couple of dozen people I've fired face to face. They were
sitting where you're sitting now. There's another fifty at
least I've let go. There's at least another fifty who know that
their job may well be casualized, or they may be made
redundant, or reassigned. Are you sure it wasn't one of
them? Do you know what it's like to run a business, Mr
Buckland?'

'No,' said Giles. 'I don't.'

Creek stood up and walked over to the window. He looked assertive again. He clearly felt back in control. We were in his office now, not the meeting room we had been in before, but the view was much the same over the reeking piles of rubbish.

'When we moved into the new block here, I had a choice. I could have had my office on the other side with a view over to the north-east. It's beautiful. People have this idea that East Anglia is flat, and a lot of it is, inland, flat as the Great Plains in the United States. But from the other side there's a view of rolling hills and an ancient oak forest that's mentioned in the Domesday Book and beyond that you can glimpse Netherfield Hall. Have you visited that? It's the most complete Elizabethan stately home in East Anglia.

'But I chose to have my office on this side, looking inwards. That's partly a matter of corporate morality, the same reason that all of us eat in the same canteens. It's not just that, though. A few years ago, when we were planning the expansion, I went for a trip across Europe and the States, visiting different waste facilities. That's pretty sad, don't you think? I'm afraid that's what I do.

'It's probably not what you'd choose for a holiday but I had a good time. One of the places I stopped off at was a dump in central Sweden. I'm not sure how big it was but I'd guess it was at least five times the size of the Marshco facility, maybe ten times. It's a beautiful place. And when I saw beautiful I don't mean beautiful for a rubbish dump, I mean beautiful, full stop. It was surrounded by pine forests. You drove into it along a snaking country road. Inside the entrance there were recycling and reclamation facilities on a level we can hardly imagine. You could drive further in, again on a country road. I drove past a lake with reeds and lilies, with geese and swans and ducks.

'The landfill itself was tucked into the hills and was a process more than a site. The refuse was flattened and shaped and then the earth was tucked into it and the landscape was restored. As I drove out I noticed that there was a golf course running along the edge of the facility. Can you imagine that? A golf course. That's how offensive the site was. That's how unbearable the smell of the rubbish was.

'That's the main reason why my office is here. One day, in five or ten years, when I or my successor looks out of this window, it will be over a landscape that will be as beautiful as the view from the other side.' He turned round and smiled at us. 'I'm all heart, aren't I? But do you think I can bring that about just by being kind to people? Look at the landscape on the other side, outside the wire, the beautiful English landscape. Do you think those fields and forests were created by people being nice?

'And do you think I should have managed the transformation of Marshco overnight? I'm afraid that the incineration process produces toxic residues. I won't argue with you that occasionally some of our waste has been dumped in the wrong place. But twenty years ago this site was being prosecuted. We haven't even had a warning in ten years. And I'll tell you something else. Is that partly because on occasion we have managed a more disciplined management of information about certain procedural errors? Yes, it is. This is waste, for God's sake. Rubbish, trash, shit, discharge, offcuts. Let's be grown-up here. People send us the stuff they think is too dangerous or disgusting to keep in their own homes or factories and we do the best we can, and since I've been here that best has been better.

'And finally, Mr Buckland, I suspect that you were going to ask if you could see the files concerning this Mr James Preece. And the answer to that request is no, because there are no such files. We dealt with the awkward situation created by Mr Preece in the way that we have dealt with other awkward situations. Namely by clearing them up, as best we could, and moving on. This is a waste-disposal business, not the Public Record Office. If the name of James Reece is mentioned, we will deny that the matter has any importance and that will be the end of it.

'Now, is there anything more I can do for you?'

Giles walked over to the side table and fetched the coffee pot. He gestured towards Paul Creek with it and Creek shook his head. He looked at me.

'Yes, please,' I said.

He filled my mug and then filled his own, then replaced the pot on the table.

'That Swedish waste facility,' he said. 'Did it include an incinerator?'

'What? No,' said Creek abruptly. 'So what?'

Giles sipped at his coffee again, with an agonized expression.

'We could sit here all day,' he said, 'and talk about the

future of waste management. A professor of mine once told me that one of the criteria for judging any culture ought to be what it does with its waste. It's one of the last taboos, isn't it? Shit and ash and all that mush that sticks to the bottoms of our plastic bins. It would be interesting to think of a society that produced no waste at all, in which there was no word for rubbish. However, that's a subject for another day when we're all looking back on this episode and sitting around the campfire laughing about it. At the moment – Mr Creek – I don't think you seem to realize the seriousness of the situation you're in. This isn't a question of just not having files and telling stories of landscaped rubbish dumps. You're facing the very clear possibility of having your expansion put on hold until we're all dead. Another possibility is having this entire facility closed. I've heard all the arguments about employment. What were the figures? Fifty jobs? A hundred? It's a matter of complete indifference to me. I live in London. One day somebody with power in this part of the country may wake up and realize that they don't need a hundred jobs shovelling toxic materials when young men can earn twice as much as a plumber or a gardener and five times as much if they go to university.

'All I would point out to you, Mr Creek, is that you are in danger of missing the larger picture. There is no point in scoring this or that point if you lose the company in the process.'

All this time Paul Creek had been standing up and Giles had been sitting down. It was strange to see this lesson being delivered slightly upwards. All the time Creek was just looking at Giles, expressionless. After Giles had finished, Creek was silent for a time. He leaned back on his desk, flexing his hands on the sharp edge.

'We're talking about this group who've had a couple of meetings in a village hall, right?'

'That's right.'

'I've got one more thing to say to you, Mr Buckland.'

'Yes?'

'And that's fuck you. And you too.' That last was to me. I felt a tight, ominous feeling in my stomach. 'There are one or two things you do not understand. You are not my adviser or my conscience or whatever the fuck you think you are. You are a very lowly member of the insurance company to which we give our business. You know what I did this morning, when I heard you were coming in to see me? I talked to your boss, Walt Broberg. You know him?'

'I've met him.'

'He's an old friend. He told me your remit, which is not to come in here wasting my time. And it's not to go sniffing around, trawling for gossip in Marston Green, stirring things up. I know that your job is to come here, find out what's happening, which is nothing, and then go back to the office. Well, you can do that. You can go back to London and tell them that fuck all is happening. I will tell you one thing, my friend. If your meddling does result in anything being stirred up, I will fuck you. Do you understand?'

With a calmness I had to admire, Giles drained his coffee and placed the mug on the side table.

'I think you missed my point,' he said. 'But perhaps I wasn't clear enough in putting it across.'

'You're working for me,' said Paul Creek. 'Do you understand that?'

'What am I meant to understand from that?' said Giles.

'Our interests are the same.'

'Thank you for the coffee,' said Giles.

'This is the last time I expect to see you here,' said Creek. 'Any questions you have you can address them to my secretary. But I'll deal with London from now on.'

In the car back, Giles was as cheerful as he'd been after our last meeting with Creek. You'd think the meeting had gone well.

'Quite a character, don't you think?'

'Wasn't that a total disaster?' I said.

'What do you mean?'

'For a start, what do you think he was saying to us about Broberg? And, from the sound of it, what do you think Broberg said back?'

'I don't know, it's not as if we were caught climbing over the wire with trowels.'

'So what do we do next?' I asked.

'I don't know,' said Giles. 'Probably we should hang around for another day or so and then leave. I don't think anything's going to top that, do you?'

I had actually got around to making a shopping list and I
suggested to Giles that I go to the supermarket and do a
basic shop. He said there was no point now in going and
buying packets of butter and sugar that we'd leave behind.
And so, at twelve-thirty, we were back in the Four Feathers
where Jan had fixed a delicious lasagne, with layers of
minced beef and tomatoes, with a melted cheese sauce over
the top. And a pint of Abbot ale. We were feeling recovered
now from the previous evening.

Giles was now even more at home in the Four Feathers
than I was. He finished his lasagne with much scraping out
of the dish.

'It's at moments like this,' he said, 'that what you really
need is a cigar or a pipe.'

'You could have a cigarette.'

'It wouldn't be the same thing. At this moment I like the
idea of puffing sagely on my pipe. A couple of hundred
years ago, gentlemen used to conduct their business sitting
in coffee shops. When we get back to England ... I mean
London, although it's much the same thing, we should find
a pub with a table close to a phone connection where we

257

could plug in a laptop and we'll move out of Wortley altogether.'

'They're called Internet cafes,' I said.

'No, no, no,' said Giles. 'I don't want to go somewhere serving cappuccinos and fizzy water. I want to have an office with sawdust on the floor, where they serve tankards of foaming ale and steak and kidney pudding.'

I was almost tempted to stay silent and let Giles carry on with this monologue. When I worked in London, his lunches consisted entirely of salads accompanied by this fizzy water that he suddenly hated so much. How he was intending to drive to all his afternoon appointments after drinking foaming tankards of ale didn't seem to have been fully examined.

'Giles?'

'Yes?'

'Is it all right if I ask you a question?'

'Sure.'

'It's about last night. Without warning me in advance, you start on that complicated business of talking to those guys from Marshco and getting us all drunk – and in particular I was totally arseholed – and then you come up with that load of crap about "dodgy adventures I had in the Black Country" – and then, unbelievably, it actually works: you get them to talk about this guy Preece, who obviously must have done the most God-awful fuck-up, which they have also obviously buried somewhere without clearing up. And then we go in to see that cunt, Paul Creek, and he shouts at us, but mainly at you. We sit through that load of bollocks about the most beautiful dump I've ever seen and the view from my window and what it takes to run a business. After all that, you just say, oh, well, it's time we went back to London.'

There was a pause. Giles took a sip of beer.

'What was the question?'

'I've got several, but one of them could be: what was the point of going to all that trouble last night?'

Giles pulled a face.

'I don't know,' he said. 'Fun, partly. Sometimes it's interesting to lead people on and see what they'll tell you if they think you're on their side. Also, I got a bit pissed off with Paul Creek being so smug the first time he showed us round.'

'But you found out stuff. It may be really damaging. Why are you just letting it go?'

'You know, Mark, Creek wasn't entirely wrong. They're a waste company. What do you expect from them? They don't employ Nobel Prize winners to move the crap around, so I'm not surprised that it sometimes gets tipped into the wrong place.'

'I've got another question. If that's your attitude, then why did you do this in the first place? Last night may have been quite fun, if you weren't me, but the result is that you had a massive row with Paul Creek, he's your enemy, he's phoned our boss to complain about us. I could just about understand this if you were going to take Marshco on, but from what you've said, the plan is to slink back to London and just tell Donna that everything is fine.'

'I wouldn't say "slink", exactly,' said Giles. 'And I'm not going to say that everything is fine.'

'But we're not going to take a position.'

'What position would you suggest?'

'I wouldn't suggest any position. We don't have enough information.'

'That's roughly the position I'm going to take in my report, which will cover one side of a sheet of A4, which is the maximum amount that Walt Broberg's famously limited attention span will tolerate.'

'We could also gather some more information.'

Giles took a tissue from his pocket and wiped his mouth.

'There are all sorts of ways of gathering information,' he said. 'We could take blood samples from the population of Marston Green and compare them with our own blood. We could climb over the fence at Marshco with a Geiger counter and search for illegal dumping. We could break into their office and search for incriminating files. We could hack into their computer system and read their emails. Is that what you want?'

'I don't want to sound like I'm not seeing the funny side of this,' I said. 'But I don't think there really is a funny side.'

'Oh, come on,' said Giles. 'There was Paul Creek ranting at us this morning. That was pretty funny. And from certain angles, Kevin Seeger and his amazing collection of filing cabinets has its amusing side. Which reminds me.' Giles's smile faded and he looked serious. 'Kevin Seeger has been gathering information for years. Hannah Mahoney is in the process of collecting data which could be important. We can

leave our phone number with her and she can get in touch.
There's nothing else I can think of that's realistic.'

We fell silent for a time. For me it was as if everything
had gone just a little grey. I wasn't sure what it was I'd
expected of the visit to Marston Green but I was starting to
realize that that there was a real possibility that it wasn't
going to amount to anything, that we were going to go back
leaving everything much as it had been before we arrived. I
also felt that I didn't have the capacity to enjoy that as much
as Giles did. Geoff brought coffee over to us and we bought
one for him and we sat and chatted for a while. Geoff liked
us very much. We were the best customers he had ever had.
He took quite an interest in our activities, though I think
this was very largely so that he could gauge how long we
would be staying. Just as he got up to get back to work,
Hannah Mahoney walked through the door and looked
around.

She saw us and came over.

'Don't you teach at the school?' Giles said.

'It's the lunch hour,' said Hannah. 'I thought I'd find you
here.'

'This is our new office,' I said. 'For the time being. Giles
has decided it's time to return to London.'

'Why?'

'He's in a bad mood,' I said. 'This morning he was
shouted at by the head of operations at Marshco.' I looked
over at him. 'What was it he called you? A very lowly
member of an insurance company, wasn't it?'

'That's right,' said Giles cheerfully.

Sean French

'What was it about?'

I wondered what Giles would say. Would he tell her?

'He's a prickly man,' Giles said. 'I don't think he liked having insurance people interfering.'

I looked at Giles again. He was talking casually and humorously and yet he was in control, he wasn't going to give anything away by mistake.

'I didn't know you were going,' said Hannah. 'This may not matter, then. I came to say that there are a couple of people you could come and see, if you wanted.'

'You mean people with cancer?'

'Yes.'

'Mark can go,' Giles said. 'If that's all right.'

Hannah looked at me, surprised.

'All right,' she said. 'I'll pick you up at six.'

I had invented a rule for myself in my time with Giles, which was never to contradict or question him in front of other people. I even tried to avoid looking surprised at the unexpected things he said, though this sometimes took a supreme effort. I made up for this, however, by allowing myself complete freedom when we were alone together. When Hannah had gone, I said:

'Now what was that about?'

'I felt the same. I wonder why she's suddenly giving us access. She may be worried she's losing us.'

'I didn't mean that. I mean, why aren't you coming? Why just me? What do I know?'

'Because I believe that it is almost certainly pointless,' said Giles. 'A great writer said about the laws of probability

262

that they are "so true in general, so fallacious in particular".
I can't think that there is anything that could possibly be
learned from visiting one or two or three sad cancer
sufferers.'

'What if you're wrong?'

'That's why you're going.'

'Are you sure that's the only reason?'

'What do you mean?'

'If you actually met some of these people, it might be
harder to be funny or detached about it.'

'You underestimate me. But being detached isn't such a
bad thing. I could come and cry with you if you want. And
then when we get back to London you could come with me
to see Susan's Aunt June, who's got metastasized breast
cancer. We could cry about her.'

'I won't cry,' I said. 'I only cry in movies. Second question,
why didn't you tell Hannah about Preece? That would be a
great help to their campaign.'

'We're not here to be a great help to their campaign. Also,
I don't want to recklessly compare insurance-claims investigators with doctors or priests or lawyers, but our clients
might not be very happy if we were reporting private
conversations to their opponents. I suspect that Paul Creek
would, in his words, fuck me.'

'The campaign group might be able to defeat Marshco if
they had the information we had.'

'Maybe,' said Giles. 'But anybody should be able to beat
Marshco, if they're not hopeless amateurs. Honestly, I sometimes think I should retire from insurance and offer myself

out as a professional activist. Like those ambulance chasers in America who fight cases for – what is it? – a mere forty per cent of the damages, just to cover expenses.'

'What are you going to do when I'm out working?'

'That's none of your business,' said Giles. 'I'm the boss, you are the exploited worker. In fact I'm going to write emails and go through some papers that Kevin Seeger lent me. Is that acceptable?'

'Maybe we can meet for steak and kidney pudding later?'

'I'll talk to Jan about it.'

Liza Barry was a friend of Hannah's. She was forty-eight years old, with dark-brown reddish hair, streaked with grey. She was thin, so that her cheeks were caved in, her clothes flapping on her. She would have been a striking woman, but it almost looked as if all that radiation, from the outside and the inside, had made the colours run out of her, had made her almost transparent. Her eyes were grey, watery. Hannah told me on the way over that Liza had been one of the pioneers of the campaign and that she had a lymphoma in an advanced stage. Hannah explained to Liza who I was and where I was from. That I worked for Marshco's insurance company. It sounded unpleasant when it was said aloud.

'So you've been there?' Liza said.

'I was there this morning.'

'They'll never meet us,' she said. 'We've been trying to talk to them for years.'

I didn't say anything. I felt constrained. I started to say I was sorry about it, but it wasn't for me to say. And if I was sorry, then what was I going to do about it?

'You don't mind me being here?' I said. 'It's an intrusion.'

'At the moment, I haven't got much to do except tell my story.'

She made us tea and then led us out into her small back garden. She had herbs growing by the door: rosemary, tarragon, different shades of thyme. At the back, by the compost heap, there was a small vegetable plot. I recognized lettuces, cabbages, green strawberries, a ragged patch of rocket. I picked a leaf and chewed it, hot, peppery.

'I've lived here all my life,' Liza said. 'Things are a bit better now. About twenty years ago, when the wind was in the right direction, the direction that it's usually in, down from the sea, it was like wispy snow. You'd come out in the morning and it looked as if the world had gone grey. You left footprints on the lawn and you had to do your washing all over again. We brushed it out of our hair. We used to joke about it. It's funny the things that seemed harmless once that we used to surround ourselves with, like asbestos.'

'Did you work with asbestos?' I asked and then immediately wished I hadn't. She looked round at me, a little sharply. She may have thought I was trying to catch her out, trying to find another possible cause.

She shook her head.

'I'm an officer at the council,' she said. 'The only hazardous substance I've dealt with at work is typewriter fluid. I just meant the asbestos tiles we all used in chemistry lessons at school and lined boilers with. The funny thing is that I've

265

been a vegetarian for twenty-five years. I do yoga. I go on long walks. I drink two litres of filtered water every day. I've never smoked. I've never taken drugs. I went to great lengths to keep toxic substances out of my body. What was the point?' She gave a sad smile. 'It seems a little unfair. But then I suppose it always does.'

I didn't ask questions. I felt it wasn't my right. I just stood with my cooling tea and waited for her to say what she needed to say.

'I hardly ever used to get ill,' she said. 'Two years ago I'd never even spent a night in hospital. I got a swelling in my neck and I went to the doctor. I felt silly doing it, but it was quite big. I had had swollen glands before, when I had colds. I remember telling him that this one couldn't be a problem, because it wasn't even sore, the way the others were. And that was almost the moment I knew. His eyes just gave a flicker of interest. But of course he couldn't have known. You give things a pattern when you look back at them.

'They did some tests and they found that I had an intermediate-grade lymphoma. They were pretty buoyant about it. You'd almost have thought it was good news. They told me that aggressive treatment was very often successful. Do you want to hear this?'

'If you want to tell me,' I said.

'It's so extremely interesting to me that I sometimes forget it might be boring or embarrassing for other people to listen to. I had the aggressive treatment but the lumps came back and so they gave me an even more aggressive treatment, chemotherapy and some radiotherapy. I was so, so sick. And

now there are some symptoms that the doctors are concerned about and I'm very concerned about. What I'm now
being offered is a form of radical bone-marrow transplanta-
tion. The odds are interesting. You work in insurance so you
know about odds. The odds are one in three that the
treatment will kill me, one in three that it will do nothing,
and one in three that it will cause a remission. What would
you say to those odds?'

'I don't know,' I said.

'The funny thing, or maybe the sad thing, is that to me, at
the moment, knowing what I know, standing here in my
garden with my courgettes and my peas, they sound like
good odds. The only problem is that I've been having rather
bad luck with odds. When they first diagnosed me, the odds
were very good. They told me I had a ninety-five per cent
cure rate. Unfortunately I was in that five per cent and I've
been in it all the way along. But that's the gambler's fallacy,
isn't it?'

'What?' I said.

'Just because I had bad luck last year and bad luck the
year before, that doesn't mean I'll have good luck this year.'

She paused. She seemed to have finished.

'Liza,' I said. 'What is it you want?'

She coughed slightly.

'If you're giving out wishes, I'd like to be cured. More
realistically – or maybe *less* realistically, I sometimes think –
I would like to be listened to, I would like all of this round
here to make sense. You know, when I first found out about
other people in Marston Green who were ill, it was terrible

of course but it was also good, in a way. Because I felt we were part of a story.'

I shook her long, thin hand. I could feel the bone under the skin.

'Thank you,' I said.

'Do something,' she said.

It was another short drive to our second destination. This was a smarter house. We drove along a curved gravel drive. The stones sprayed like water. It was the sort of place you expected horse-drawn carriages to pull up in front of. Hannah's Fiat looked definitely shabby beside the gleaming Range Rover and BMW saloon that were already parked there. We crunched over to the front door and Hannah rapped the heavy doorknocker. We hadn't spoken on the short trip over and it hadn't even occurred to me that I might know the person we were going to see. The door opened and it was Charles Deane, the chairman of the campaign. He was wearing a brown sweater, corduroys, brown shoes, and he looked ill at ease, completely different from the golf-club bore who'd introduced the meeting I'd gone to. Hannah introduced me and we shook hands.

'I feel awkward about this,' Deane said. 'I don't want to display Ella like a freak show. Perhaps we can just say hello and then we can talk somewhere else.'

At that moment I felt in a cold rage against Giles, who had sent me to go through this while he was sitting back at the pub sending emails. As we walked up the large staircase to Ella's bedroom, I felt that this was just a sign of their desperation and sadness. I knew, and Charles Deane knew, that I was low, low down on the list of people who could do anything for his daughter. I wasn't a doctor, I wasn't a representative of Marshco. Did he maybe think that I would tell someone who would tell someone who would tell someone who would do something? And what is it that they could do?

We knocked on the door and there was a grumpy 'come in'. Presumably I was expected. We all walked in, three adults looking awkward and clumsy in a fourteen-year-old girl's bedroom with its posters and strange drapes and crystals hanging from bedposts and piles of books and funny cheap little bottles arranged on bookshelves. Ella Deane was sitting at her desk. It was quite dark in the room, so I could hardly see what she was wearing. But I could see that on her head she was wearing a merry little skullcap made out of silk triangles, gold and black. It didn't conceal that she had almost no hair.

'Ella, this is Mark Foll.' She looked round. 'He's from an insurance company.'

'Hi,' she said.

'Hi,' I said, hoping that she would see that I was young like her and not just another man in a suit. Except that she probably didn't want me to be someone like her. She wanted someone who could make all this go away.

'How are you feeling?'

'All right.'

'No, really, Ella.'

She pulled a sulky face.

'I'm just a bit tired, all right?'

'Have you been sick today?'

'Oh, for God's sake, Dad.'

I felt my cheeks burning with the embarrassment of this. Hers mainly but mine as well. I thought of circuses a hundred years ago, going into booths to see the hairy woman, the dwarf, the man with no legs. We backed out of her room, leaving her to her homework. That was it, that was the part I had played in Ella Deane's life.

Charles led us along the corridor into a large sitting room with large sofas and a chandelier and bookcases with carved scrolls on them. He asked if we would like a drink. I looked at Hannah and she gave the tiniest hint of a nod, so I said yes. Charles took a decanter of whisky from the shelf and poured us each a drink in a cut-glass tumbler. We sat on the sofa and I fidgeted with my drink and Charles took a deep gulp of his. He said that he was sorry that his wife wasn't here but she was out playing bridge. It had hit her particularly hard and he was trying to encourage her to get out of the house, develop her interests. Ella was their only daughter, so sometimes things got a bit . . . you know.

He walked over and topped his whisky up from the decanter and he sat down. We were facing each other on two sofas divided by a low coffee table. Hannah was sitting beside him. They didn't seem the sort of people who would ever have found themselves in the same room in normal circumstances.

He started to talk. He talked about Ella when she'd been

younger, how she'd loved riding and gymnastics and how good she was at playing the piano.

'Does she go to Hyland?' I asked.

It was the only smile I saw from Charles Deane.

'No,' said Hannah. 'She goes to Chalmers. It's a famous private school over on the coast.'

I looked again at the chandelier and the scrolls on the bookshelves. It was my famous imitation of an idiot again. Charles Deane described how Ella had become lethargic and how they'd thought she was becoming a problem child. They'd shouted at her for a while. She used to sulk in her room, lie in bed all evening. She used to get sudden nose-bleeds. They thought it was all part of her hysteria. Then she got a throat infection, and when she hadn't shaken it off after a fortnight they took her to the doctor. He took a blood test. Acute lymphocytic leukaemia. The doctors were very positive, he said. A better than half chance of a cure. He and his wife had spent the past year accompanying her to treatment. It was very intense, it was important to do it all on schedule. And they had sat with her while she was injected in her spine and while she vomited and while she cried.

As Charles talked I gradually had the feeling of sinking into blackness and feeling cold, even with the fire burning in the grate, and thinking: what is real apart from fear and pain? I wondered if Hannah was planning to take me to see any more of these sufferers, because I thought if I saw more of them I might go mad. Or maybe I wouldn't go mad and would get used to them. I thought of being a doctor. The first few would shock and distress you and then after a few weeks or a few months you would be secretly looking at your watch and wondering what video to rent that evening. I thought of Ella up in her room doing her homework.

'What are the doctors saying at the moment?' I asked.

Charles started to say something, coughed, shook his head, looked away. I could see that there were tears running down his face. He wiped them away clumsily with his hands. I didn't know what to do. Hannah put her hand on his knee. If I were going to do anything, I would have to get up and walk around the table and lean over. It didn't seem like a good idea.

'I'm sorry about that,' he said. 'I didn't want to embarrass you. What you probably want to know about is the campaign, how it got started.'

'No, that's all right.'

'We met another child at the hospital. She came from Marston Green as well. That made us think. And it started from there.' He drained his glass and stood up. I placed my own untasted drink next to his. He led us to the front door. As he opened it, I felt he was searching for something appropriate to say.

'What we feel, Mary and I, is that something good must come out of this.'

I shook his hand. Hannah gave him a hug and he shut the door. She looked at me.

'Don't worry,' she said. 'That's all for today.'

When we got back in the car, Hannah said she was in a hurry. A friend was babysitting Bruce, but she had to get back and take over from her. It was a very short drive. She'd drop me off at the Four Feathers on the way. We were moving through Marston Green quite quickly and I suddenly had the feeling that this was it, that this was it and if I didn't do anything I would leave Marston Green as I had everywhere else, without touching the sides, without a trace, unless I did something.

'So what did you think?' she asked.

'Hannah, there's something I've got to tell you.'

'What?'

'I know about your cancer.'

She stopped the car. It wasn't at the Four Feathers. To drop me at the pub, she needed to drive across the village. She hadn't. She had stopped outside her house. She was looking out of the windscreen, away from me, so I couldn't see her expression. She was touching her lips with her right forefinger. She bit on it.

'I'm sorry,' she said. 'I don't . . . I . . .' She seemed to have lost her train of thought completely. I could see her face

273

very much more closely than I had before. I could see the soft down on the edge of her firm jaw. 'I'd better take over from Gina. Do you want to come in for a moment?'

I followed her to the door. She introduced me to Gina as a man from an insurance company. As usual that was a quick way of getting rid of someone. People don't look at insurance men, just as they don't look at postmen. Hannah seemed to be finding it difficult to speak coherently. She seemed confused.

'I need to check on Bruce,' she said. 'Pour yourself something, if you want.'

I wasn't at all clear what I should be pouring or where I'd find it, so I stood and waited. When she came down, I was standing in the same place. I suddenly thought how different she was from her friend, Liz. Hannah had a fierceness about her. The light was catching her eyes making them look as if they were glowing.

'Is he asleep?' I said.

When she answered it was with an effort, as if I were distracting her from something else.

'Pretty much,' she said. 'He mumbled something and I gave him a hug and he rolled over. He'd have noticed if I hadn't been to see him, though. What was it? Was it the map?'

'What?'

'My cancer.'

'Oh,' I said. 'No, it wasn't the map. I'm really sorry about this. Giles is a compulsive spy. It's what makes him good at his job. When he went to your lavatory, he noticed some sort of pill that you've been taking because of, you know . . .'

'Breast cancer,' said Hannah. 'You're allowed to say it out loud. I won't faint.'

'I might,' I said.

'Sit down over there,' she said. 'On the sofa.'

She walked over to a cupboard and took a bottle of Scotch and two glasses. One of them was coloured like the sort of children's glass you might serve a fizzy drink in. She gave each of them a good splash of Scotch. She came over and sat by me on the sofa and handed me one of the glasses – not the children's one. We both took a sip. As usual, I had to resist the temptation to cough.

'So what did Giles say after he'd been poking around in my bathroom? I suppose he saw me as a hysterical woman who had started a campaign because she was angry about getting cancer.'

I felt an odd pang of disappointment that she was focused on Giles. Giles adored her, of course.

'That's not what he said. He was impressed that you'd done all this without putting your illness at the centre of it.'

Hannah took another sip of her drink, almost a gulp.

'What do you think, Mark?'

I looked at her.

'I don't know,' I said. 'You have this fantasy of being very ill and dignified and everybody saying how brave you are. But maybe it would be a real pain after a while, everybody asking about it.'

'A real pain?'

'You see, that's what I mean. I know you've been through real pain. When somebody's got cancer, I guess that other people start worrying about saying the wrong thing. You know, should they mention it, does the person want to talk about it or not talk about it. Do they want to explain their treatment to the milkman? So people might avoid you altogether.'

We looked at each other. I found myself looking at her breasts. I couldn't help it.

'It was two years ago,' she said. 'A lump in my right breast. I guess you've probably had enough by now. Do you want to hear this?'

I took a gulp.

'Sure.'

She pushed a strand of hair behind her ear.

'I didn't find it. It was found by my boyfriend, Don. Apparently that's quite common.'

'I didn't know . . .'

'That it's common?'

'In fact, I meant that you had a boyfriend.'

'We broke up. He found it difficult. You want to hear this?' Why should I not want to hear this? What was she going to say? 'He was very apologetic. He cried. He cried more than I did. And then he couldn't touch me. He tried, but it was impossible. He said he couldn't think of me in that way any more.'

As Hannah spoke, it felt all the time as if she was putting something strange and unexpected on the table in front of us and seeing how I reacted, seeing if I was shocked.

'I find that hard to believe,' I said.

'The lump ached slightly, but my doctor told me it was almost certainly benign. You remember Liz talking about how the odds were so good. I feel that's what the doctors do. Unless there's no hope at all they pretend it's going to be all right. They say the odds are in your favour, they say the lump will be benign. I think it's just to get you out of their office. I had a biopsy, which showed I had breast cancer. The doctor told me that it would almost certainly need nothing more than a small operation. There would just be some scans, X-rays, blood tests. These showed I had invasive breast cancer. It was bigger than they had thought and it had spread, so I needed quite a big operation. It's called a modified radical mastectomy. They removed the whole breast and some of the lymph nodes in my armpit. That was a big deal.'

Yes, I thought. Too much detail. I took a gulp of whisky and coughed once more. She continued.

'Don was out of the picture by that time. My mother came down and lived here on and off for a year. You see, it wasn't just the operation. I had a few courses of chemotherapy and I spent days throwing up. The really funny thing was that after a bit I didn't just get sick after I'd taken the pills. I started feeling sick in the days leading up to it. Once I drove past the hospital and the sight of it was enough. I had to stop the car so I could throw up in the gutter. I thought I was going to be so strong, for Bruce, and for other reasons. But I wasn't. I spent days lying in bed with a bucket on the floor. And then of course my hair fell out, so I spent a few

277

months wearing all kinds of scarves and little bobble hats and tea cosies, whatever. So the fact that I had cancer wasn't exactly the best-kept secret in Marston Green. I think that over the next few days someone would have mentioned it to you.'

I looked at Hannah. She was wearing a brown cardigan with small square buttons. You couldn't tell. There, apparently, were her two medium-sized breasts. Her right breast. Her right, my left. Maybe she wore a normal bra with the right half stuffed with something. Or was it a fake breast? I also imagined her throwing up in the gutter, like a bag lady. Funny, the things that people have done. We try and pretend that we're in control, like politicians, but we've all had moments where we're in a gross-out comedy or a horror film, puking up hopelessly, blood everywhere, crying, screaming.

'How are you now?' I said.

'Waiting,' said Hannah.

'What for?'

'For nothing to happen,' she said. 'If I wait five years and there's nothing, then that's good. And in the meantime I'm looking after Bruce and doing my job and I've got involved in this campaign.'

Another long gap. There were all these embarrassing silences.

'You think it'll work?'

Hannah finished the last of her whisky. She stood up. Maybe it was time for me to go.

'What I want,' she said, 'what we all want, is some sort of acknowledgement. There are a lot of people ill in this village.

You've just met Liza and Ella. Liza will be dead within a year or so. I've got about a fifty–fifty chance of being alive in five years. Ella about the same. I don't want it all to mean nothing. You've met the people at Marshco. Did you like them?' I didn't answer. There might as well be another silence. 'I want them to face up to what they have been doing in this area. I want them to admit what they did. The alternative is that we'll all just disappear and the world will continue.'

'But the world just *will* continue.'

She gave a sad smile.

'Sometimes I forget which side you're on.'

I stood up as well, which brought me quite close against her, almost awkwardly.

'I'm not sure I'm on any side,' I said. 'Not anymore.'

'It doesn't matter,' she said. 'I'm not expecting anything from you. I don't want some huge expression of sympathy.'

'Didn't I say that?'

'I don't want you to say it. I've had enough of people's sympathy.'

I felt confused by the situation. I didn't know what I was doing here. I could hardly think of what to say or what to do.

'So when did your boyfriend leave?' I asked.

What a stupid question. Hannah's expression hardened slightly. The room chilled.

'I said, didn't I? He didn't just walk out. He became uncomfortable and gradually he wasn't here so often. In the end I was the one who said we should stop seeing each

279

Sean French

other. I've never seen anyone look more relieved. Maybe he thought he could catch cancer from me.'

'That's ridiculous,' I said.

'It's not really any of your business.'

Another silence. She had been open with me and I don't think I'd ever felt so awkward. Like that hopeless Don I was just going to run away mumbling something. We couldn't just stand here looking at each other for ever. I felt like I was thirteen years old at my first party.

'I'd better go,' I said.

'Yes,' she said.

I walked to the door and she walked with me. I felt her shoulder brushing on mine. She was quite tall, just a couple of inches shorter than me. I opened the door and then turned to her.

'I'm sorry,' I said.

I put out my hand and touched her shoulder, as if I were brushing a piece of dust. She moved away just a step.

'I've told you,' she said. 'I don't need that.'

'I mean sorry just generally.'

I walked out and I heard the door close softly behind me. It was colder than I expected. It was a cloudless night with more stars than I could ever remember seeing before. I looked up and there was nothing but sky in my field of vision. Suddenly I had the feeling that I was falling upwards into them. I felt dizzy and almost stumbled. I put my hand out and I steadied myself on the wall by the garden gate. It was old, made up of rough, irregularly shaped stones.

I stroked them and then, suddenly, I clenched my right hand into a fist and brought it down hard on the wall two times, three times, four times. I muttered something under my breath and had the crazy sensation of not being able to hear what I was saying.

I turned and leaned back on the wall and looked at Hannah's cottage. I knew it was a quiet night, but it seemed noisy. I felt that I was in a railway tunnel with a train rushing past, inches from my face. I could feel the pulse in my neck, my chest, my head. There was no point in thinking. I walked back up the path and knocked on the door. It opened almost immediately and I wondered if Hannah had been leaning on the other side of it. She had a questioning look, as if she was waiting for me to say something else stupid.

There was nothing I could say that wouldn't be another disaster so I just stepped forward and put my hands on either side of her face, and paused just for a moment to think properly for the first time how lovely it was, and then kissed her, first softly and then deeply. I stopped and pulled back to look at her. Her lips were half open, glistening. She gave a release of breath which could almost have been an expression of pain. She looked almost groggy and passive, but she leaned forward towards me. It was about a millimetre but I saw I hadn't been wrong and I felt a ripple run through me which was almost pain and we kissed again. I moved my arms around her back and felt her arms holding me. Still holding her, I leaned against the door and nudged it shut. I pushed Hannah back so that she was against the inside of the door. We kissed and when we stopped we were both gasping as if the air was thin in the room.

I stroked her cheek and then kissed her and undid the top button of her sweater. She pulled her head away from me.

'No,' she said.

I gulped. I could hardly speak.

'Is it too early?'

'Not my sweater,' she said. 'The rest.'

I surprised myself by how intensely relieved I was by that.

'Shall we go upstairs?'

She shook her head.

'Bruce comes into my bed sometimes. Down here.'

Entangled in each other, we hobbled across the room and actually fell over on to the sofa. It was all very fast and flailing and desperate in a way I wasn't used to. I pulled her trainers off. Her trousers were tied at the top with a cord. I pulled the knot undone and she eased herself off the sofa so that I could pull her trousers and her blue knickers down and over her feet. Her pubic hair was lighter and softer than the brown hair, still loosely fastened up on her head. It was almost golden. Her feet were over my shoulders and I looked up her body at her face. Her left arm was across her face as if she was trying to silence herself. Her right hand was stroking my head. Then she flinched and I felt a shiver through her body. Her fingers gripped my hair. I raised myself up. I was still fully dressed. She was naked only from the waist down. Her head was moving from side to side. I took my jacket off and eased my trousers and boxers down below my knees and I was on top of her and inside her and my mouth against hers and kissing her softly now, always looking at her. I felt her come, her face pushed into my neck to silence herself, her fingers digging into my back so that I could hardly stop myself crying out, and then I came and we lay there, entangled. It was a bit farcical. My trousers were almost inside out, over my shoes.

'I don't know whether to take my clothes off or put them on,' I said.

'Take them off,' said Hannah. 'I want to look at you.'

With some awkwardness, I tugged my trousers over my shoes and then kicked the shoes off and unfastened my shirt and pulled it over my head.

'It feels unfair,' I said.

'What?'

'You've got half your clothes still on.'

'I'm sorry,' she said. 'I can't.'

'That's all right,' I said, and lay down beside her on the sofa where, about half an hour earlier, I had been listening to her tell me about her cancer. I stroked her stomach and her warm damp pubic hair. 'I can't believe this.'

'Why?' she said.

'I thought you liked Giles,' I said.

She smiled drowsily.

'Giles?'

'He's the clever, interesting one. He's married, but he thinks you're wonderful. He keeps talking about you.'

She stroked my hair.

'Do you remember when we met in the High Street? I said that awful thing about you being the *pretty* face of your company, instead of the public face.'

'I thought you despised me.'

'Well,' said Hannah. 'There was the problem that you were part of the enemy. Are part of the enemy.'

'I keep saying that's not true.'

She looked at me with a tired, lovely smile that I hadn't seen before.

'If you could go back to London with a killer fact that let Marshco off the hook, you'd be a hero, wouldn't you?'

'Giles says it's not like that. It's all too messy and hard to make connections that really stick. That's your problem.'

'Is it?' she said.

Then she pushed me down onto my back. She smiled down at me then kissed me on my chin and on my chest and my stomach and on and on until she took me in her mouth. As I lay back and felt myself grow hard, the curious thought came into my mind that this was the first time in my life that I had had sex with a grown-up woman.

Afterwards, we lay together. I felt her, was wrapped in her, but I didn't see her. I looked up at the low ceiling, whitewashed, with heavy cracked old beams across it.

'I'd like you to stay the night,' she said, and I was about to say 'yes' when she added: 'But you can't. Because of Bruce. You don't mind, do you?'

'I don't want to move,' I said.

'What's the time?'

I looked at my watch.

'One-thirty.'

'Bruce gets up. He wanders around.'

'I'm not so frightening,' I said.

'Confusing,' she said.

I stood up and put my clothes on while Hannah lay sprawled on the sofa and looked at me, with a smile. I couldn't tell if it was resigned or sad. She walked over to the door with me for the second time that night. We kissed in the doorway again. I tried to think of something to say that wouldn't be a disaster.

'That was . . .' I said and then the sentence trailed away.

'Yes,' she said. 'And please don't say something like I'll call you.'

'What do you mean?'

'I don't know. I don't know what I mean. My life's a mess and I don't want to make it any worse. And I'm probably going to start crying in a moment, so you'd better go.'

As I walked back under the stars, I thought that this hadn't been meant to happen and I felt confused. It was as if I had been on my way somewhere and had my pocket picked. Except that it was sort of the opposite. Someone had brushed against me and I'd felt something strange had happened; I'd put my hand in my pocket and found that something had been put there without my knowledge. There was also the further question of what I was going to say to Giles. What I was going to say to anyone. And then there was the further question of what it was exactly that I would say if I said anything.

It was a short walk back to the Four Feathers and I had made sense of nothing by the time I arrived at my room. I opened the door and something fell to my feet. I switched on the light and saw that it was a note that had been wedged in the door. It said: 'Come and see me. However late you get in. Geoff.'

I couldn't take any more confusion so I just numbly walked over to the back door of the pub and rang the bell. It took many rings before there were sounds of movement from the first floor and footsteps on the stairs. Geoff appeared in a dressing gown looking awful. I started to apologize and then he told me that Giles was in hospital.

Geoff offered to give me a lift but I managed to get Giles's car keys from his room and I drove myself to the hospital in Melwarth along winding dark lanes.

The hospital looked abandoned, the paper shop and cafe in the entrance hall were shuttered up. There was a man in a uniform at the front desk who gave me the name of a ward but apart from him I saw nobody as I walked down an immensely long corridor through a wing that looked as if it had been left over from something in the war. I arrived at the Martin Guy ward and found a nurse sitting in a cone of electric light just inside. She directed me halfway along. It was all wrong. Ten hours earlier I'd been sitting with him in the Four Feathers and now he was installed here, his name on the system, a nurse who knew him by name. I padded along the ward looking left and right at people in various stages of damage until Giles swung into sight and although I was prepared, I felt shocked.

I would hardly have recognized him if his name hadn't been on a label at the end of the bed. There was a plastic tube into his nose and a cord leading to a machine but it wasn't just that. His face looked as if it had been inflated with a bicycle pump and it was livid and raw with purple bruises. Plasters and cotton wool were taped crudely along his nose. I could see that his right hand was bandaged and two fingers were attached to strips of plastic like miniature rulers. It was such a dreadful sight that I looked for some movement and saw the sheet above his chest rising and falling. I pulled a chair over and sat down. Suddenly I heard a splutter from Giles that sounded as much like a death rattle as anything else.

'Giles,' I said. 'It's me, Mark.'

'Ark.'

'That's right.'

'Eef.'

'What?'

'Eef.'

'I don't understand.'

'Fucking eef. Idey mash my fucking eef?'

'Do you mean teeth?'

There was a slow groaning clearing of the throat.

'Yes,' he said at last. 'My teeth.'

'I don't know,' I said. 'I'll ask the nurse. Are you all right? Is it hurting?'

'Up.'

'What?'

'Cup,' he said, as if the word had several syllables.

I looked around and there was a small plastic cup by the bed.

'You want a drink?' I said.

'Spit,' he said.

I held the cup under his mouth and he spat in a splattery way, saliva streaked with yellow and red. I wiped his mouth.

'They've given me stuff,' he said. 'Strong fucking stuff. Heroin, probably. I'm speaking from somewhere far away. I'm in the corner of a cloud.'

He wasn't looking at me. I don't think he could move. He did indeed sound as if he was speaking from somewhere distant, but his voice was becoming stronger and clearer. I just didn't understand what he meant.

'Is there protection?' he said.

'What?'

'They'll be coming for me. Need police at every entrance.'

'I don't think there's anybody,' I said. 'But I'm here.'

'Fuck,' said Giles.

'Do you know what happened?' I said. 'Geoff said you were attacked along from the pub.'

'Got hit,' said Giles. 'Didn't see anything. Heard something from behind, started to turn, things went bright, lots of flashes. Fell on the ground. Stamped on my hand. Which hand is it?'

'Your right hand.'

'From my point of view or yours?'

'Yours.'

'Fuck.'

'I'm so sorry, Giles.'

'Does it look bad?'

'Pretty bad.'

I heard a strange snuffling sound. It was Giles.

'So how was your evening?' he said.

'All right,' I said.

'Depressing?' he said.

'Sort of mixed.'

'Did you tell her?'

'What?'

'That we knew.'

'Yes, I did.'

'What she say?'

'It didn't matter,' I said. 'She said it wasn't a secret.'

There was a silence. I raised my fingers to my nose. I hadn't had time for a shower or anything. I was conscious of being there with Hannah's smell on me. I was aroused and guilty at the same time. I looked around. It sounded crazy, but maybe he really ought to have some sort of protection. This wasn't just a brawl in a pub. Somebody had gone for Giles deliberately. But then if they wanted to kill him, they would have done it on the spot, there in the dark. They just wanted to hurt him. But they really wanted to hurt him. Looking at the dismal figure in the bed, I could see that they hadn't just set out to rough him up a little. He was really smashed up.

'Beep,' said Giles.

'What?'

'That fucking machine,' he said.

I looked at it. I assumed it must be something to do with his heartbeat, but the beeps were too irregular for that.

'Got this electric cooker at home,' Giles said. 'Electric. Got a clock. Timer. Never worked out how to use it. What's the point? Put something in the oven and fucking cook it. Don't need timer. But it's got a beep. Pressed every button, did every kind of programming, couldn't stop it. Every fifteen, twenty seconds, another beep. Drove me mad. Did. Where was I?'

'Your cooker,' I said. 'It's got a beep.'

'Drove me mad. Did everything. Random as well, did I say that? I timed it once with my watch. Fifteen seconds, twenty seconds, eleven seconds, seventeen seconds. Like pi. No pattern emerged.'

'So what did you do?'

'Wanted to smash it with a sledgehammer. Take it out onto waste ground and bury it. But I just shut the kitchen door. Shut the bedroom. Could sleep. Can't sleep now. That beep. Keep listening for it. If it stops, it means I'm dead.'

'I'll go in a minute,' I said. 'You can sleep.'

There was another unidentifiable sound from Giles and then I saw tears running from his eyes down the side of his face onto his pillow. I took another tissue and dabbed at his face as gently as I could manage. Then I stroked his face on an unbruised spot on his left cheek.

'I'm so sorry,' I said. 'I should have been there.'

Another snuffle.

'Yes,' said Giles. 'Should have been you.'

I leaned over him.

'Giles, we'll talk about this tomorrow, but do you have any idea who they were?'

'Didn't see.'

'Did they say anything?'

'Didn't hear.'

'But what do you think?'

'Dunno. Can't think now. Tomorrow. Next year.'

'People who thought we were going to close the plant down, maybe.'

'Dunno.'

'I'll be back tomorrow morning. Can I get you anything?'

'Call Donna.'

'All right.'

'First thing. Call . . .'

His face tipped and then I saw that Giles was asleep, although the machine was still beeping. I walked as quietly as I could down to the nurse on duty. She didn't know whether Giles had lost teeth. She didn't know what the doctors had done or were planning to do. She was from an agency and had arrived at the hospital for the first time the previous day. When I asked about police protection she just looked completely baffled, so I didn't pursue it. I briefly toyed with the idea of sitting guard on Giles all night but I assumed I had probably been right about the motives of the attackers. If they had wanted to kill him, they would have done it out on the street. In any case I was dizzy with tiredness. On the drive back I was pinching and slapping myself to keep awake.

I set my alarm for eight the next morning and woke up still in a fog of tiredness. First I phoned Hannah, who was in the middle of breakfast with Bruce. I told her about Giles and at first she sounded more intrigued than sympathetic. She started asking questions about what had happened and I wondered if she saw some sort of campaigning opportunity.

'I saw him at the hospital in the middle of the night,' I said. 'He's badly hurt.'

'I'm sorry,' she said. 'What do the police say?'

'I don't know,' I said. They weren't there by the time I arrived. Also, I'd like to see you.'

'I'd like to see you as well.'

'Are you around in the day?'

'I've got a job, Mark.'

'In the evening, then.'

'Come at nine, when Bruce is in bed. If you want. It's not compulsory.'

'I want to.'

Then I phoned Donna Kiely and was told she hadn't arrived yet. After some pestering I was given her mobile number. When she answered, she sounded as if she was in the car.

'It's Mark Foll,' I said. 'The guy who's up in Marston Green.'

'Yes, I know which Mark Foll you are.'

'Giles is in hospital.'

'I'm very sorry to hear that. What happened?'

'He was beaten up. Badly beaten up.'

Even over a bad mobile-phone line I could hear that her tone had changed from dutiful concern to alarm.

'What? Who by?'

'I don't know. It happened last night and he's really banged up. From what he said, he was attacked from behind. He didn't see anything.'

'Jesus.'

'Ms Kiely . . .'

'Shut up.'

I waited.

'Has this anything to do with Marshco?'

'Probably.'

'Is it quicker to drive or go by train?'

'I'm not sure. About the same. Driving may be a little bit quicker, especially if you're going to the hospital, it's a bit awkward to get to Melwarth . . .'

'I'll drive. I'll head out of London straight away. I'll see you at the hospital when I arrive.'

'Ms Kiely?'

'Yes?'

'Somebody should tell Giles's wife. Have you got the number?'

'I'll get on to it. I'll ring you back for the directions. Are we allowed to visit him?'

'I guess so.'

'I'll see you when I get there.'

That was going to be fun.

I wasn't sure what I could bring to Giles. I looked in at the village shop but the only fruit they had was some very green bananas and the only newspapers they had were a couple of weird tabloids which were completely about a missing toddler. So, on the way to Melwarth hospital, I did what I had been meaning to do over the past few days and had never quite got around to, which was to go to the massive supermarket, which was almost identical to the one in Camden I sometimes dropped into late at night on my way home from work. I bought some grapes and nectarines, a bottle of freshly squeezed orange juice and an armful of newspapers and magazines, and I bought a sandwich for myself. I hadn't eaten for almost twenty-four hours.

When I arrived at the hospital, everything was different. I had to drive around the huge car park searching for a space and then feed coins into a machine. It seemed morally wrong for the relations of desperately ill people to have to pay so much money to visit them. The corridors were bustling with doctors and nurses. Where had they been in the night? Did people only get ill between nine and five?

In the ward, the curtains had been opened, trolleys were

being pushed back and forward but somehow it looked worse now that I could see the split lino and the awful light-blue paint on the walls. Most of the patients were sitting up in bed but Giles was lying in the same position I'd left him, fast asleep. In the morning light I could see more clearly what had been done to him and I stood for a while and looked at the bruises and the swellings and the stitches. There was a bruise on his forehead that was so swollen and purple and glistening that it looked like a boil caused by bubonic plague.

He seemed peaceful so I sat on the chair by the bed and read the paper and ate some of the grapes and one of the nectarines. I didn't touch the orange juice, though.

'Mark,' said Giles in his distant-sounding voice.

'Yeah, I'm here. I brought you some stuff. Would you like a nectarine or some orange juice?'

'Can't. Might be operated on.'

'I don't think so,' I said. 'I talked to the nurse.'

'Uh?'

'I'll go ask her.'

I found a nurse in authority and learned that as of this morning and the doctor's visit there were now no plans to operate on Giles. She walked over with me and picked up two files attached to the end of his bed. Giles had suffered broken ribs, dental damage, two broken fingers, concussion and then a whole stack of more superficial bruises and abrasions. There were going to be further investigations later in the morning for suspected ligament injury, possible damage to one eye and a few other things. But he could eat and drink. So I poured some juice into a polystyrene cup and I tipped it into his mouth. He moaned a bit, saying it stung his mouth. I offered him a choice between grapes and nectarine and he chose nectarine, so I cut one into chunks and fed them to him chunk by chunk. It was a slow process.

'Fuck,' he said when we were done. 'Been thinking. Thought maybe they thought I was you.'

'That's not very likely.'

'That girl. One you seduced. Abandoned.'

'Sandy? I didn't exactly abandon her. You don't think she could have . . .?'

'Her father. Met him in the pub. Him and friends taking revenge.'

'Giles, this isn't Sicily.'

'They don't like it. Men coming from London, violating their women.'

'You're about three inches shorter than me. If it was planned, then they must have seen you earlier and followed you. But it might just be a mistake. Maybe this is what they do for fun in Marston Green when the pub closes. Find someone and beat them up.'

There was a low mooing groan from Giles.

'No,' he said. 'It's to do with Marshco. It was me. People thought we could shut it down.'

'Do you think they did it to warn you off?'

I could hear Giles breathing deeply, long slow breaths.

'Hurting a bit more,' he said. 'Reduced the good drugs. Don't need to warn me off. Don't give a fuck. Have I lost teeth? Doctor was here earlier. Said something about teeth.'

'I think a couple, maybe. The nurse was talking about dental damage.'

'Oh, fuck.' He groaned. I thought he was going to start crying again. 'What a fuck-up. The plan was ... What was the plan?'

'To get in and out very quickly. Do a quick report.'

'That's what we were doing. We were about to go. Oh, bother.'

'I'm sorry, Giles, but I don't understand you. You were the one who found out about Marshco dumping things in the wrong places. You were the one who threatened Paul Creek. I don't see how you want to just walk away from it.'

A coughing sound from Giles. I leaned over and decided it was a gloomy laugh.

'Can't fucking walk. That's one. Two. Doesn't matter.'

I took a grape from Giles's bunch. I peeled it very delicately, in strips, and then chewed on it slowly.

I spent twenty minutes with my mobile sitting on the front steps of the hospital with a map on my knees, guiding Donna Kiely through the back lanes towards Melwarth until, as if by magic, her blue BMW glided into the car park. She saw me without the tiniest flicker of greeting. She was in her office uniform and she behaved as if she was in the office, as if I had just come back from the coffee machine. We walked briskly to the ward.

'Is he in any danger?' she said.

'Not at all. He was badly beaten up, he's in pain, but there's nothing really scary.'

'Can he talk?'

'He was smashed in the mouth, so it hurts, but he can physically say words. I think the drugs are making him ramble a bit.'

Donna looked at me properly for the first time.

'What have you clowns been up to?' she asked.

I was going to say nothing, and then I thought this wasn't strictly accurate. I gave a shrug that I hoped wouldn't commit me to a particular version of events.

As Donna entered the ward and caught sight of Giles, she stopped and visibly flinched. Then she gave a warm smile and stepped forward. She sat at the bedside and took Giles's good hand between hers. She leaned across and spoke softly into his ear.

'It's Donna. How are you, Giles?'

'Crap,' said Giles.

'Mark just told me this morning and I drove straight here. But I've made some calls and we're sorting things out. We're driving Susan here and she should be here by lunchtime. We're checking with the doctors and the plan is to transfer you to the Middleton in London as soon as possible.' She paused, maybe waiting for an expression of gratitude, but Giles said nothing. 'Are you in pain, Giles?'

'OK,' he said. 'Not that bad.'

'I am so sorry this happened.'

'Me too.'

She stroked his hand absently. Her thoughts seemed to be

elsewhere. His hand could have been one of those executive playthings that you squeeze in moments of stress.

'Giles,' she said, 'I know this is the worst time. Can we have a brief talk about Marshco? If you feel you can't, that is no problem at all. It can wait. And I can get what I need from Mark.'

More snorting and croaking and wheezing. I think he might have been laughing at the idea of me being able to provide any information at all.

'I can talk,' he said. 'Bit slow.'

'Jesus, Giles, this may seem like the wrong question to ask at a time like this, but have you any idea why this may have happened?'

Giles proceeded to give a halting, slow, wheezy precis of our activities in Marston Green. I was surprised at first that he didn't just ask me to give Donna the low-down, but then I realized that he was giving a judiciously edited version. He talked about certain concerns about Marshco's dumping practices and he said he had raised them with the management. But he didn't properly describe Creek's response and made no mention at all of our encounter with Tony, Ewan and Steve at the Four Feathers.

'Forgive me for being dense,' Donna said. 'You raised these concerns with the Marshco management. What precise concerns were these?'

Giles described the problem of Marshco not being straight with him and the effect of the information coming too late if Wortley weren't prepared. Donna was silent for a long time.

'Of course,' she said, 'it could arguably be said that your

job while in Marston Green was just to garner information about the status of the protests and extent of the implications the campaign might have with any policy with which we are associated. Forgive me once more for being stupid, but I'm not quite sure why you were confronting Marshco's management over questions of their practice.' Giles didn't reply, so she continued. 'Before this happened, did you have a next step?'

Now Giles spoke slowly and clearly.

'We were returning to London. The next step, if any, would be a full assessment of the evidence on dioxin contamination. You would need to take scientific advice on this.' He paused, as if he needed to concentrate on the act of breathing for a few seconds to control the pain. His skin had gone pale and he looked damp. 'In a nutshell, my view is that such evidence is not compelling enough to be a risk in itself. That was why I considered other factors that might be used to muddy the waters in a legal case.'

'I see,' said Donna. She gave his hand a stroke. 'I just want to say, Giles, that we're going to make sure you get better. You can have all the time you need to make a full recovery. I'll talk to you later.'

She walked away from the bed and gave me a look, signalling me to follow her. We walked out of the ward. A young woman in a white coat happened to be beside us and Donna waited until she was out of earshot. Then she turned to me.

'What the fuck have you two been up to?'

'I don't know what you mean.'

I immediately regretted that I hadn't just said sorry, anything, just so that she wouldn't have that scary expression on her face.

'You want to know what I mean? If you cast your mind back to the meeting we held just a few days ago, the idea was for you to come up here and assess the situation without creating any waves. You've hardly been here and already you have been involved in a major argument with the company we're supposed to be representing – yes, I heard about the call he made to my boss, who's your boss as well. And now you have become so embroiled in this dispute – which hardly was a dispute until you arrived here – that somebody out there has decided that you two are a part of the problem and has done something about it.'

'Something?' I said. 'You mean they almost killed Giles.'

'Are the police involved?'

'Of course.'

'Oh, shit.'

'How could they not be?'

'Have you talked to them?'

'I haven't even seen them.'

Donna's eyes flickered from side to side.

'They might think it was just a couple of drunks having fun.'

'Maybe,' I said.

'No, they won't. They'll know it's something to do with Marshco. They'll have to investigate.'

I knew what I should have said. I should have asked if that was such a bad thing but then I also knew what the answer would be. It was a bad thing because it might be embarrassing or worse for Marshco. And in that case it might be expensive for Wortley.

'You think I'm callous, don't you?' said Donna.

'I'm not sure, I . . .'

'I feel terrible about this. It was at least partly my idea to send you two up. The basic idea was keep everything as quiet as possible, everything nice and easy. Now we have a colleague in hospital and maybe a criminal investigation. We need to make this go away.'

I looked thoughtful. I was pretending – but under my pretence I was being very thoughtful indeed. Mainly I was thinking about what would happen if Donna learned about the meeting in the pub with the Marshco workers. Giles had taken a risk in keeping that quiet, but then he could claim that he was confused after all the blows and kicks to his head. I had no such excuse. Then there was Sandy, which was irrelevant but which could possibly be made to sound relevant in the context of what happened. And Hannah. I remembered her, lying on her sofa with a peaceful smile on her face, looking at me. The thought of describing my activities aloud, in front of people in suits, filled me with intense horror. It occurred to me, in the midst of everything that was happening, that I wanted to be with her again.

'Make it go away,' I said.

'That's right,' she said.

'You might say that there isn't really an "it" so far. As yet, nothing has happened.'

'I'm driving straight back to London. Is there anything that needs sorting out here?'

I thought for a moment.

'I'll finish a couple of things off,' I said. 'Say goodbye to people.'

'Fine,' she said. 'We'll need to talk. But no more trouble, OK?'

'No,' I said. 'I mean OK.'

I walked down with Donna to the car and saw her off. It wasn't exactly a big romantic parting. She got into her car, switched the motor on and then the window hissed down.

'I don't want any more surprises,' she said.

'Even nice ones?'

She didn't smile at all, not even the tiniest bit, just drove away. I watched her disappear and then didn't immediately walk back to see Giles. I couldn't bear it. I walked around the outside of the hospital. I was feeling plunged in self-pity for the situation I was in, but the sight of all the different departments, and the thought of all the different kinds of disease and pain and fear that I wasn't suffering from, made me feel a little bit better.

Giles had been given some fresh medication while I'd been away and he was drowsy. I sat with him, mostly in silence, until Susan arrived a couple of hours later. She looked terrible and even worse when she saw the state of her husband. I remembered how she hadn't wanted him to go and I thought of how the plan had been that she and the children could pop up for lovely days in the country and I felt that it really hadn't worked out very well for him at all. She actually gave me a hug when she saw me. She hadn't eaten, so I went down to the canteen and bought her a salad and some coffee and then I told Giles that I would leave them. He asked Susan if he could have a moment with me before I left. She looked at me, a little concerned, but took her salad to a table in the middle, further down the ward.

'That cunt,' said Giles.

'She's just come all the way up to see you,' I said.

'Not Susan,' he said. 'Donna. That fucking power-suited cunt.'

'Giles, you're not feeling well.'

'I can't believe it. What did she say to you?'

I gave a brief account of what she had.

'Oh, fuck,' he said. 'What a fuck-up. I told you, didn't I? I said if anything went wrong, they would hang us out to dry. And here I am in a fucking hospital bed and that bitch lecturing me in her suit. You know, when I go off to sleep, I can't stop myself dreaming of when I was on the ground and they were kicking me. Except that in my dream, I keep trying to explain to them that I'm about to go back to London and there's really no point, but when I speak nothing comes out of my mouth. Oh, fuck.'

I looked at him and now he really was crying. It was an awkward manoeuvre but I managed to put my arms part of the way around him and give him a partial hug, patting the side of his head. It hurt slightly. It really was difficult to find an uninjured part of his body, but I think it was appreciated.

Susan saw what was going on and she came over and hugged him from the other side of the bed. I started to disentangle myself, saying goodbye. Giles looked at me fiercely.

'I'll probably be going back to London today,' he said hoarsely. 'I'll call you. Wait for my call.'

I'd made plans about what I was going to say to Hannah. I thought that she might be feeling awkward about what had happened, regretful even. I would need to tell her about going back to London and that we would need to talk about things. This was something that we had both stumbled into. I was still surprised by it when I went over it in my mind. There was so much to talk about but when she opened the door to me, we didn't talk at all. The sex was even more urgent than it had been the day before. It was more relaxed as well, if that's possible. We knew each other's bodies now, we knew what to look for. We had sex on the floor. We didn't manage to get more than a few feet away from the front door.

'I thought about you all day,' Hannah said, when we were lying in each other's arms.

'Wait,' I said.

My clothes were half off and I stood up and took them off. I kneeled, looking down on her. I kissed her on the lips and on her neck. Then I started to undo the buttons of her sweater.

'No,' she said.

'Shut up.'

'Mark, I've told you . . .'

'I'm stronger than you are.'

I wondered if we would actually have a fight. She looked as if she was ready for one. Her jaw was set, her eyes shining. She looked magnificent. I undid the last button and pushed the sweater off. She could have fought it but she didn't. She had a heavy-duty, old-fashioned-looking bra. She looked straight at me as if she was daring me. Then she gave a little shrug and put her hands behind her back and unclipped it and let it slide down her arms and off. I pushed her down so that she was lying flat on her back.

I'd thought that I was going to be all casual and cool about it but it didn't work out like that at all because I wasn't the same person anymore. Something had happened to me. There was one quite normal breast, with a large dark pink nipple. On the other side of the chest it wasn't just absence. There was a long scar that began just above her armpit and crossed her chest to the centre, like a line drawn in pale lipstick, ending in a gentle curve.

'So if you're going to say I look beautiful anyway,' said Hannah, 'you needn't bother.'

I touched her nipple with the tip of my ring finger. It swelled noticeably. She gave a little gasp.

'That's amazing,' I said.

'You sound like you're on a school trip. It's just gone, that's all there is to it. They cut it off and probably put it in a jar somewhere.'

'Do you feel the nipple that isn't there?'

'No, I don't.'

'People who have a leg amputated sometimes have pain in the leg that isn't there.'

'I know. And apparently some women do feel the nipple that isn't there. And yes, if that's what you want to know, they sometimes feel the non-existent nipple become erect.' She leaned up on one elbow and looked at me. She smiled. 'You're aroused. I don't believe it. You're turned on by looking at me where my breast has been surgically removed.'

I stroked her leg and then between her legs and then pushed a finger inside her.

'So are you,' I said. 'You're turned on by the idea of me looking at where your breast has been removed. Or something like that.'

'That's not true,' she said. 'That's left over. From last time.'

Sex that time was slower, more gentle, better really. We couldn't just lie together on the floor all the time, though. Eventually we had to do something. So we took a shower together, with the door to the bathroom locked. We helped each other dress and then Hannah cooked a very basic pasta meal with sauce out of a carton. We ate hungrily, drinking red wine.

We didn't talk about our relationship. I didn't say anything about going back to London. There was no discussion about its suddenness or where we were going to go from here. There was no need. I felt as if I'd dropped off a cliff and I knew exactly where I was going. I was going to keep falling and falling. Eventually, no doubt, I would hit the ground. What was the point of talking about it?

Instead we talked about Giles. I told her about my day at the hospital, about my encounter with Donna. When I mentioned that Giles had already been taken down to London, I thought that she would ask me about when I was leaving but she said nothing. Didn't she care? She only asked me why I thought it had happened. I gave her a detailed account of what had happened on our evening in the Four Feathers with Tony and Ewan and, yes, Steve Yates.

'That's the father of Sandy,' Hannah said.

'I didn't mean to bring it up,' I said. 'I'm just telling you what happened.'

'I don't mind,' she said. 'More than that. When I heard about you and Sandy ... I'm sorry, I quite like the idea of sex with someone who picks up nineteen-year-old girls in pubs.'

'You shouldn't say that.'

'Are you shocked?'

'You make it sound like I'm doing you some kind of a favour. It's not like that.'

'It certainly isn't,' she said. 'You're lucky to get me.'

'Don't joke,' I said. 'I *am* lucky.'

'Did Steve know about you and Sandy?'

'No idea,' I said.

Then I told her about the row at Marshco.

'So what do you think?'

I took a sip of wine.

'I think you look beautiful,' I said.

'What do you think about Giles?'

'I reckon there's about a one per cent chance that some mad drunk attacked Giles at random. There's about an eight per cent chance that Paul Creek got a couple of heavies to teach Giles a lesson. He really got Creek angry and Creek threatened to fuck him. That was his word. But I reckon it's about a seventy-five per cent chance that those guys realized that Giles had tricked them and they panicked. They may have thought that would discourage him from taking it any further.'

'I think you've got a few per cent left over.'

'I was never any good at arithmetic.'

'So what are you going to do?'

'Not much. I guess the police will investigate. I doubt they'll find anything. If they didn't catch anyone straight away, they probably won't find anyone at all.' Hannah looked thoughtful. 'I know what you're going to say,' I said.

'What?'

'Not exactly at this moment. But at some point in the near future you'll say that I have to leave. But I'd like to stay the night.'

'No,' she said. 'Definitely not. And this isn't like taking my bra off. Bruce isn't ready.'

We argued for several minutes over this. Hannah yielded a bit and said that maybe I could sleep in the spare room. I said I would only do that if she would sleep there with me, which she said was ridiculous and defeated the point. We compromised by saying that she would spend a bit of the night with me.

'I'm not sure it's a good idea,' she said. 'It's Saturday morning tomorrow. Bruce is going to his football.'

'That's fine,' I said. 'I'll take him.'

She looked as if I had slapped her.

'You're not serious,' she said.

'Why not? I'm an expert on football.'

After all we'd been through, all the different settings I'd seen her in, it was the first time I'd seen her look baffled and indecisive. I really didn't think she knew what to say. When she spoke it was as if she had just tossed a coin.

'All right,' she said.

I felt relieved and alarmed at the same time. We went together and made up the tiny bed in her ridiculously poky spare bedroom and both got into it. I won there as well. Hannah fell asleep and snored in a very comical way and didn't wake up until she heard the sound of Bruce blundering around at six-thirty the next morning.

'What's your favourite team?' asked Bruce sternly.

'You mean football team?' I said, playing for time.

'Course *football team*,' he said.

I was a man. There was meant to be a football team that I was emotionally attached to. I'd never in my life watched sport. Looking at people playing a game. It seemed as much use as watching people eat. I tried to think of the name of a team that I could be sure really existed.

'Manchester United,' I said.

'What's your favourite player?'

'Who's *your* favourite team?' I asked, and Bruce was away. His favourite team was Arsenal and he had an encyclopaedic knowledge of all of the players. He named them one by one and identified them by position, and they weren't even positions I'd heard of. I'd played a bit of sport and I'd even played football a bit. But there were no right halves or centre forwards. There was still a goalie, though.

It was a short walk from Hannah's cottage to the football pitch and Bruce was barely halfway through the team by the time we arrived. As soon as we left the house I became very nervous. It was as if Hannah had suddenly said: here's this priceless Ming vase. Carry it around the park and bring it back safely. It seemed too intimate a thing for me to be doing. But Bruce was apparently untroubled. He had agreed as if it had been previously arranged and as soon as we left the house it was as if he was resuming a conversation we had been having for days. Perhaps all large men were the same to him.

Around the football pitch there were various groups of small boys and fathers, and even a few small girls and fathers. I was carrying a black bag. From it I removed shin pads, football boots, juice bottle. Bruce needed a lot of preparation for the game. I helped him tie the laces.

'Under or behind?' I said.

'Under, course,' he said, as if he was starting to have suspicions about this person disguised as a man who was accompanying him. So I wound the lace under his boots and tied each one in a neat little bow on top. Bruce was a goalkeeper, so he put on a green shirt which was decorated on the back with a number one and a name that wasn't his. When I asked him why the back of his shirt didn't say 'Mahoney', he looked suspicious again.

It was curious that Bruce was so passionate about football, because he wasn't very good at it. He was incredibly agile, throwing himself like a cat at even the most feeble, bobbling shot. But he seemed to have very little sense of where the ball really was. A few times it actually looked as if he was blind. The ball would sail past him into the goal and he didn't seem to see it, or dived in an odd direction which suggested he was only guessing, like in a spot the ball competition.

On the other hand, he wasn't particularly outshone by his fellow players. 'Team' wasn't the right word for them, because none of them ever passed the ball. They just ran blindly for the opposition's goal, wherever they were on the pitch. Because they knew that they were never going to get the ball unless they won it for themselves, the players all gathered around it, like a very tight, slow-moving swarm of bees. The only exception was a very small boy in glasses who stayed hopefully next to the opponents' goal. But nobody ever passed to him.

At half time Bruce came over to me. I gave him his juice and his chocolate digestive.

'Good game,' I said.

'It's five–six,' he said.

'Is that right?' I said. 'You had a good first half. Well done.'

'Did you see my save?'

'Excellent,' I said.

'He tried to bend it round the wall.'

'Fantastic. One thing, Bruce. When the ball is coming straight at you along the ground, maybe you should get your body behind it. So that if you miss the ball with your hands, it will still hit your legs.' Or was that cricket? Bruce wasn't paying attention anyway. 'Is someone else going in goal in the second half?'

'What?'

'You could have a bit of a runaround.'

'I'm a goalie,' Bruce said. 'I've gotta go. Team talk.'

I walked up and down the touchline roughly following

the progress of the ball and a man in a tracksuit engaged me in conversation.

'Which is yours?' he said.

'Bruce. He's in goal.'

'Mine's Tom. He's upfront.' Suddenly he shouted so loud that I jumped. 'Get stuck in, Tom.' He turned to me again and spoke again in a normal tone. 'The ref's a father from the other team. He's blatantly biased. It's a bloody scandal. I mean, look at that. That was never their throw. It destroys all respect for the game.'

Fortunately my phone rang and I excused myself. It was Giles. His voice sounded stronger.

'They've got me in this private ward,' he said. 'I've got colour TV, my own phone, incredible food. I don't want to go home. Susan's out of the room at the moment. The kids were just in here playing hide and seek. Are you still in Marston Green?'

'Yes.'

'Poor you. I've got time on my hands. This afternoon they're going to wheel me off and give me a fucking brain scan. But in the meantime I've got time on my hands and I've been thinking. You know why I gave up working in genetics?'

'It was something to do with your aunt, wasn't it?'

'Do you know how many people in the world today are descendants of Genghis Khan?'

'No, I don't.'

'Sixteen million. One in every two hundred men in the world.'

'When's your scan?'

'Because he was Genghis Khan, he could have sex with anyone he wanted, the pick of every captured citadel and castle. And you can see the result by sticking a cotton bud in the mouth of almost any man in Central Asia.'

'I'm sorry, I'm watching a child's football match. It's a bit hard to concentrate.'

'That's why I gave up. When you study Darwinian genetics you realize that nothing matters except transmission of genes. All the people who tried to live good lives, none of that mattered. All that mattered was to fertilize as many women as possible. What I realized was that we're all the descendants of rapists and pillagers and murderers and I decided I wanted to get into another line of business so I wouldn't have to think about that on a daily basis.'

'I'm sorry,' I said. Giles sounded very down. And then an idea came to me. 'Giles?'

'Yes.'

'That aunt of yours.'

'What?'

'The one you said was the cleverest person you'd ever met.'

'Aunt Frankie, yes.'

'Is she still alive?'

'Yes. She's pretty old, though.'

'I've been thinking,' I said. 'Kevin Seeger has a ton of information in his spare bedroom but what he doesn't have is a plan. He doesn't have a story. If he thinks he's going to stumble on the process by which Marshco's dioxins are giving children cancer in Marston Green, well, he fucking isn't. What I was thinking about in the middle of the night was Hannah Mahoney's map.'

'And?' Giles sounded interested now. He saw where I was heading.

'I wondered if someone who knew about this sort of thing, who had no connection to any of this or to Wortley, might be able to look at it and, well, you know . . . come to a conclusion.'

There was a long silence and I wondered if we'd been cut off.

'Do you think that there's any way you could get a copy of her map?' he asked finally. 'I know that Hannah's pretty scary.'

'I'll talk to her.'

'Interesting idea. If all else failed, you could break in and steal it. Do you remember where she kept the maps?'

'I'm not sure that's such a good idea. I'll talk to her. But do you think that aunt of yours might be a help?'

Another long silence was followed by what sounded like a cackle on the other end.

'She might,' he said. 'She just might. Unfortunately she lives over near Oxford, so it'll be a bit of a trek.'

'Have you got her number?'

'I'll get it and call you back. And I'll phone her, tell her to expect your call.'

'Will that be all right?'

'She's a bit old. Her hearing isn't very good. You'll have to say things quite slowly. Is this going to be all right?

Would it be better if I came and saw Hannah Mahoney myself? I'm not too well, though.'

'I'll talk to her.'

'Tell her you're speaking on behalf of me, if there's a problem. She doesn't trust us. We're the enemy. So you're going to have to tell her a bit about what's happened. You need to make it clear to her that this will benefit the campaign. That's the whole point of it.'

I looked over at Bruce, who was flying through the air, totally missing a long-range shot.

'I'll try to convince her.'

Giles said he'd ring me straight back with the number. I watched the rest of the match in a fog of indecision. While we had been talking on the phone, I had considered telling him about Hannah and me, but then I decided that the fewer people who had this incriminating piece of information the better.

The rest of the second half was pretty exciting. The ball kept hitting the post or Bruce and bouncing away. Parents on the sidelines were frothing at the mouth. Men were swearing at the referee. At the end the score was nine to Marston Green Junior Rovers and eight to the collection of waifs from a nearby village. On the way back, Bruce was torn between his excitement at having won and his anger at the ref.

'That was never a free kick,' he said. 'It was a fair shoulder barge.' And: 'Did you see the one I tipped over the bar? Did you think that was my second-best save or my first-best save?'

'Your second best.'

'Which was my first best?'

'The one where you dived at that girl's feet and she kicked you.'

'What about the header that bounced off my legs?'

'That was your fourth best.'

'What was my third best?'

When we got back, Hannah had made lunch, just soup and cheese and salad. She asked if I wanted to stay and I said yes, I needed to talk to her about something. She gave me a suspicious look. Hannah and I ate mainly in silence while Bruce maintained a monologue which was almost a minute-by-minute account of the match. He only stopped when Hannah gave him an ice lolly after he had finished his cheese sandwich.

'I've arranged for you to go round and see Nicky this afternoon.'

Bruce gave a very loud slurp on his lolly.

'I can't,' he said. 'I want to stay here.'

'Sorry, love, I've arranged it. I'll pick you up later.'

In a pre-emptive strike, Hannah told me to make coffee and she scooped him up and led him out of the house, still protesting. I'd only just poured it into the pot when she came back through the door.

'Nicky must live close by.'

'Everyone in Marston Green lives close by,' she said. 'We've got about two hours. I thought you might like to try my bed. It's better.'

*

She was suspicious when I told her about my conversation with Giles.

'What sort of state is he in?' she said.

'He sounds rough. He was hit on the head, so sometimes he's a bit off the wall. But he was always like that, even before he got beaten up.'

Hannah was lying beside me in the bed. She had taken all her clothes off without saying anything, which I liked. She was stroking my stomach.

'What does he feel?' she said.

'He's angry, I think. He feels that his boss – not even the top boss, the immediate boss – came up here and treated him like shit while he was lying in a hospital bed.'

'You think he's willing to go along with this as some sort of revenge?'

'I think he's considering it.'

'Does that sound sane?'

'Why should that bother you?'

She looked up at me with her large dark eyes.

'It's not very inspiring,' she said. 'You came to Marston Green to do a little report and get out as quickly as possible. Now you've come up with this plan and Giles is going along with it because he wants to get back at his employers. What is it? Didn't they give him a nice enough hospital room?'

'It's just information.'

'Giles asked for my data before. I was dubious then and I'm dubious now. You say that he wants to revenge himself on Wortley. There's another possibility. From what you say, he feels he's in trouble. He might be going along with your suggestion because he thinks it will bring him back into favour.'

'He didn't sound like that,' I said. 'He sounded like he was happy to go down in flames.'

Hannah leaned over and kissed me.

'And you may go down with him,' she said.

'I'm just interested,' I said. 'I want to know. Don't you want to know?'

'I do know. I've got all the information. Anyway, who is this aunt? What can she do?'

'I don't know. I'm meant to phone her. But there's no point in talking to her if I don't have your maps.'

'Maps? Not just the Marston Green map?'

'The others as well.'

'The others aren't ready yet. I've got the responses but the maps aren't finished.'

'Will it take long?'

'It's none of your business, Mark, I haven't said I'll let you have them.'

'Let me talk to this woman. I'll help you with the maps.'

'I don't need your help,' she muttered. She was frowning with concentration, but it is hard to look grim and business-like lying naked on top of a bed in the middle of the afternoon. 'Phone this woman,' she said. 'It may be a dead end anyway.'

'I'll do it now,' I said.

'What? Here?'

'Why not?'

The number was on a piece of paper in my trouser pocket.

I dialled it and it rang for a long time. When it was finally answered it sounded as if the phone had been pushed off a table onto a hard floor.

'Hello?' I said.

There was no answer but I could hear the sound of something. It could have been many things but I guessed someone was making a fumbling attempt to pick the receiver up.

'Hello?' said a voice. 'Is that Gerald?'

'Gerald?'

'Would two o'clock be all right?'

'Is that Frankie McDonald?'

'Gerald?'

I had been mistaken for somebody and it took a long time to make my identity clear, while Hannah lay sprawled across me looking amused. It was Frances McDonald and she was fairly deaf so I had to explain things slowly and very loudly. I managed to convey to her that I knew Giles Buckland.

'My nephew,' she said.

That was a start. Very slowly, feeling this was going to be pointless, I started to explain about Marston Green and the cluster of illnesses.

'Giles told me about that,' she said. 'He said you're coming to see me. Would you like to come for lunch?'

'Mrs McDonald . . .'

'Call me Frankie.'

'Do you need just the figures of illness?'

'You have maps, don't you?'

'I've got a map of the affected village.'

'Giles said you had other maps.'

'There are two or three others that are being prepared. They're of adjacent villages. They were done as a sort of control.'

'Excellent.'

'So you want those as well.'

'They're essential. Would you like to come for lunch tomorrow?'

'They aren't ready just yet. Excuse me for just one moment.' I covered up the receiver and looked down at Hannah. 'She wants to know when I can come.'

'I haven't agreed,' said Hannah.

'Hannah, I've seen your map. It's dynamite. And anyway, what have you got to lose?' She looked hesitant. 'Take the chance. Throw the dice.'

'What's she going to do?'

'I don't know. It took me long enough to tell her my name. Why not try it?'

She looked doubtful but she nodded.

'All right.'

'When?'

'A couple of days.'

I thought for a few seconds.

'Hello? Are you still there, Frankie? I'll have the finished maps by Tuesday. Is that all right?'

'What do the maps look like?'

Sean French

'What do you mean? They're just maps of the villages with the addresses of people suffering from cancer marked on it as dots.'

'Can you do something else for me, Mark?'

'What?'

'You need to draw a grid over the inhabited areas. These should be a quarter of a square kilometre each. The squares should also have roughly the same density of population in each square. It doesn't have to be exact but you could cross out squares that are mainly playing fields or woodland or farmland, that sort of thing. Can you do that?'

'I guess so. What's it for?'

'And I'll expect you for lunch on Tuesday.'

'I'll be there.'

We had to start almost straightaway. Hannah began to unpack her files and I went down to the Four Feathers to buy a bottle of wine. Geoff didn't generally sell drink in that way, but he was very understanding with me. I noticed Ewan further along the bar, having a drink with someone I didn't know. I thought, fuck it, and walked over.

'How are you doing?' I said.

'All right,' he said. 'How's your friend?'

'What do you mean?'

'Heard he got banged up.'

'Yes,' I said. 'He was badly beaten up. He's in hospital.'

I looked at Ewan's florid face, the face of a pale, red-haired man who had spent too long in the sun. I just

324

couldn't tell whether he was hostile or just the basic indifference we feel when something bad happens to someone we don't much care for. I tried to push it a bit.

'Why do you reckon someone in Marston Green would do something like that? He wasn't robbed. He hadn't been arguing with someone.'

'Maybe he'd scared people,' Ewan said, taking a sip of his pint. 'People don't like people coming in from outside, interfering. So what about you? Going back to London?'

When I got back to Hannah's house, there were files and filled-out forms spread out across the floor. I poured us each a glass of wine and we took a sip. It was a dismaying sight.

'You know what worries me,' I said. 'Apart from the thought of getting this done in about two days and you've got to go to work on Monday and you've got a son to bring up. What Giles always says to me is that it's always about the quality of the data. It doesn't matter what wonderful things you do to it, if the information isn't reliable. Isn't it a problem relying on people who just happen to fill in a form?'

Hannah gave her slow smile, which I'd started to like and thought about when she wasn't around. She walked over to me and took my wine glass from my hand and put it on the table. Then she gave me a long slow deep kiss. I could taste the wine, cold, sharp, on her tongue. She stepped back and looked at me as if she was checking the effect of what she'd done.

'One of my best friends works as a GP,' she said. 'She also has a young son who has been treated for leukaemia. She's played no public part in the campaign. But she has obtained for me the epidemiological details I needed. Completely off the record. Now, I've told you that, and I haven't insulted you by asking you not to tell anyone else.'

I kissed Hannah on her face and neck, feeling her body through her shirt and her trousers.

'I just talked to Ewan,' I said. 'One of the guys I think beat up Giles.'

'What did he say?'

'He said that some people didn't like people coming in from outside and interfering.'

'Do you think he was threatening you?'

'He was being fairly unambiguous,' I said. 'And then he asked me when I was going back to London.'

'That's a good question.'

'I'll have to check in at Wortley soon,' I said. 'They'll be wondering what I'm up to. Which I'm wondering myself.'

It didn't take two days. It took one very long Sunday, with quite a lot of the Saturday evening before. Hannah carefully drew the map of Heiston, Lingham and Chapel Willow that formed an almost continuous slug-shaped mass heading north-east from Marston Green. She had street plans and I used these to plot the incidences onto the map. It was laborious and fiddly and after a few hours of it my eyes were throbbing. Meanwhile Bruce lay beside us on the floor with a large sheet of paper drawing his own giant map of an imaginary country.

At six o'clock we ate pizza and beer, Coke for Bruce, and then Hannah read to him and got him into a bath while I worked and then I read to him while she worked and then Hannah lured him into bed and we worked together. After the map was finished, we made a tracing of the whole thing and then Hannah of the steady hand drew the quarter-kilometre squares over it. She quickly crossed out the uninhabited areas and – just before nine – it was all finished. We propped the map against the wall and proudly surveyed it, as if it was a huge canvas we had painted together. I remembered when I had seen the first version of this map, in the village hall, and I felt the same now. There were dark nasty clumps of speckles. There was also one in Chapel Willow and a few scatterings in Heiston and Lingham but there were clearly more specks, and more concentrated specks in Marston Green.

I started to unfasten my shirt and Hannah pulled her sweatshirt over her head, both of us still looking at the map.

'So what does that say to you?' she said.

'It's devastating,' I said.

'Are you won over?'

'In all sorts of ways.'

I walked over to the fridge and fetched two glasses and a bottle of sparkling wine I had bought earlier in the day for this moment. In her underwear now, Hannah was gathering our clothes from the floor. There was a new exhilaration in our sex that evening, as if we were flying together high up in thin air and bright sunlight. Later we lay exhausted, but I couldn't stop caressing her warm, damp skin.

'I think I'm going to leave Wortley,' I said.

'I thought you loved it.'

'I do. I did. I'm not sure if it's right.'

'Why? Maybe we'll get them to pay out lots of money to people who deserve it.'

'Maybe,' I said.

All of a sudden I felt distant from my own life, as if I could hide from it in Hannah's bed. I kissed her breast and then stroked it, around the nipple and then down and around. Suddenly I wanted to stop the moment. Stop it and go back. Not go through what I was going to have to go through, not say what I was going to have to say.

'Hannah?'

'What?'

I touched her breast slightly more firmly, at the point underneath where it met her chest.

'I think I can feel something.'

It was a long and tiresome journey to Frankie McDonald's cottage in High Shapland. I checked on a road map and the village was almost directly a hundred miles west of Marston Green. But this is England and everything is designed for people travelling to or from London. This suited me most of the time but not now. I took a cab to the station and caught the train down to Liverpool Street. Then I went by Underground to Paddington and took a train out to Didcot and then changed on to a smaller local train that took me through small towns and villages with picturesque names. By the time I got out of another taxi outside Frankie McDonald's cottage, I had been travelling for five and a half hours.

On the other hand, High Shapland was a more beautiful village than Marston Green. Marston Green had been messed up by having new houses built there for people who were doing actual jobs, and it was obvious that these people didn't want old cottages with thatched roofs and honeysuckle round the door. They wanted driveways, garages, gravel paths, picture windows with double glazing, conservatories.

In High Shapland the houses were made out of the rough

329

biscuity local stone, the windows were tiny, the walls bulged and curved. Frankie McDonald's house was right on the High Street, without even a pavement separating it from the traffic. I knocked on the door, but there was no answer and I walked up an alley that led along the side of the house to the garden. A woman was on her knees by the side of a bed, doing something fiddly to some sort of flower. I called over the fence but she didn't look around. Finally I had to let myself in through the gate and tap her on the shoulder. I helped her to her feet. She was almost white-haired with a leathery wrinkled face. She was incredibly shabbily dressed, in rough brown paint- and mud-spattered trousers and a sort of rough navy-blue smock.

'Frankie McDonald?' I said.

'Are you hungry?' she asked.

'Quite.'

'Lunch is cooking away.'

'I brought you this,' I said, handing her a bottle of red wine.

'Oh, goody,' she said. 'Excellent. Come inside.'

I followed her inside. She lived in a real old-fashioned cottage, floorboards that were almost black with age, except for the kitchen, which had a floor of smooth stone flagging. It was full of what looked like nice bits of furniture and pictures and things on sideboards, but there was a basic sense of a grip having been lost, of faded paint, dust and dirty cups and things that had fallen over and not been picked up.

'Now, what have you brought me?'

I unrolled the map on the floor and placed a book on each corner to keep it flat. She looked down at it.

'These are the four villages?'

'That's right.'

'Excellent. Have you heard of the Texas sharpshooter problem, Mark?'

'No.'

'Hmmm. Shall we open your bottle of wine?'

'What is it?'

'Sorry?'

'The Texas sharpshooter problem.'

'Oh. Someone empties their gun into a barn door and draws a target carefully around the bullet holes.'

'I don't understand.'

'Hmm,' she said. I wasn't sure whether her 'hmm' was a statement, a sign that she was thinking, or whether it was a sort of burp. 'It suggests that people are doing things the wrong way round. You ought to define an area and then look for the incidence of disease inside it. Instead, they sometimes find a number of cases in an area and then draw a line around those cases and it can look alarming. But this doesn't apply in this case. This is excellent.'

'Don't you think it looks convincing?' I said.

'Shall we open your bottle of wine, Mark? There's a corkscrew somewhere around.'

I found the corkscrew after a search through several drawers and opened the wine. I poured two glasses and Frankie seized hers hungrily. Her hand trembled slightly.

'Your good health, Mark,' she said and took a large gulp

and then another, so that her glass was already half empty.

'So you've been visiting cancer sufferers?'

'I've seen a couple,' I said. 'A few.'

'Very sad,' she said. 'I never did any of that.'

'You worked in insurance, didn't you?'

'Yes. I was an actuary.'

'Doesn't that deal with illness and death?'

'Oh, absolutely. But just with figures, you know. I think I would have found it terribly off-putting if I had actually gone and met people with dreadful illnesses.'

'I don't know,' I said. 'It's easy just to sit in an office. I feel it's important to get out there and get a smell of it.'

'Smell? What do you mean smell?'

'When you go out in the world, there aren't numbers. Just people.'

Frankie drained her glass and with slightly mixed feelings I filled it again.

'I'll prepare lunch for us, Mark, and in the meantime I'd like you to do something for me, if you would be so kind.'

'What?'

'I should like you to count up the number of squares on your map.'

'There are five hundred and seventy-six,' I said.

'Jolly good. Then I should like you to count up the number of squares with no dots, the number with one, with two, three, four and lastly five or more. It will be frightfully boring, I'm afraid.'

It was, but at least it took my mind off lunch, which I had

already glimpsed. In an old saucepan there were a couple of carrots, a couple of potatoes and a strange and very bony fatty cut of meat boiling away in some water. While I totted up the figures, I heard a clattering of plates and cutlery being placed on the table in the kitchen. I was finished in twenty minutes and Frankie spooned her strange casserole out onto the plates.

'I think we're going to need some more wine,' she said. I had barely touched my glass but the bottle was almost finished and when Frankie helped herself to another glass, it was finished. 'You'll find some in the cupboard. Choose whatever you like. Whatever.'

I opened another bottle of red wine.

'The Texas sharpshooter problem. Did I tell you about that?'

'Yes,' I said.

'But it's not a problem.'

'What?'

'That map. Excellent. Was it done by your girlfriend?'

I was stunned. Did Giles know something? How could he possibly? Had he told something to Frankie?

'She's not exactly my girlfriend.'

'Are you sexually involved?'

I took a deep breath.

'Well, yes.'

'You see, it's all about figures. What you have to see is that disasters have to be seen as deviations from a baseline of routine background tragedy. Do you know what I mean?'

'No, I don't.'

'You see, the truth isn't something that you can just go and look at.'

'Why?'

'The truth is a product of the statistical analysis of trained professionals. Do you want some gravy?'

'Yes, please.'

Unfortunately the gravy turned out to be nothing more than the water that the meat and vegetables had been cooked in.

'Have some more wine.'

'I'm all right, for the moment.'

'The war,' she said, taking another sip of wine. 'Was I talking about the war?'

'No.'

'Wasn't I?' She looked puzzled. 'Did I say I worked in insurance?'

'Yes.'

'I was a statistician.' The word 'statistician' was now rather hard for her to say. 'But in the war, I mean the second war, I worked in something frightfully secret.'

'Maybe you shouldn't tell me about it.'

'I worked for an intelligence division that was connected with Bomber Command. Oh, now I remember, sex. You were talking about sex.'

'Not really.'

'There was a lot of sex. Do you know, people talk about the sixties, but there was a lot more in the war. It's to do with death. It's a well-known psychological phenomenon.'

'Phenomenon' was also a challenge. 'When people think they are going to die next week, then why not have sex now? My husband died about five years ago, ten years ago. He was already my fiancé but we slept with other people. He was in the army. I slept with pilots and soldiers and people in my department and all sorts of people.'

Frankie was drunk, but she caught my eye and just for a second I had a glimpse of the beautiful, brilliant, naughty, sexually adventurous young woman she had been fifty-five years earlier. That's probably what she still felt like, on the inside.

'On VE-Day we all ran out of our office and people were dancing and hugging and drinking. Hours later I was in St James's Park and an American GI came up to me and we kissed each other and we went behind a bush and I sucked him off. Is that what you say? "Sucked off"?'

'That's right.'

'I haven't said it out loud before.'

I chewed slowly and many times on my piece of meat. I tried not to think about where it might have come from.

'It sounds amazing,' I said. 'But I wanted to talk about these figures. What are you going to do with them?'

I had to wait some time for an answer. Frankie had fewer teeth than me and was taking even longer to chew her meat.

'Your figures,' she said. 'I'm going to apply the Poisson frequency distribution to them.'

'Obviously that means nothing at all to me,' I said.

'The war,' she said. 'Did I mention Bomber Command?'

Conversation with Frankie moved in the shape of a spiral.

She would circle back to a previous subject, but just a little further along.

'Yes, you did.'

'We did the maths,' she said. 'We did the calculations for trajectories and flight paths and whether one big bang was better than two small bangs. Once, towards the end of the war, we worked on the flying bombs. Do you know about the flying bombs?'

'A bit.'

'Wonderful things. Brilliant German invention. Streets ahead of anything we could manage. They were unmanned rockets that flew to London. Then the engine would cut out and they would fall. I heard them sometimes. It was a funny thing. You may have heard the story that people used to hear the motor and pray and pray that they would keep on hearing it, because if it stopped, then it would land on you. Nonsense, of course. Obviously, the momentum would carry it far away. For a flying bomb to land on you, the engine would have to have cut out miles before it reached you and you would hear nothing. The bombs were falling on London in quite large numbers and people started to claim that the bombs were falling in clusters. Now this might have meant that they were tending to cut out at certain points. But there were even rumours that particular areas were being targeted. There were the wildest rumours. So some of us were asked if we could test this mathematically. Funny thing, isn't it? Bombs falling, families being killed, and a group of us responded by sitting at our desks with pen and paper and slide rules. And we did what you did. We selected an area of South London and we divided it into squares and counted the impacts.'

'Won't you need a computer or something?'

'Just a calculator,' she said.

Just under an hour later, the cab arrived to take me back to the station. We stood on her front step while the driver waited in the car.

'I was hoping you'd stay to tea,' Frankie said.

'I've got to get back,' I said. 'This is important.'

'That was great fun,' she said. 'Let me know what happens.'

'All right.'

'Quite like the old days.'

'I'm glad,' I said. 'Thank you very much.'

'You know, the world is so complicated with all the things in it, sunsets and forests and people making decisions, falling in love, making jokes, it's all noise, fluff on the surface. It can all be reduced to figures. As long as you get the right figures. Take the problem with negroes, for example.'

'Sorry?'

'Are negroes stupider than the rest of us? My friend who lives in London was robbed by a negro.'

'You're not really meant to say "negro" any more.'

'Why? That's the polite word, isn't it? People argue about whether they're naturally the way they are or whether it's the way they're brought up.'

'What do you mean "the way they are"?'

'You know what I mean. One's not supposed to say it but everybody knows. My point is that there's no need to get all het up about it. It's just a matter of finding the figures. Mark, you're clearly good at gathering information. Could you find some figures on negroes for me?'

I pretended that I was in a desperate hurry to catch my train and I didn't reply.

Things seem clearer when I'm thinking about them in the middle of the night, when the curtains are just starting to turn grey. It's in the daytime, with all the noise and distraction, that it gets complicated. Giles used to talk about making decisions under conditions of uncertainty. He meant constructing factories and organizing building sites but I felt the same about simpler things. I guess you make about three basic decisions in your life. Where you work, where you live, who you live with and who you love. That's more than three but they're not exactly separate. But I felt like I had Kevin Seeger's filing cabinets in my head. Kevin had everything you could possibly get hold of about dioxins and fucking furans whatever they were, and he sort of knew where everything was, but if you asked him the basic question about whether he could show that Marshco were responsible for the cancer, this funny look came on his face. And I felt like that about almost everything.

When I saw Hannah again, late that evening, I told her about Frankie.

'She was completely mad,' I said.

'In what way?' said Hannah.

'Babbling. And she was pissed. I brought her a bottle of wine and she drank that and then another. She's also some kind of weird racist. Her big plan is to do some statistical project to demonstrate why white people are cleverer than black people.'

'So why did Giles send you to her?'

We were sitting in Hannah's living room. I was on the sofa and she was in the easy chair, facing me. It felt strange talking to her without touching her. It made me nervous.

'She's done stuff like this before.'

'What sort of stuff?'

'She was an actuary. And in the Second World War she was attached to Bomber Command.'

'Bomber Command? What's that got to do with anything?'

So I told Hannah the flying bomb story, as well as I could remember it.

'People thought they were falling in clusters. They got paranoid that they were aiming at certain areas. It looked like it. She showed me a report on it. There was a map with the impacts marked on it. It really looked as if somebody had tried to hit particular areas and avoid others.'

'And had they?'

'No,' I said. 'It was an illusion. The impacts were entirely random.'

There was a very long silence. Hannah's expression didn't change at all. Her eyelids fluttered a little, as if there was some dust in her eyes, that was all.

'How could they be sure?'

'It's some incredibly complicated theorem. It made my head ache just looking at it. But if you have a certain number of squares and a certain number of, well, in this case bombs, it tells you, if the hits were random, how many squares you would expect with no hits, how many with one, how many with two, and so on. And then they compared that with the distribution of the actual hits. It was an amazingly close fit.'

There was another long silence.

'Did it prove that the bombs were *not* being aimed?'

'No. She spent a lot of time explaining this to me. It was hard to get my head around. All it proved was that it didn't need to have been aimed. There was no pattern, except for the pattern you get from randomness.'

'So does it prove that the cancer in Marston Green doesn't come from an environmental cause?'

'No,' I said. 'It just proves that there is a random spread across Marston Green, Heiston, Lingham and Chapel Willow. What is certain is that there is no special cluster in Marston Green.'

There was a long silence and Hannah looked so alone.

'I assume this woman is right,' she said finally, hopelessly. 'You said she was drunk and mad.'

'I didn't understand the formula, but the agreement between the expected figures and the ones on your chart are amazing. I've got them here.' I took a piece of paper from my jacket pocket and unfolded it. 'You can look. She said the figures indicated . . .' I looked at her handwriting on the

bottom: ' "perfect randomness and homogeneity of the area".
But I've faxed a copy to Giles and he's going to get someone
to check the figures. But they're right.'

'You gave it to Giles.'

'Yes.'

'I guess he would have got the report from his aunt
anyway.'

'I suppose so. Did you go to the doctor?'

'I called him. I'm going in for a scan tomorrow.'

'There's a possibility that it might be nothing.'

'That's true.'

At that moment, I had a stinging sensation in my cheeks
that was both hot and cold. I tried to think what it was. It
seemed familiar, like something I had felt long ago and then
I remembered. It was the feeling of being eight years old
and being about to start sobbing, not because you were sad
or in pain but because you were confused and it was all too
complicated. I didn't cry. That was the one good thing. I
went to the cupboard and got the whisky and two glasses
and filled them both. I handed her one and took a deep gulp
from my own which made me cough. I sat next to her. I
wasn't going to defend myself. I wasn't going to say anything on my own behalf. I had nothing to be ashamed about.
I hadn't betrayed her. I'd done nothing wrong.

'Were you trying to prove something?' she said.

'To you?'

'Giles thought it was the only way you could win.'

'I don't care what Giles thought. What did *you* think?'

'Do you want me to say that I did it for you?'

'You could say something.'

'It didn't work out the way I wanted.'

'You found the killer blow,' she said. 'They'll be very pleased with you.'

'That's not what I've been thinking about,' I said.

'What have you been thinking about?'

I took another burning gulp of whisky.

'The plan was that I was going to come back with these findings from Frankie and that would make up for the bad things that are happening. But on the train back I was thinking about being afraid.'

'I'm not so afraid,' Hannah said.

'I can't believe that.'

'I'm angry,' she said. 'When Bruce was born and when I was left on my own with him, I didn't mind because I knew I'd save him from anything. I didn't need anybody else. I'd stand in front of a hurricane to protect him. And now there's this.'

'You'll beat it,' I said.

She looked at me sharply.

'Are you an oncologist?' she said. 'Oh no. I forgot. You're making yourself feel better.' I put my hand on her arm but she shook it away. 'Do you want to have sex? Is that what you want? Take our mind off things. You'll excuse me for having other things on my mind. I'm thinking of Liz and Ella and the others and how it looks as if it's all been for nothing.'

I started to say something and gulped and stopped myself and then didn't stop myself and said it anyway:

'It wouldn't have cured them,' I said. 'If the campaign worked, some of them would live and some of them would die anyway.'

Hannah leaned towards me. I thought she was going to touch me, kiss me, but she took the glass from my hand and placed it on the table.

'I think it's time you went back to London,' she said.

Maybe originally I had hoped that Giles and I would return in triumph, but, even though it looked as if we had achieved what they wanted, now I just wanted to sneak in unnoticed and get back to work. Giles was even more paranoid than I was and he made elaborate arrangements to prepare the report without attracting the attention of anybody from the office. He summoned me to his house on a day when Wortley assumed I was still in Marston Green.

He had just left hospital and he still looked rough. His face was discoloured and he did something funny with his mouth as he talked, as if he was testing the mobility of his lower jaw. His movements were generally slow and accompanied with much groaning.

'What do they need to know?' he asked.

'There's Frankie McDonald's stuff about the cluster.'

Giles looked suddenly sad and I wondered if there was more bad news for me to hear.

'I'm tormented by the image of my aunt giving a blow job to an American soldier in a public park.' I had given Giles a detailed account of my conversation with Frankie, with all its weird detours. Maybe this was wrong, but I

345

couldn't resist the temptation. 'Furthermore, why did she tell you? Nobody tells me things like that. Is that a problem I have? Is it something about me? Mark, would you confide in me?'

'It depends,' I said.

'I haven't got a confiding face,' he said. 'I talk too much. That's probably it. They're about to tell me their equivalent of the blow-job story and I'll interrupt them and carry on talking. That's why I have to go and spy in people's bathrooms.'

'I was saying,' I said, 'that Frankie's analysis of the cluster will have to go in the report.'

'Obviously,' said Giles. 'In fact they already know about it. I sent her figures to Ross Cowan to check.'

'You didn't tell me that.'

'No.'

'You should have done.'

'Why?'

'You didn't know what I'd said to Hannah. I might have promised her to keep the results secret.'

'I didn't think about it,' Giles said. 'But if I had, I wouldn't have asked you. I wouldn't have been bound by a promise like that. In any case, if you remember, the point of getting the figures was to use them as a weapon against Wortley. But once we'd found out the truth, we couldn't bury it.'

'I agree,' I said. 'But you should have told me.'

'How did you persuade Hannah to give you the figures, by the way?'

'I asked her for them.'

An expression of pain slowly spread across Giles's face.

'Don't say it,' he said.

'What?'

'Say it isn't true,' he said. 'You and Hannah. It's not true. Just remove one potential source of misery from my already miserable and frustrated life by saying it isn't true. Please say it.'

'It *is* true.'

'That's not allowed. It's against the rules, it's forbidden.'

'Why?'

'Lots of reasons. One, it's unprofessional. Two, she's a generation older than you.'

'Six years.'

'Three, she was on the other side. Four, she has a disease.'

'What are you talking about?'

'Five, she has a child, who is presumably psychologically vulnerable to strange men appearing on the scene. Six, you were meant to be working. Seven, you have already seduced and abandoned one Marston Green girl. Eight, you laid yourself open to blackmail. Nine, she is a sensitive and intelligent woman and deserves better than a bit of meaningless, exploitative sex and ten, well . . . I could go on. And there is certainly going to be no mention of this so-called relationship in the report.'

'Obviously,' I said. 'And you don't know what you're talking about.'

'It's a pity we didn't stay another few days. There was that girl with leukaemia you saw. What was she? Fourteen? You could have tried someone younger.'

'Shut up, Giles.'

'I'm wondering if we need to mention my business in the report.'

'You mean the assault? Of course you do.'

'I could probably make it work for us. Ill-feeling in the town against anything that could impact on employment prospects, even to the point of violence.

'We'll need a brief report from you on the campaign. Very brief. The cluster profile has now been authoritatively discredited. Not much more than that. That wretched schoolteacher probably isn't worth mentioning at all. A bit pathetic, isn't it? I think that poor old Kevin Seeger thought that this was going to make him famous. As it's turned out, he's not even a fly worth swatting.

'There should be a mention of our meetings with Marshco. Cooperative and helpful briefings from the management and technical staff, blah blah blah. Anything else?'

'What about the allegations of illegal dumping?'

Giles frowned.

'You're right. We'll need to cover ourselves with a reference. How shall we put it? Associated allegations of bad practice. Reports of illegal dumping. Bit strong. Allegations of undocumented disposal. No corroborating documents or testimony found. That should do it.' Giles wrote something illegible on his notepad. 'Anything else?'

'Should we mention meeting some of the victims?'

Giles sucked the end of his pen.

'I really can't think of any way it's relevant,' he said. 'Even if we had discovered that the cluster was authentic, the experiences of individual sufferers wouldn't matter one way or the other. I guess that sort of thing might become relevant if it ever came to court, which it won't. If one of them had seemed particularly touching, it might have been worth mentioning.'

'I thought they were all pretty touching.'

'Needless to say,' said Giles. 'But as you helped discover, they are not part of a cluster. Throw a stick out of a window and you'll hit someone with a touching illness.'

'Frankie called it the background of general human suffering, or something like that.'

'Don't mention Frankie to me. The name simply makes me think of her doing that thing behind a bush on VE-Day. The image haunts me.' He looked down at his notebook. 'I'll type it up tomorrow morning, send a copy to Donna copied to Broberg, Cowan and Vicki Hargest and it will go into a file, never to be seen again.'

'Is that it?' I said.

'If we're lucky,' said Giles.

'Don't you think it's a bit ironic? Marshco's an awful company and you were badly beaten up by someone connected with them, and you were treated with contempt by Donna. And you're writing a report letting them off the hook. I won't even mention the people with cancer that we're cutting adrift.'

'You just did,' he said.

'What?'

'Mention them. I know what you want me to say. You want me to say that I'm worried about my mortgage and my children and I can't afford to take a stand. But I'm not going to. You know what I think about the people with cancer? Fuck them. That's what I think.'

'You don't mean that,' I said.

'All right,' he said. 'I'm exaggerating for rhetorical effect. But the truth is, they're ill. And some of them, or some people on their behalf, couldn't just accept it. It needed to be someone's fault. They needed to be compensated for being ill by being given money.'

'So you reckon that we've taught them a lesson?'

'It's not our job to teach people lessons.'

'Is that what you think of Hannah?'

'Do you want my approval of Hannah?' Giles said. 'Do you want me to tell you she's all right?'

'She's not all right,' I said. 'There's another lump.'

Giles started at that.

'I'm sorry,' he said. 'Are you . . .? I don't know how to say it? Are you really involved?'

'I don't know,' I said. 'It feels too hard for me.'

I'd phoned Hannah during the day but there'd been no answer, so I tried her again when I got back to my flat and this time she answered. It felt wrong on the phone, like talking through a narrow crack in a fence. I asked meaning-less questions about how she was and how Bruce was and all the notes seemed wrong because there was only one thing to talk about.

'Did it go all right today?'

'How do you mean?'

'At the hospital.'

'What do you think?'

I wasn't sure if she was playing some ridiculous game because I hadn't been there. I mean 'there for her'. The question of why I should have been or what I would actually have done or that if she wanted something from me, she could have asked for it, all that, was something that wasn't at all clear to me.

'Is it back?' I asked.

'Yes,' she said. 'They're doing some further tests but yes, it's back. Next question.'

'What's happening?'

'What's happening is that on Monday I go into hospital to have more bits of me cut out, including my other breast. And then I have another course of chemo, so I've got another few months of sleeping next to a bucket.'

'I'm so sorry, Hannah.'

'So what are you going to do?'

'I don't know.'

'To prove to me that you care.'

'That's not fair.'

'Not fair? Oh, I'm so sorry. I'm going to have another breast cut off. Am I not being sufficiently sensitive to your needs when I talk to you on the phone? I'm so sorry. How's work?'

'It's . . . it's nothing really.'

'Are they pleased with you? I bet they are.'

'I haven't talked to them yet.'

'They will be. I'm sorry, Mark, I've got to go. I'm tired. I'm sorry.'

'We'll talk soon.'

'Sure.'

She put the phone down. I held the receiver for a few more moments, as if it had something extra to communicate. I replaced it and found myself looking at my own reflection in the window. At first I had a puzzled expression and then I smiled at myself. What was there to smile about? I'd known absolutely for sure that the cancer was back, so there was no shock about that. I'd been entirely prepared for that. I think that what would have depressed me would have been if she had been all friendly and civilized on the phone. It hadn't been like that at all. She was scratching at me like we were two people horribly entangled and she didn't know what to do.

Giles was wrong about the file being buried and everything being forgotten. Within an hour of his delivering the report we were both back in the conference room at Wortley, barely ten days after we had met there before. The circumstances were not exactly the same. We were ordered up with no notice. Nielsen wasn't present. He was in the States. And nothing had been prepared. There was no coffee in silver pots. Donna hustled us into the room and Broberg, Cowan and Hargest were huddled in a group at the end. I saw copies of the report on the table. It all looked a bit chaotic. Broberg was in his shirtsleeves with no jacket in sight. Vicki Hargest was in an overcoat and carrying a bag. She looked as if she'd been caught on her way somewhere. They looked up when we came in. There were odd smiles on their faces but it wasn't exactly a friendly welcome. It was more as if the circus had come to town. Giles limped along the table like Quasimodo, which must have been a feeble bid for sympathy.

'Guys,' said Broberg. 'Welcome back.' We murmured something. 'Normally I would ask if you've had an interesting time, but I already know.' We murmured something else to the effect that it had actually been incredibly routine, but Broberg continued without listening. 'We thought you were going to sit in the back of a village hall and take some notes, just a quiet sniffing around. But this, this was quiet like the Vietnam War.'

'You've seen our report,' said Giles. 'I'm not sure what else you need.'

'I've got to hand it to you guys,' Broberg said. 'This old woman from the Second World War. Cowan showed me those figures. Fantastic.'

'I know there was the odd incident,' said Giles.

'Incident? You mean a possible attempted murder? A stand-up row with the boss of the company we represent? Have I missed anything?'

Yes, he had. I stayed silent and looked at the floor. I wondered if Giles might toss me to them, the way you might throw your pet dog to a wolf pack to keep them off you for a few extra seconds.

'I don't see the point of this,' said Giles, falling into his lawyer-speak. 'As our report clearly states, the issue of the alleged cluster in Marston Green is now settled. I don't know what else there is to talk about.'

'Do you two gentlemen know the name Simon Tierney?' asked Broberg.

Giles and I looked at each other and shrugged. I had never heard the name. But I was also completely and utterly sure that he wasn't going to be good news.

'Mr Tierney is the solicitor representing the Marston Green campaign,' said Broberg. 'He contacted us earlier today. He claims that Marshco made physical threats against you, Giles Buckland . . .'

'That's just rumour,' said Giles.

'And that the men who assaulted you were employees of Marshco who then made further threats against Mr Foll here. And here's the interesting bit. I mean, a further interesting bit: Tierney tells us that they intend to call Mr Buckland and Mr Foll as witnesses. Do you gentlemen have any comment on that?'

I almost laughed, but didn't. Fucking Hannah. Shafted. Utterly shafted. I was like a beetle that had had a needle pushed through it and was being displayed on a card. But didn't they kill them first? My legs were still waggling, with the needle through my chest. I looked at Giles, who had gone a curious colour. He clutched his broken ribs as if they were a war wound.

'It's not relevant,' he said. 'The issue of my severe injuries is utterly marginal to this case.'

'We'll leave that question to our legal department, if that's all right,' said Broberg. 'But I'm intrigued. These alleged threats. If they were actually delivered, this was in a private meeting with the three of you, correct?' Giles nodded. 'And the further threats made to Mr Foll. Were you alone at the time?'

'The landlord, Geoff, may have been around,' I said.

'Mr Tierney didn't mention a "Geoff". He talked of calling you two as witnesses. Mr Foll, if you were cross-examined on this question, what would you say?' Vicki Hargest made an attempt to interrupt but Broberg gestured at her to be quiet.

'It depends what I was asked.'

'Would you testify that threats were made against Giles Buckland by Paul Creek?'

'Yes,' I said.

'And were threats made to you by the people you believe to have assaulted Mr Buckland?'

'That's the way it seemed to me.'

Broberg seemed slightly at a loss for anything to say. He looked at his colleagues.

'Ross? Vicki?' he said. 'Any questions?'

They shook their heads. They seemed in a state of shock.

'That went more quickly than I expected,' Broberg said. 'I think we can resume this at another time. I believe that we're in a poker game, gentlemen. You can go now.'

3 1

We were told to stay in the office until further notice. I didn't know whether they wanted us where they could see us or whether they were worried about what other trouble we could cause out there in the real world. I hardly dared to catch Giles's eye. As he had limped down from Broberg's office, he had looked like the way that people in films look like when they have suffered a trauma. He had stary eyes and was almost unable to speak. We spent a grim day and a half completing paperwork and signing off on cases over the phone.

I tried to stay out of Giles's way but he came and found me and said we had to go somewhere. He was looking around as if he thought we were under surveillance. I thought he might take us into the toilets and switch all the taps on so that we couldn't be overheard.

'We need to go out,' he said.

'Is that all right?' I said.

'You think we might get into any more trouble?'

He led me out of the office and along the road to an upmarket snack bar. He looked at the list of coffees on the wall.

'Do you just have coffee?' he asked the woman behind the bar.

'Caffé Americano,' she said.

'Can't they fucking speak English,' he said, as he led me to a table. 'Understand, this is not a point about immigrants. It's about coffee.'

It wasn't something I could get worked up about at a time like that. Giles looked at me warily.

'I'm not sure it was such a good idea to be so clear about the way you'd testify,' he said.

'What else could I have done?'

'Almost anything else,' he said. 'You could have lied. That's always a good tactic. If you can't lie, just be vague or boring or unintelligible.'

'Sorry,' I said.

'I suppose there's no point in my even asking you how this lawyer heard about a conversation that took place in an office with only three of us present.'

'I told Hannah,' I said. 'She trusted us with her research. I felt I owed it to her to be frank with her.'

'And she shopped you.'

Suddenly I felt light-headed. I didn't care.

'Didn't we shop *her*? We took her data and used it to destroy her campaign.'

'What does that say for her feelings for you, that she'd betray you like that?'

I looked out of the window. It had been raining when we came out. The rain had stopped but the air was misty and grey.

'I don't know,' I said. 'Maybe it means she knows me.'

'I don't suppose there's any point in my saying that you let me down?'

'I was trying to do the right thing.'

He took a sip of coffee.

'I'm sorry, Mark,' he said. 'I didn't hear you properly. I was preoccupied by the picture of us in court appearing as witnesses against Marshco and Wortley. I try to keep it out of my mind but it stubbornly forces its way back in. It's like telling you not to think of a purple cow. You're thinking of a purple cow, aren't you?'

'I've got other things on my mind,' I said.

'You're passing through, I suppose. You think you can go off and get another job?'

'I didn't think about it.'

'Let me tell you, Mark. These guys play a tough game. We need a plan. One possibility is that we should get a lawyer. Or lawyers. I'm not sure if we're on the same side.' He looked thoughtful. 'But that might just make them angry. Or we could ask to talk to their lawyer.'

'Stop,' I said. 'I'm not interested in any of this. If you want, I'll walk into Donna this minute and resign.'

Giles didn't seem to hear me.

'The question is whether Wortley might sue us.'

'I don't care.'

'I admit, there's a funny side to this,' said Giles. 'But I wish it was happening to somebody else.'

'Are you worried about getting fired?' I said.

'It was all going to be so simple,' said Giles. 'And then I

got beaten up. Even after that, we tied it all up brilliantly and now we're going to court in order to extract damages from our own company. I think firing us is down the list of the things they're going to do with us.'

I only gave a sort of shrug in response.

'You see,' said Giles. 'This is the problem I have with you. I get this impression that you are planning to immolate yourself as a matter of principle. But you're doing it on behalf of a wrong cause. You saw the figures. You saw the chart. There is no cluster. It's like looking at shapes in the clouds. It's not there.'

There didn't seem anything left to say. We stood up. I told Giles that I couldn't face going back to the office. Giles looked concerned.

'Don't destroy yourself,' he said. 'Leave that to Donna and Broberg.'

'They know where to find me.'

It was drizzling now but I walked back to my flat. It took about forty-five minutes and by the time I arrived the trousers of my suit were sticking to my thighs and itching. When I got inside and took my suit off it smelled like a dog that had jumped into a pond. I phoned Hannah and a woman I didn't know answered. She told me that Hannah was in hospital. I wondered if it was Hannah's mother, looking after Bruce, or maybe it was a neighbour. I couldn't think of what to say and said something feeble about calling back later and put the phone back. Immediately I realized I should have asked at least about which hospital Hannah was in. But what would I have done, even if I had asked?

I took off the rest of my clothes and had a shower. I put on some jeans and a T-shirt. It was only the mid-afternoon and now I regretted coming home. I'd spent weeks wandering around London, working late into the night. I'd been perched in a rented chalet in Marston Green. Now I was back in my home and I didn't have anything to do. My mind was buzzing. I should read a book or go shopping or make a decision about my life or do something. Then I found something. That picture, the boat in the sunset that looked as if it had been knitted out of something. I pushed the sofa over and stood on the arm and finally, after all this time, I straightened it.

Afterwards I pushed the sofa back, away from the wall, and sat on it. There was a buzz of traffic from outside but inside the flat it was quiet. I felt for just a moment that I could sit here for ever, but I knew it was an illusion. Soon the world would come to get me.

The next morning I went to work but it wasn't like real work. I was like a robot that had been brilliantly designed to imitate work. I arranged files and moved papers around and took some calls and noticed people looking at me in a funny way. I once read something horrible about being guillotined. Back in the eighteenth century, some psycho did research on people who were guillotined. They were interested in how long, if at all, people who were guillotined remained conscious as their head tumbled into the basket or bumped down the steps of the scaffold. The problem is I don't know anything more about what the research consisted of. I assume that they weren't able to hold a conversation with the head. I don't think the mouth would work. Maybe they just said, blink once if you can hear what I'm saying. I have to say I don't know what's more nightmarish. The idea of being aware of your head rolling away from your body and seeing the world gradually switch off like an old-fashioned TV. That's bad enough, but what about being grabbed by a researcher and asked to blink if you can hear what he's saying. If your mouth were still working, you'd say, look, I've got about two seconds left before my brain shuts down and do you think I'm going to spend it answering a questionnaire? Except that you'd be cut off about a quarter of a way through the sentence.

That morning I was like a guillotined head bouncing through the Wortley office. I was an object of curiosity. Look, that's the severed head of Mark Foll. He's the one who's going to be appearing in court testifying against his own company. He looks as if he's actually still alive and functioning, but his artery has been severed and any second now his eyeballs will rotate and he'll be pronounced dead.

I knew it was only a matter of time, and that afternoon, Donna Kiely appeared in the door of our office.

'Both of us?' asked Giles.

'Just Mr Foll,' said Donna. 'Mr Broberg wants him on the seventh floor.'

All these misters. We all knew each other but suddenly it had become formal. It sounded like a bad sign.

'Come on, Donna,' said Giles. 'What's up?'

'I'm just the messenger,' she said.

'This is bullshit,' said Giles. 'If there's any trouble, I was in charge. It's down to me.'

'Write a memo,' said Donna. 'Except I wouldn't, if I were you.'

I followed Donna along the corridor and into the lift. She didn't speak to me, or even look at me. There was one very, very small good sign. I'd seen really brutal sackings before. I'd seen two security men arriving at a desk holding a black binbag and sweeping the contents into it before escorting the ex-employee to the front door. I'd heard of people who discovered they'd been terminated when they swiped their card downstairs and a beep told them it didn't work any more.

It wasn't a great deal of comfort. I also knew that if you were going to be fired for gross misconduct, they had to do it face to face. I tried to think of something I could say in my own defence but my brain wouldn't work properly. My perceptions were hyper-sharp. Everything around me seemed clear and brightly coloured. But I couldn't think. But I made myself some quick promises. I wasn't going to cry. I wasn't going to beg. I wasn't going to say sorry.

When Donna led me into Broberg's office, I expected to find him on the phone to someone or in the middle of a meeting, but he was sitting still at his desk, his jacket on, like a king in his throne room. He didn't seem to be doing anything except waiting for me. He spoke first to Donna.

'Donna, will you step outside and set up the call?'

'The call?'

'Marcia will fill you in.'

She gave me a curious look and backed out of the office closing the door. I was still a long way from Broberg's desk, so I padded over towards him on the thick carpet. Broberg stood up and walked towards one of the great windows. The late-afternoon sun was streaming in and he almost seemed to glow in it. I took a deep breath and suddenly felt calm. Perhaps it was the high altitude.

'I'm happy to resign,' I said.

'What?' said Broberg.

'If there's some problem, then it's probably best if I just leave.'

Broberg looked thoughtful.

'You like football, Mark?' he said.

'I don't know much about it,' I said.

'Did you know that we have an executive box at Highbury?'

'No.'

'It's a major asset. Like with our modern art. Football's not really my game, but it's something we guys are meant to do. You know it's funny, the kind of men that we entertain on match days are chief executives, finance directors, actuaries. They weren't captain of the first eleven when they were at school. They were the boys with thick glasses who sat at the front and paid attention. They were the ones who were pushed around behind the bike sheds and joined the electronics club. Now they come to our box and eat our smoked salmon and drink Montrachet and shout like hooligans and talk about who's sitting on the subs bench and pretend that they're all guys together.'

'It's part of being a man, I guess,' I said.

'So the beautiful game doesn't interest you, Mark?'

What the fuck was this about? I'd assumed I was stopping off here on my way to being thrown off the premises. Was Broberg trying to recruit me for the company football team?

'I never really saw the point,' I said.

'The phone lines have been burning over the last twenty-four hours.'

'Are we still talking about football?'

Broberg greeted that with a forced smile.

'No, Mark, I'm talking about Marston Green now. As you

can understand, we've been exploring the various legal implications and ramifications.' I didn't reply. 'Now, none of us believe that senior executives at Marshco directly ordered the attack on Giles Buckland, do we?' Again, I didn't reply. 'Well, do we?'

'I'm out of this now,' I said. 'I've tried not to speculate.'

Broberg looked at me closely as if he was trying to assess which side I was on.

'Be that as it may,' he said, 'Marshco has been conducting an unofficial enquiry into what happened. One issue that arose was that Giles and you were considered hostile to the company and its activities.'

'Why should that be?'

Broberg gave an impatient gesture.

'This and that. Comments you made, questions you raised, the emphasis of your enquiry. Oh, and one other thing. It's the reason I asked you about football. One of the employees allegedly involved takes his son to football on Saturday mornings. He told Paul Creek that last Saturday he was surprised to see you there. He claims that you were accompanying the young son of one of the leaders of the protest campaign. Is that true?'

'Yes.'

'Is that all?'

'What else should I say?'

Broberg took his jacket off and draped it over his chair. It had a beautiful silky rose-coloured lining.

'I was staggered,' he said. 'Marshco is a significant client. We send two representatives to investigate an issue that threatens their entire existence and one of them forms a liaison with their leading opponent. Is that an accurate account of what happened?'

'I've been seeing her. It was from her that I got the map which we used to disprove the cluster hypothesis.'

'There's another thing, Mark. I'd like to assure you that we are already off the record. I would now like to move even further off the record and ask you, when you got possession of this crucial data, which incidentally was a damn good piece of work, why the hell did you take it to an eighty-five-year-old woman in Oxfordshire? I'm paying six-figure salaries to a bunch of actuaries two floors down. Why didn't you give it to them?'

'The only way of getting Hannah's data from her was to promise that it would be looked at independently.'

'I almost don't want to ask you what would have happened if this woman had found that the cluster was genuine.'

'As you said at the beginning, Mr Broberg: if the cluster was genuine, it would be good if we were the first to know.'

Broberg put his hand across his forehead as if he could feel a migraine coming on.

'There's so much I want to say, I don't know where to start. You say that it was through Hannah Mahoney that you got the crucial data. Just to get it out of the way, I take it that you gave her the information which she then passed on to her lawyer.'

'I didn't do it on purpose.'

Broberg looked puzzled.

'Did she drug you? Did she read it in your diary when you weren't looking?'

'I mean that I didn't mean her to make use of the information. She was being open with me, I wanted to be open with her.'

'You're in a relationship with this woman, then?'

'Yes.'

'A sexual relationship?'

'Mr Broberg, I really don't think . . .'

'You may find yourself answering questions on this in court, Mark.'

'All right. Yes. I am in a sexual relationship with her.'

'Have you anything to add?'

'You were the one who called me here,' I said.

'You realize, I assume, that you have been guilty of gross negligence in your behaviour at Marston Green.'

'I don't know,' I said. 'It was a complicated situation.'

'It's complicated *now*,' said Broberg. 'Jesus.'

The phone rang and Broberg picked it up as if he was expecting it.

'Yeah,' he said. 'Good.'

He pressed a button and replaced the receiver. Immediately a booming voice came out of a speaker. It was a man who sounded as if he was speaking at the deep end of an empty swimming pool.

'Hello?'

'Fergus, good to hear your voice. I have Mark Foll here with me.'

'Mark. I heard about the old lady. Good job.'

'Thank you, sir.'

Suddenly I'd forgotten the second name of the head of Wortley's parent company. 'Sir' would have to do.

'When I'm next over, we'll get together and I want to hear the full uncensored version. Is that a deal?'

'Sure,' I said, bemused. Did this mean that for some bizarre reason they weren't going to let me resign?

'So where are we, Walt?'

'What do you say to five million?'

'What does that buy us?'

'The whole deal.'

'Any other claims against Wortley?'

'Forfeited.'

'Any restraints on Marshco?'

'Any beneficiaries will sign binding restraining orders.'

'So we have closure?'

'It's a done deal, Fergus.'

'All that for just five million?'

'Pounds, not dollars.'

'Fantastic. I owe you guys. See you.'

There was a click and the line went dead. Broberg looked at me as if he had just produced a rabbit from his hat and an ace of spades from his ear simultaneously.

'Jesus, Mark,' he said. 'The next time there's a lightning storm or a nuclear bomb or we're attacked by terrorists, I'm going to stand next to you. You are one lucky fucker.'

'I don't understand,' I said. 'Has this all been sorted out?'

'What do you think we've been doing since yesterday?'

'Have the people on the campaign agreed to this?'

369

'Through their legal representative, yes.'

'So all the problems about Marshco's expansion. The cancer.'

'They'd lost anyway. If you're sitting there with a couple of deuces and someone offers you a few chips, you'd better take them.'

'What do Marshco think?'

'Their premiums will be a little higher but they can plan for the future now.'

'You've paid five million.'

'It's a small price to pay for ruling out any nasty surprises in the future.'

'You mean if the cluster were to turn out to be genuine?'

'These cancer sufferers will receive their money now. Otherwise it would be in twenty years. Or never. Would you turn that down if you were their lawyer?'

'What about the attack on Giles?'

'I'm about to talk to him about that. It's our view that nothing more will come of that investigation. We realize that Giles has undergone a traumatic experience and we will offer an ex-gratia payment to reflect our concern.'

'Ex gratia,' I said. 'Is that Latin for "bribe"?'

'Hey, Mark, let's not be prim about this. I'm sorry for bringing you up here and scaring the shit out of you but you've got to realize that fucking the opponents of our clients isn't always going to be an appropriate way of working. However, on this occasion, it's all worked out. Everybody has won. Everybody is happy. That's the way things are supposed to be and never are.' He held his hand out. With some hesitation I shook it. 'As for you, Mark, you're either very, very stupid or you're someone I should be keeping an eye on.'

'Can I ask you one question?' I said.

'Sure.'

'What do you think of Marshco? I mean as a company.'

There was quite a long pause. Broberg gave me an appraising look, narrowed his eyes.

'Mark, you don't know the half of it.'

'I kind of thought so.'

'It'll all be sorted out by an appropriate authority on the Day of Judgement. But until then we're living in the real world. You did good, Mark. Congratulations. You're an insurance man.'

Hannah had nothing to do but wait and I had nothing to do but wait with her, so we had time to talk properly for the first time for weeks.

'Do you know how much you're getting?' I said.

'That's all being hammered out,' she said. 'It's between about forty and seventy grand and there's some very technical sliding scale based on age, dependants, that sort of thing. I'll probably get about sixty because of Bruce.'

'Who gets it?'

'It's limited to the original list we had, drawn up for the campaign group.'

'That's a bit tough on the cancer sufferers in Heiston, Lingham and Chapel Willow.'

Hannah swallowed hard. I knew she was already feeling nauseous and the treatment hadn't even started. She had started to change colour when we walked in through the main entrance.

'They were only chosen as a control,' she said. 'You know that.' She took a couple of deep breaths. I thought of times I had been on ferries, sitting on deck staring at the horizon, counting down the hours, and I felt so sorry for her. 'I'm not going to argue about the justice of this. I didn't achieve anything I wanted. I didn't stop Marshco.' Another deep breath. 'In the end – thanks to my own figures, which I killed myself getting – we had nothing to bargain with. So I just did what I could. Sorry. Hang on.' She clutched my hand hard, the nails hard in my palm. I found the sensation intensely pleasurable. That it was me she was reaching for out of her fog of sickness. 'It was a last desperate throw. We got all we could. We were recognized. It was something.'

A nurse came over and told Hannah they were ready for her. We walked with her and she sat Hannah down in a chair surrounded by screens. Next to it was a stand on wheels with a transparent bag full of liquid that was clear but somehow had a thick, gluey look to it. After her second mastectomy, Hannah had had a second operation in which a reservoir system was implanted under the skin near her collar bone. This was an incredibly clever way for all the intravenous drugs and liquids and things that Hannah now needed to get into her body but it depressed her. She said she felt she was being turned into a machine for the administration of drugs. The nurse casually pushed the needle through the skin, high in her chest, into the reservoir. She said it would be about forty-five minutes.

'It's funny,' said Hannah. 'I always had to avoid alcohol because it made me ill. When I first went on the Pill when I was a teenager, it made me feel sick and I gave it up. Meat made me feel bloated. And here I am sitting here poisoning myself. You know, if they gave me a ten per cent overdose of this stuff, it would kill me. That's an interesting fact that Dr Leonard told me. That's the whole point of it. To poison me as much as possible without killing me.'

I sat and held her hand.

A little bit more than two hours later I was sitting next to her in her bathroom. Her head was over the bowl.

'I'm feeling a bit . . .' she started to say and then a shudder gripped her body, a spasm and it was as if she was trying to turn her mouth inside out, a horrible tearing sound. All that came out of her mouth was some slime, not even enough to fall. It just hung from her lips. I wiped it with my hand and then rinsed my fingers under the tap. I dried my hand and then stroked her naked back. I rubbed my fingers on her spine and down between the cleft of her buttocks.

'The amusing thing,' she said, 'is that Dr Leonard told me that the two chemos I got today rarely cause nausea. That's a comfort.' Even her voice seemed to move in sickening £lurches.

There seemed to be nothing more that was possible to be vomited out and I led her to her bedroom. I fetched a bucket from downstairs. She lay naked on top of the covers. She couldn't bear to have anything weighing down on her. She lay with her right arm across her eyes. The other breast had been removed now and she should have looked like a man but she didn't. She might not have been able to feel the breasts that weren't there, but I could. I ran my fingers over her stomach and chest and legs and in her pubic hair. Sometimes she flinched and sometimes she gave a slight groan that signalled it made her feel just a bit better.

'There are some good things,' she said. 'Dr Leonard is upbeat. The odds are surprisingly good. No distant spread. There's a fifty per cent chance I'll be alive in five years. The bad thing is that there's a fifty per cent chance I'll be dead in five years. Are you going to London tomorrow?'

'I'll be back in the evening.'

'It's not a civilized way to live.'

'I'm better off than some people.'

'There are other good things,' she said. 'Do you want to marry me?'

'I was the one who asked you,' I said.

'I wasn't proposing. I was asking whether you really want to. I'm not much of a catch. I'm probably dying. I've got no breasts. I'm probably sterile. I'm an ageing hag. I throw up all the time.'

'It's your money,' I said. 'I'm after your money.'

'I'm putting it in a trust fund for Bruce. You won't be able to get your hands on it.'

'I work for an insurance company,' I said. 'I can get my hands on anybody's money.'

She was getting drowsy now.

'I never thought I could fall in love with someone who worked in an insurance company.'

'It's the drugs talking.'

'Can you say it?'

'What?'

'Can you say that you love me? It makes me feel better. Just a little bit.'

'I love you,' I said. But she was already asleep. I looked at her gaunt breastless body that had taken so much punishment, and I saw her chest and stomach rising and falling in sleep. The heart was still pumping, the lungs filling and emptying, struggling against it all.

I switched the light off and walked to the window. It was a full moon and the outline of the trees was hard against the sky. There was a squeaking sound from outside, loud and insistent. Was that an owl? Was I gradually going to learn things like that? Was it possible that I might end up living in Marston Green? Was that what growing up might mean? It was a sobering thought.

I turned and looked at Hannah's body, dimly illuminated in the moonlight. I thought of what it would be like if her body was dead and suddenly, for some reason, I thought of the *Titanic*: people escaping, people desperately trying to escape and failing, people hopelessly trapped and drowning. Now the ones who had survived and the ones who had drowned were all dead. I thought of being dead. Being dead is not being here, but, as Giles had said, even when we're alive we're still equally absent from almost everywhere. It was a thought that confused me. I couldn't think if it was a comfort at all.

Hannah was one of the dots on her own map. She was one of the figures who in Frankie McDonald's application of the Poisson distribution had not formed a pattern. She was part of the noise, the fluff on the surface of reality, the mess, the non-digital part of existence. I walked across the room and lay down next to her.